OBJECTS IN MIRROR
ARE CLOSER THAN
THEY APPEAR

OBJECTS IN MIRROR ARE CLOSER THAN THEY APPEAR

a novel

KATHARINE WEBER

Crown Publishers, Inc.

New York

*This is a work of fiction. The characters, incidents, and
dialogues are products of the author's imagination and are not
intended to represent real people, living or dead.*

Published by Crown Publishers, Inc., 201 East 50th Street, New York,
New York 10022. Member of the Crown Publishing Group.
Random House, Inc.   New York, Toronto, London, Sydney, Auckland
CROWN is a trademark of Crown Publishers, Inc.

Manufactured in the United States of America

Library of Congress Cataloging-in-Publication Data
Weber, Katharine.
Objects in mirror are closer than they appear / Katharine Weber.
p.   cm.
I. Title.
PS3573.E2194025   1996
813'.54—dc20   94-38571
                                                                          CIP

ISBN 0-517-59890-6
10 9 8 7 6 5 4 3 2 1
First Edition

For Nick
O.l.i.h.t.s.

Always there lurked the fear that one's own view of truth was merely a small window in a small house.
　　　　—Thornton Wilder, The Eighth Day

Part I

Geneva

July 3

Oh, Benedict,

It's been five days since your touch. Your touch, hell, your rib-crushing hug at the security checkpoint. I think I have a bruise, Dr. Heimlich, would you mind taking a look at my clavicle? Have I told you how easily I bruise? How easily I bruise: Once, when I was maybe seven and I was walking with my grandmother, my marvelous grandmother, Gay, across 59th Street to the Park, I darted out into the street at an intersection. She grabbed my wrist, for fear of what she called Come-Arounders—cars turning the corner at a high rate of speed and disregard and by the next day I had developed a perfect set of her fingerprints. I thought it looked as though a freshly printed felon had taken my wrist in the middle of a booking. (Did you know that when I was little, I wanted very much to be an FBI agent?)

That same afternoon, when we were waiting for the light to change at Second Avenue, a little boy darted into the street in front of us, with traffic streaming close by, and Gay let go my hand to trot right after him so she could whisk him back up onto the sidewalk with a quick underarm hoist. And then the little boy turned around and hissed, "Fuck you, lady!"

It was no little boy at all, but a dwarf, a middle-aged dwarf with acne scars and a Don Ameche mustache. He and I were about the same height. My grandmother grabbed my arm and we backed away together as she murmured, "So sorry, so sorry," in a tone that suggested a limited command of English. She hustled me into the nearest doorway as the dwarf advanced, shouting horrible obscenities at us still. This was fortunately a luncheonette, and we backed into the doorway as if that had been our intention all along, and we sat at the counter, Gay and I, and had coffee frosted milk shakes and the dwarf went away and we kept looking at each other and laughing.

I still can't believe she is gone. I wish you had known her. I dream about her. God, I miss her. Even when she was dwindling away with encroaching senility, she was still there at the core in some tiny way. One of the last times I saw her, about a week before she curled up to die—I just realized she died exactly six months ago today, which is perhaps why I find myself thinking about her now—she seemed to have no idea who I was. But she tugged at my sleeve and kept saying, "What's this?" until I figured out what she was asking and said, "I'm Harriet."

"Are you really?" she asked. "Are you really Harriet? In that case, I love you!"

Funny: that moment with the dwarf. Horrifying, but reassuring. Something about Gay always made me feel protected, almost magically so. Though God knows she was impossible, judgmental, full of rules for others to live by. She's in my thoughts all the time. And I carry her with me in other ways, too. She was, of course, English, as you know. But she was *really* English. I wish you could have heard her voice. Even though Gay emigrated as a young child and lived in New York for the rest of her life, she had all sorts of her mother's habitual gestures of speech, which I absorbed osmotically, without even knowing that certain phrases or words weren't ordinary American talk.

Was it Alexander Portnoy who thought *spatula* was Yiddish? When I was small, Gay read to me a lot (possibly because she wasn't particularly adept at making conversation with a toddler), and what she read included some books from her own childhood, as well as books she had read to my mother when she was little. Consequently, when I was about six (the story goes), I asked my mother for a sixpence for the gumball machine in the shoe store. (My mother thought this was a bit much and instituted an embargo on Enid Blyton books.)

So. My own use of language, spoken and written, ends up somewhere halfway over the sea, unless I'm mindful. There I go. (I notice when you raise those eyebrows over some of my more uncommon utterances, don't think I don't.) Maybe it's one of my connections with Anne. Though I insist that I come by my affectations more honestly.

I wouldn't say that Gay was affected, exactly. Is it an affectation if the things you say and do run deep, through and through? But you know, even though I ended up living with Gay for most of a year, I was never completely at my ease with her, I never felt that I knew her, not really. Maybe that's why I soaked up what I could, mimicked her as a way of trying to figure her out.

After our milk shakes that afternoon, we went, as always, to the Park and watched the seals catch those silvery fish flung by keepers, one fish after another; life could be so sardine-y and simple. I always wanted this moment to last forever; it never did. The disappointed seals would slide into the watery murk and swim in urgent revolutions. Ritually, the disappointed child would feed greasy peanuts to squirrels, feeling guilty for eating some.

We would laugh at our reflections in the glass of the monkey house and make monkey faces. (This was always a thrill, as Gay was at other times quite perfectly ladylike.) Then we would hunt for a balloon man so we could buy my requisite green balloon, and then we would walk back to Sutton Place. So it was on the way back, I guess, that I darted and she clutched. She had to rescue somebody. I had to let her rescue somebody. I had those fingerprints for a long time. I regretted their fading away; I liked them.

★   ★   ★

So here I am. Anne worries me. Imperial, imperious, impera-
tive. Still the Anne Gordon of Eighth Street days, but not. Wan,
thin, pale as a graduate student who hasn't emerged from library
stacks to find out the season. She has developed something far
beyond her old queerly tentative self that I suppose you might
call a style. But you wouldn't call it a style; I'm not sure what
you would call it. Tootsishness. Isn't that one of your words? A
toots on wheels, you might say if you passed her on the street.
Her new look seems to derive from scarves and boots and sunglasses in the hair and eyeliner and I don't know what else. She's
frighteningly accessorized.

Anne's arms, for instance, are racked with silver bangles. At
first I thought she was wearing Slinkies on her wrists. She didn't
know what a Slinky was, though, when I suggested this. You
probably think women should wear one bracelet per wrist.
Which makes me think of that day when you stroked my arm
for an hour and described all the muscles and nerves under the
skin. I hadn't noticed my arm in years. Not since I was little and
used to lick the sun-salt from my arms at the beach when I lay
on a towel waiting for the hour to be up after lunch. But I had
never seen my own arm through another's eyes, loved my own
arm. The anatomy lesson of Dr. Thorne. Was it three or four
hours? (I discovered that evening, in the bathroom mirror, that
my face was pinked from the sun. For the next couple of days,
people kept asking me if I had gone to Vermont for spring
skiing.)

We sprawled on that rock in Central Park and talked all afternoon, and we weren't touching except for that one place where
your fingertips brushed up and down on the inside of my left
arm. That tiny electrical point of connection, those molecules of
skin touching. I wanted that moment to last forever. It was only
the second time we were together. We had never even kissed. I
embarrass myself even now when I think of it. (The smile you
are smiling you were smiling then.)

Anne has acquired an edge that was not there in New York. She is even more impossibly affected than she used to be, with her Lauren-Bacall-as-Alistair-Cooke delivery, always amusing in light of her Westchester origins, although she did, inexplicably, go to that hoity-toity Swiss boarding school. Thus her immunity to whole chunks of popular culture.

She loves old movies, for instance, has an uncanny memory for entire scenes, especially the Bogart-Bacall or Tracy-Hepburn ones, and yet she simply has never heard, or never noticed, the music of that vintage you'd think she would also love. The music we love. Anne's not literally tone-deaf, but she claims that she just can't remember a tune, not even for five minutes, not even while the song is being sung.

At a Shippen Gallery opening someone once tried to get everyone to sing "Button Up Your Overcoat"—I don't remember quite why, though I'm sure it made sense at the time—and Anne just wouldn't do it. Reluctantly, she mouthed the words, but no sound came out.

I've tried to fill in some of the lacunae. On Eighth Street, I would endure Anne's schmaltzy Chopin, and Anne would listen as best she could to my Lee Wiley records. Remedial Show Tunes 101. She had got to the point where she was really taken with some lyrics, though she was still comparatively immune to the music itself; Anne still seemed unable to hear the connection between words and music. It's a curious deficiency. Now, with Victor, she's probably done some backsliding into Viennese waltzes and I'll have to start over.

Even as I write these words, I worry that you won't like her, that it doesn't even sound as though *I* like her very much. I adore Anne. And—outside of family—I have never felt as loved by anyone, until there was you. We are so alike and unalike at the same time. And, though I feel these changes in her that I can't quite pin down, we always used to enjoy our samenesses and differences, if you know what I mean.

How can I describe a friendship in more precise terms? You've heard so much, but in bits and pieces. It's much more than mutual eccentricities and passions for cultural artifacts. We can —or used to be able to—finish each other's sentences. We just *knew* each other as women can, as men so rarely do, at least heterosexual ones.

Anne's a terrifically loyal friend, one of the smartest people I know, and she's not just interesting, she has that rarer capacity of being interested. And she has a very droll side that unbuttons at unexpected moments, though those moments don't usually survive in the telling. One of the things I mean to say is that she's not like anybody else. A teacher at l'Ecole Prétentieuse, or whatever it was called, apparently used to habitually say to her, *"Mademoiselle Gordon, vous êtes une drôle d'originale!"*

That's why Anne in Geneva is such a puzzle to me. I don't feel that I know what's going on with this person with whom I used to feel almost telepathically connected. For instance: Benedict, what do you call the meal you eat in the middle of the day? Same here: lunch. One of the most beautiful words in the English language, *n'est-ce pas?* I could swear my old pal and roommate Anne used to call it lunch, too. We used to eat it together sometimes and it never went by any other name. (Certainly not the dreaded b-----, though if it was late enough, we called it "lupper.") Nowadays she calls it luncheon, as it must be known among the Geneva intelligentsia. But she doesn't seem to eat it, oh, no, not our Anne, because during the luncheon hour she is consorting with her married lover.

Even in New York days, when she worked at Shippen, she didn't exactly always eat lunch in the manner of a normal person, I admit. Unless you call an entire bunch of raw carrots a normal lunch. She did it to save money for going to the movies, she told me. Gloria pays her people slave wages, I know, but still. The first time I ever laid eyes on Anne, she was in that little back workroom scrubbing away at a bunch of carrots over the sink in the corner where the coffee things are. Gloria was showing me the gallery; we were at the nerve-wracking point when she was thinking of putting me in a group show, and I was grateful for the distraction when Gloria introduced me to this odd creature, so angular and Vermeerish at the same time. I was particularly struck by her unusual voice. I didn't know if I liked it or hated it, but I wanted to hear more. We shook hands, and her hand was wet because of the carrots, and she apologized too much about that. I developed an instant sort of crush on her; she fascinated me.

Once, before Anne left, I met Victor. She and I were room-mates by then; it was about six months before she actually left New York to come here. This falls under the Had I But Known category of meeting people. Just as we figure you probably encountered Anne in the course of your own gallery wanderings in those prehistoric days before you and I met, but didn't know to pay attention. (I still can't believe I've known you only—what? —three months.)

I wish you knew Anne. I wish you could help me figure out what is going on here. When you wandered through shows at Shippen, you probably passed within a few feet of her, when she was filing invoices, or she was stashed away in the back washing carrots and making telephone calls in various languages. You would be more likely to have chatted up the more visible woman who worked at the front desk there, named Marjorie Something, also known as Our Favorite Anti-Semite. ("A nice fellow," she would sniff about some client, "although one of the Chosen, I believe.")

So I met him a long time ago, as it turns out. Victor Marks, I mean, speaking of the Chosen. Anne's nonlunch date. But at the time I could swear he was represented to me as yet another mere Friend of the Family, an enormous category of humanity known to Anne that seems to embrace half the Eastern European refugee population of the greater New York area. He came to Eighth Street to take Anne out to dinner one night early last winter. I only vaguely remember the evening, and vaguely remember him as some old guy in a blazer standing in our hallway, winded after three flights of stairs. It didn't occur to me to notice him. It didn't occur to me in all these months that *that* was Victor.

He even *looks* a little bit like "Daddy" (a dour, retired Austrian baker with a flour allergy whom Anne addresses as Henry, who lives alone with his bitter memories in deepest New Jersey), whose life Victor is credited with saving in a children's barracks (where they shared a bunk) at Auschwitz. Something about a potato.

How long has this been going on? It was only last winter. Anne says Victor is fifty-nine. He looks older to me. He has a wife, who from Anne's descriptions has got to be the Polish Julie Andrews, and three young children, whose names, if you can believe it, are Lucien, Otto, and Minerva.

So, after four days here, the routine is more or less this: Anne gets up and does things to her hair and walks into the sharp corners of furniture and mutters, *"Merde,"* and leaves at about eight. (The *merde* habit is a leftover affectation from her New York days, and she needs to fix it because here it is of course not a charming expression in another language.)

I have the flat to myself for the rest of the day, as she had promised in her letters of enticement this last spring, so I can read and write, or go out and take pictures, and otherwise squander time in splendid solitude. But: every day, Anne and Victor come here, to this flat, for what I believe is quaintly called a "nooner." And here I am.

So of course here I am not, rain or shine, at the appointed hour. This is a bit much, despite all the thick and thin I've been through with Anne. For one thing, and it's a big one: I am sleeping with her in her bed, as there isn't a couch, and Anne refused to let me sleep on bedding on the floor. It's a big bed, and I sleep very much on my own side—you know how little I move in my sleep—but I feel like a voyeur; the bed feels crowded. Much is made of ostentatious sheet-changing on my behalf. But: did Anne tell me about Victor when I won the Swift and we made plans for my month in Geneva? She absolutely insisted that I must stay here with her. So I feel a bit boxed in. I suppose I could look for another place to stay, but that would be insulting and impossibly expensive, and I have no idea how to go about doing it. And I'm not here forever, anyway, just until the end of the month. And I return to the thought that Anne wants me right here with her, for reasons I can't quite grasp that go beyond any discussed or so far discussable reasons.

And: it turns out that the reason she left her job as the only trilingual staff member at Shippen Gallery (essential slot she filled; they're bereft without someone to translate foreign auction catalogs and place telephone orders at the Czech deli over on Second Avenue) was Victor. Her job at UGP is a piece of cake, a lot of financial paper shuffling and occasional simultaneous interpreting of meetings between the polite and cold Swiss men in dark suits who run the front office and the hostile and sneering Arabs— known, I regret to say, as "towel heads"—who secretly control everything. This is according to Anne, who has never before had a grasp of or interest in world politics or oil markets.

UGP seems to be an enormous consortium of petroleum investors. I can't even determine what the initials stand for, and I have no idea what it is or does. The Arabs speak terrible English that's mostly strange slangy metaphors, and the Swiss speak equally terrible unidiomatic English that's entirely correct and formal, and it's their only common language, so Anne has to convey in French whatever she thinks the Arabs mean to say. Meanwhile the Arabs transmit to her in a not particularly gracious polyglot of German, English, Italian, and street slang they pick up here and there.

The Arabs have provided no opposite number for Anne, as is often the custom in these situations, so when these meetings occur, she has to strain to make both sides feel understood as well as feel that they understand. If world oil prices collapse or something, I think it will be safe to assume that Anne was more concerned with the former than the latter.

All the Arabs have three-day beards and funny smells, according to our representative in the field, who is herself obsessed with funny smells because she is convinced that colleagues around the office—there are about fifty other people there, doing something or other with computers and fax machines and telephones—can tell when she and Victor have been At It. (My theory is that she and Victor are At It so regularly that if there is any sort of clue, no one would notice. Come to think of it, Anne is a bit, well, Clorox-y. I assumed it was her deodorant.)

Anne herself seems to spend a lot of time on the phone, pecking away at a computer, or hovering over a fax machine. When Anne showed me around the office yesterday, after hours, I could hardly believe that she knew what she was doing there, it's such an alien setting. Anne has always seemed more a member of the quill pen and sealing wax set. Watching her fax a document was like watching someone rehearsing the stage business for a part in a play.

Yet she appears to do her job perfectly well, and she seems to be making a fortune at this so-called profession (annually, about ninety g's, at which don't sneeze), which is just as well because she is giving away the best years of her life, and meanwhile a tiny cup of admittedly excellent coffee costs four dollars in a café here. Victor is her boss at UGP, you see. Have I said that? I'm not sure I'm explaining this very well. I'm just trying to sort it out myself.

He's the head of the division, or something. He created the job for her after they slept together in his hotel room in New York that fateful winter night. He sat on the edge of the bed and calculated and formulated and ruminated and made her a job offer on the spot. I remember her coming in at around four in the morning, after dinner out with "Daddy's old friend from Auschwitz," but naive me thought they had stayed up talking about the potato. I never connected her decision to go to Geneva, to take a mysterious job for an oil cartel, with the soon-forgotten (by me) events of that night—her hot date with an old, balding, Hungarian refugee.

And Anne can play her cards pretty close to the vest, when I think back on all the heartfelt conversations we had about her decision to leave New York, leave that which we call the art world, bail out of our apartment, move to Geneva. It never occurred to me to cross-examine her about how exactly she came to be offered this high-powered job while cutting the occasional mat, scrubbing carrots, and ordering Eastern European takeout at Shippen Gallery.

I knew that it wasn't the first time they had met; Anne had told me before he came to get her that night that she remembered meeting him once when she was ten and he came for dinner, in Hastings-on-Hudson. He hadn't seen Anne's father since the war ended, and both men wept and hugged each other and spoke (in what Anne insists is some obscure variation of a Yiddish dialect from the Austro-Hungarian Empire that they both know) about many dead people.

Victor has since told Anne, and Anne told me just this morning, that what he most clearly recalls about that night fifteen years ago is going into the kitchen where Anne was helping her mother do the washing up. Victor chummily put his hand on Elizabeth's shoulder, which caused fierce little Anne to brandish a paring knife in his direction. He thinks this is a funny story, according to Anne, and says it was the moment he fell in love with her. Isn't it romantic?

Anne's apartment—she always calls it the flat—is small, but somehow even in the dark you would know where you are;

it's totally Swiss. I cannot forget for one moment that I am in Switzerland; whenever I raise my head, something Swiss-ly efficient strikes me, like the tiny little kitchen across from where I sit. It's in an alcove, a sort of open closet, and has no oven and looks like the sort of stewardess-packed kitchen on a Boeing 757 that you glimpse on your way to the toilet.

This is the perfect very grown-up and very modern mistress's apartment. It faces out onto an anonymous courtyard. Everybody's shutters are closed but ours. Who are those people in the other flats? KGB agents, smugglers, characters from Françoise Sagan novels? It's a third-floor walk-up; there are clean but grimly institutional stairs of gritty marble. Every time I've been up or down them an elderly woman all in black has been on her knees washing them. There is an elevator, which I have used once, the day I arrived. I may be the only person to have used it since the War. (Oh, yes, Switzerland. What war? Well, you know what I mean.) It creaked up the three stories in about twice the time it would have taken me to walk with my two suitcases. I was already confused about which floor I wanted because in America when we say first floor we mean it. Then I cut my hand rather badly on the folding gate contraption, and I arrived at Anne's door with blood dripping in a trail behind me down the dim marble hallway. When I went out with Anne to get milk for the tea an hour after I had come in, there was no trace of it.

There is very little furniture in this L-shaped room; Our Lady of the Perpetual Milk Crate has reformed. Anne has a table with two chairs; that's where I am now. There is a high chest of drawers, with a large mirror over it, and the bed, or should I say The Bed. It's very low and modern, the only expensive item in the place. Victor has a bad back—Victor has many infirmities— so when Anne arrived, she spent all her money on it. She doesn't seem to notice how impersonal the place is. Or maybe she likes the ambience of a hospital room. It does have that feeling of a place where some sort of procedures are performed on the human body. Which I guess you could say is the case.

The ceiling is so high that I think the room may be taller than it is wide. It's like being at the bottom of a box. The scale is so odd, in fact, that when I look at the very tall doors in their very tall doorframes, I feel diminished and am reminded of being a child in my room, looking up at the tops of doors and wondering what the top of my head might look like from up there on the lintel.

The only good light is here at the table, where I can see the blank shuttered faces of those other apartments. If I duck down, I can see a little slice of Swiss sky; I guess that's the allotment that comes with the flat.

Yesterday I had lunch in a café around the corner, and when the waiter offered me a dish of extra little pickles—two had come with my ham sandwich—I accepted. Then the bill came and I saw that I had been charged four francs for *"cornichons supplémentaires."* So the Swiss are a pickle-counting people, and I must remember to count my pickles before they go down the hatch. (Did I really eat six? I wonder.)

When I faxed Anne my flight information last week, I added, WILL YOU BAKE A CAKE? (Now that she knew I was coming.) But I always forget how charmingly unknowing of popular culture this girl is, how much she missed by going to school abroad, by having a European father and, after seventh grade, a deceased mother, and she had never heard of the song—she thinks that maybe she has heard of Jimmy Durante, but she's probably got Will Durant, or Asher B. Durand, in mind—and so she went out and bought a cake (a dense poppy-seed one from a Viennese bakery of which Victor approves) because, as I have said, she has no oven. Just a very literal mind.

I do love her though, and I am cross with myself for my impatience with this strange new mistress-person. Anne of Cleavage. It makes me doubt what I thought I knew. What did

I know? Who was that in New York with whom I shared those two rooms on Eighth Street for a year and a half? We were practically living in each other's pockets, and maybe I mistook a mutual love of so many books and movies and a million other things for something else. Have I told you that we once sat through *The Philadelphia Story* twice when it was shown at the Modern? We both know most of the good lines. We both used to want to be Katharine Hepburn. If Tracy Lord had had a best friend, the George Kittredge alliance would never have got so out of hand.

Anne used to have a certain kind of rational, if not practical, approach to life. But this new Anne seems to have no good sense, and no good sense of herself. I want to shake her, slap her, wake her up from this fugue state. And then I'm impatient with my impatience.

She also has no good records. I just got up for a stretch and a prowl, and I see nothing worthwhile except for the Django Reinhardt album I gave her for her birthday last year, which she doesn't seem to have opened. Too much Rachmaninoff, way too much. Also odd books: very *affettato* fiction (*The Name of the Rose,* an unread-looking Pynchon, dog-eared Du Maurier, and strange quantities of Ann Beattie and Paul Theroux), three different How to Improve books (sex life, complexion, thighs), and, of course, your basic, up-to-date Survivor Guilt Library: *The Abandonment of the Jews, Holocaust Testimonies,* the *Annotated Diary of Anne Frank, Eichmann in Jerusalem, Children Without Childhoods, Nazi Doctors, Wartime Lies, Sophie's Choice, The Painted Bird,* and every book by Primo Levi. (I wonder if I could make money with a Holocaust Book Club. You bet. People would be too guilty to return any of the monthly selections.)

Oh, maybe I'm just jealous of Victor and feel left out, relegated to a more distant role in Anne's life. And Anne knows me well enough to discern my lack of enthusiasm for him. (The Gay

Gibson term for my response to Victor is *modified rapture*.) For all I know I made Anne feel left out in my letters to her about you. But this is more than the dislocation and adjustment between the best of friends, each of whom thinks she has met the love of her life. Something about this makes me uneasy.

But I'm rambling. Maybe life doesn't have to be as complicated as I always seem to think it is. So. Please forgive these platitudes. Benedict: you are my You. This month ahead of me is more than a little bit alarming, and not just because of Anne, and this peculiar situation with Victor. I am, because of you, squaring off to account for myself, in some ways for the first time. You showed me the way. You make me see that I really have to think about my photographs. Your relationship to your painting is so solid; you have incredibly high standards for your own work. You make me want to assess and revise everything in my work. You make me realize how much of my work isn't good enough, how tempted I am to coast. I worry that you are too confident, not in yourself but in me. This is hard to say: You don't know the half of it, dearie. Maybe you don't even know the quarter of it.

So I'm in Geneva, city of watches and illicit romance, the measly grant from the Swift Foundation covering my plane tickets, and, if I'm lucky, maybe one good meal out with Anne while I'm here, but it's nice work if I can get it. Gloria tells me that the prestige of winning a Swift is worth far more than I realize. I certainly hope so. Meanwhile, I'm stewing over several ideas for some groups of pictures. And I do have the commitment from Gloria for a small back-room show at Shippen in late winter.

I mean to take a lot of pictures based on reflections in shop windows. This is perhaps too neat a sequel to my self-portrait series, but what can I say? Does it strike you as too pandering, too commercial, too expected, too Harriet Rose? It will be more subtle than it sounds, I promise.

So here's hoping for an astonishing month, Benedict. It seems wrong that I have gone away from you right now. But this trip was arranged for several weeks before we met, as I keep reminding you in order to remind myself that I haven't just flown the coop, that you're real and you'll be there.

You've become part of me, you're inside me all the time. When I think of you, I think about the future in a different way than I ever did before. The important things are starting to be clear to me, some for the first time. I feel balances shifting, in good ways, in major ways.

With you I can begin to care, and to stop caring. I mean: there is a freedom, for the first time, to think about the sensibility in my work in a pure way.

There's a song stuck in my head. Remember the night we drank rusty nails and listened to the entire score for "Of Thee I Sing"? I had never really paid attention to the words before. Now I can't stop thinking about Mr. and Mrs. Wintergreen, at the beginning of "Who Cares?":

> *Who cares what the public chatters?*
> *Love's the only thing that matters.*

I miss you in all ways. I passed a walled garden yesterday on my way back from my pickle lunch, and I could hear a tennis game, and it made me think of you in that New Hampshire air teaching tennis to overprivileged monsters.

Do you know, the first person scares me, Benedict. The very photographs for which I am known, the pictures that put me squarely in the middle of the Brat Pack for better or worse, the photos that in a sense made me, those self-portraits: they were torture.

It's all done with mirrors. And how. Have you ever really looked yourself in the eye? Your self-portraits are so stripped: of course you have. It's part of what makes you so different from me. I hardly dare to catch my own eye.

Maybe I've arrived too soon in my work. The journey, not the arrival, matters and all that. Gloria Shippen chose me for that "3 Under 30" show because of what she called the "authority" of those self-portraits. What Shippen Gallery, what the critics who boosted me along by singling me out for praise, what even those check-writing collectors who suddenly needed to own a Harriet Rose thereafter, what they all don't know is that any so-called authority lies in the eye of the beholder.

And I count myself as a beholder. I don't mean to say my work isn't good. It's damned good. But time and again, when I was printing those pictures, I would see something in the darkroom that I hadn't seen when I was setting up those shots. I take credit for those things, but it makes me uneasy. How can I own those inadvertent plays of light or the random objects that made Sanford Schwartz analyze the Balthus references in my oeuvre, for God's sake? Before last year I didn't know I had an oeuvre. (Why does a Frenchman have only one egg for breakfast? Because one egg is *un oeuf.*) Has my life changed because *The New Criterion* loves me? I really don't know. I really don't even know with certainty about my own criteria for my work, old or new.

In short, Benedict, my photographs mean more than I knew I meant. Does that make sense? Is this what art is?

I think of my pictures as decisions about what to show, a diagnosis of what's beneath the skin: a slice, a biopsy. A pathology report. It's art that scares me.

At the moment, I'm not sure I could ever do another series like those relentless mirror self-portraits. I know too much. By that I mean: I know how little I know. I could never put myself out there again like that. But in this month here I intend to call my own bluff. I mean to sneak up on myself, in those shop windows. I'll be there, if you know where to look.

But now it's nearly noon. I've got to vacate the love nest. I wish I could hear your voice. I wonder if we have made a mistake, agreeing on this mutual meditative transatlantic silence. I wonder if I have broken the rules, in writing to you this way. I wonder if I will ever have the nerve to show you these letters or journals or whatever they are.

I just took out the little red-striped-shirt portrait of you that I took two weeks ago. Oh, Benedict. Getting sentimental over you.

Noon: Love you and leave you—

July 4

I just realized the date—no big deal here—and picture you at
the most uncompetitive tennis camp in New England, surrounded by rich children in tennis whites scarfing down hot dogs
while you sweat over the grill. Luckies. They are sunburned and
demanding. You are sunburned and patient. There is red clay
staining your sneakers and the left pocket of your shorts. You
wish you could have a beer. A camper with a bee sting cries.
Smoke gets in your eyes.

Benedict, do you remember everything? Absolutely everything that ever happened to you? In the exact words people
used? I do, or at least I believe I do. It is only with you that I
forget things, such as whether or not I have told you a joke
already. (Frog goes into a bank. Did I really tell you that joke
three times? That's because I was dazed, able to let go. Very
rare.)

Certain experiences have a perpetual effect; if you drop a
pebble into water, the outward ripples continue for a long time.
Maybe they continue forever.

Do you have dreams of falling that seem like memories?

When you said you wanted to marry me, the night before I
flew, I felt a rush of love for you and a kind of gratitude you
cannot imagine. (You've got what gets me.) But I also felt a
pang. I felt like a fraud. I had won you, fooled you, persuaded
you the way I persuade the viewer with my photographs. Be-

21

cause I knew that you don't really know who I am, or you couldn't possibly want to marry me.

I was thinking about this yesterday afternoon when I was killing time at a sidewalk café, eating expensive coffee ice cream because it was the only thing I could think to order in my nonexistent French. And I realized that I have sold you a bill of goods—have sold it to myself—that I am one of the world's most honest and open and direct people.

Memories beset her brooding brain.

Last night Anne and I went out for a walk, and she led me to an open-air flower market in the Place du Molard, which, owing to the long summer days, was going full tilt at nine o'clock. Anne hunted down the vendor who had sold Victor an important bouquet of roses a couple of months ago, and then Anne proudly pointed them out to me, roses of just the same hue. I was made to admire them as if the very shade of pink transmits the significance of it all. What could I say? They're a deep, somewhat labial color, they give off a wonderful fruity fragrance, and I gather they cost fifty dollars a bunch.

I had my camera along, and I took two pictures about which I have great hopes: One was of the rose vendor, an old woman wearing a straw hat of the sort you expect to see on someone you would call Dobbin and to whom you might offer lumps of sugar. She even had copious whiskers, but did not look as though she would take kindly to being stroked on the nose. She was bending over a huge bucket of water, getting ready to fill it with some bouquets she had been assembling, and the picture I took captures her face and its reflection in the surface of the water, with her hands in the frame. She probably assumed I was photographing her flowers. On her hands were these odd gloves that matched only in that on both the fingers were missing—I suppose they were to protect her palms from the thorns. She was armed with this little stubby knife with which she stripped the thorns off every stem, very quickly, like a cardsharp dealing out a stacked deck, faster than the eye could see. The intensity of her movements I found mesmerizing. I wish I could concentrate like that on anything, anything at all. The light was ancient, molten, golden.

The other picture was of Anne. She doesn't know I took it, thanks to the Harriet Rose Method of Surreptitious Portraiture. (Put the camera up to your eye while facing in a different direction, turn slowly and appear to be interested in potential shots of entirely distant subjects, take the picture, don't advance the film, and don't take the camera away from your eye until you've turned again, at which time you are gazing into the middle distance.)

Anne was looking into the shop window of the drugstore on the corner near her flat, where a big old cat was stretched out among the toothbrushes, shaving things, hideous rubber items for personal uses I cannot begin to contemplate, soaps, nailbrushes, virtuous wooden sandals, unguents and emollients, vomit trays, syringes, hair dyes, and sundry other useful Swiss products. I framed her reflection so that her face and the cat's face were overlapped. It was a lucky happenstance of reflection and position. What I saw looked very much like a composite made with two separate images. I think I really have something. She thought I was merely taking a snapshot of the cat.

Anne has absolutely zero understanding of photography, mine or anyone else's. Her idea of art is Titian. Full stop. We've never really talked about my work, I mean about the deeper issues, but she's a loyal friend full of enthusiasm, encouragement, respect even, despite that void. She was terribly excited by my good reviews and all. I was really touched that she called, even though it was the middle of the night, thrilled out of her mind about that interview from the *Boston Globe* running in the *International Herald Tribune*. She still talks about it. But to her it's like a game, I think. She would love me if I did magazine illustration, if I worked with an air gun, if I painted by numbers. She doesn't

know the difference between Brassai and Avedon. It doesn't
matter to her. For someone so attuned to nuances of personal
appearance, she's weirdly unvisual, now that I think about it.
Well, if anything, it frees me to work with her around, as she
doesn't have the least interest in or comprehension of what I'm
up to. I can do as I please: it's like speaking a foreign language in
front of the children.

I used to take pictures of Anne in New York all the time.
You've seen a lot of them. Hell, I've *sold* almost as many pictures
of Anne as self-portraits. Some of those studies even *felt* like
self-portraits. She was always so obliging, yet completely without
understanding of what I was doing.

After the flower market, we went for ice cream down at the
lake—my second of the day; I've got to watch that I don't eat
ice cream incessantly here, as it's so good and my French is so
bad—and walked along eating our cones. Anne is capable of
walking miles; that's one thing unchanged about her. Did I tell
you that once we walked from the World Trade Center, where
we'd gone, cornily, for the view, all the way up to Columbia
University, to hear a lecture on the role of the photographer in
South American literature? Then there was the insanely cold day
when we walked from the Brooklyn side of the Brooklyn Bridge
all the way up to the Carnegie Cinema on Fifty-seventh Street
so we could see the Tati film *Playtime*.

I fail to understand how Victor can possibly keep up with her;
he seems a hundred years old, and not a young hundred, either.
She's always been so walkative, so full of energy and enthusiasms,
and she's always had a sense of adventure—I suppose that's a
tune that's unchanged, though it's transposed and now playing
in a minor key with ominous diminished fifths. But the mysterious new Anne has made this worrisome alliance with a charter
member of Hypochondriacs Anonymous—an organization that
could never hold meetings, for fear of infectious disease—and
she's beginning to develop her own complaints as well, with

headaches, and matching back pain, and otherworldly, mistressy discomforts of the "indoor plumbing" ilk, as she says. She's probably taken up douching.

Oh, I'm making Anne sound dreadful, and she's not. She was the most important person in my life before I met you. You're the two most important people in my life now.

We talk. We talk and talk, yet there's a veil, a screen. Anne is very curious about you, very reserved on the subject, almost jealous, I think. I don't think she has made any friends here, other than a few office acquaintances. You know, she had very few friends in New York, and she hasn't kept in touch with her one or two boarding-school chums. The only one she's ever talked about at length was a girl called Keggie Barnes who was born on a ferry crossing between England and Ireland. Keggie smoked Player's and wore a deerstalker cap to class and signed all her letters and notes "Love you and leave you," which is where Anne got it, which is where I got it. The other Keggie habit Anne has retained is the ladylike *merde* for all occasions. But Anne hasn't been in touch with Keggie since I've known her and has no idea if she ended up raising horses in Ireland or what.

And I don't know much about Anne's past love life, either. Other than a sordid thing with her French professor at Bennington, who was her first, I think, I'm not sure Anne has had the usual run of affairs. She has always referred to various people with whom she has done things or gone places, but never with a clear sense of a romantic connotation. I am certain that I've not met any old flames. She was always producing Friends of the Family, but they were inevitably elderly, and from someplace foreign, like Prague, or Cincinnati.

Anne talks about meeting you and worries that you won't approve of her. She also keeps threatening to show you one of my letters to her, in which I seem to have described having met you. And she keeps parroting those lines to me whenever I bring your name into the conversation:

" 'I have met a wonderful man: Benedict Thorne is his name.
I think we are falling in love. I know I am. He is a painter who
teaches tennis in the summers. I like his work, have always liked
his work since I first saw it several years ago in a show at Fox. I
would like to photograph him naked, but don't have the courage
to ask him. Yet.' " She does seem to have it memorized. Maybe
our grandchildren will enjoy that. (Oh, look what I just said.)

She talks about Victor compulsively. His reminding her of
her father. I don't see it. She makes much of Victor's having
come from similar circles, though on close examination that's a
stretch, as Anne's Viennese grandparents on that side were cul-
tured, educated people, both scientists at a university, while in
Budapest, Victor's mother sold secondhand shoes and his father
ran a little hole-in-the-wall restaurant. I gather that before the
War Victor was a tough, clever child of the streets, a thief, sort
of a barrow boy; just those nervy skills were probably what en-
abled him to survive the concentration camp and keep Henry
alive, too.

I was wrong, yesterday, when I said that Victor and Henry
had been in a children's barracks at Auschwitz. Anne and I talked
about this last night. According to Anne, there were no children
at Auschwitz. At first I thought she was speaking metaphorically,
but then I realized she was being literal, as usual: there were no
children at Auschwitz. When Anne talks about this, tears roll
down her cheeks. In the face of such turmoil, I can't press to get
the story straight, and I'm not sure that I have it right now. As
obsessed as Anne is with certain details, she's vague about others,
such as the dates.

This is what I know: Victor has described to Anne the night
he arrived at Auschwitz, exhausted, starving, dirty, crammed into
a railroad car with strangers. He had been picked up on the street
(I can't name you the street, or even the city, and I begin to
wonder if Victor Marks is even his real name), with a canned
ham under his jacket and no proper identity card.

On the platform, Victor was quick to understand the selection process that was dividing the human cargo into two groups. Mothers attended to their terrified children, bent over them, smoothed and tidied their hair in the universal ritual of mothers and children at the end of a journey. No matter how able-bodied they were, how fit to work, these women were being sent, with their children, to join the old, the sick, the crippled. Victor instantly saw why this was happening—keeping the mothers with the children avoided upset, prevented the disruptive noise and alarm of children being separated from their mothers.

Victor was not the only one to figure this out; he watched young men and women handing their babies into the arms of grandparents. Moments later the family would be divided for-ever, women to the right, men to the left, children and crippled and elderly to the middle, to live, to die. Seeing the group to which all the children were being sent, having a sharp sense of what this meant, Victor ceased being a child at that moment.

He was large for his age, which was fourteen. He announced, boldly, that he was seventeen. He had no identification that would have proved otherwise. Perhaps this was the moment he became Victor Marks. I mean that in every sense. He survived the selection, and all that followed, and spent the rest of the War at Auschwitz, working for several months in the grueling construction of a synthetic rubber factory for I.G. Farben.

Victor met Anne's father, Henry, that first night. Henry may well have been in the same railroad car; he was certainly on the same train. They happened to stand next to each other during the selection. They passed through every stage of the process together. Their numbers, therefore, are consecutive. Victor and Henry were assigned to the same bunk. They hadn't yet spoken to each other, and had to locate together their common tongue, that Yiddish dialect, the scrap of language they would share for almost two years, as they shared a blanket. Henry, who was eighteen, looked young for his age. He was still baby-faced, still had the look of a Talmudic scholar about him. He was in shock, having seen his parents shot in the head in their own sitting room just days before, having seen his sister and her baby dispatched to the other side of the train platform just hours before. Victor appropriated him, Anne says, because he thought that having a buddy of the age he claimed would help him to pass. He nursed Henry through typhus and protected him from the vultures who would steal his ration.

It's a touching story. But Anne works too hard selling the perfection of her romantic alliance with Victor on the basis that Victor and Henry are linked, fated, re-created by the War as two peas from the same unthinkable pod. (As if the obviousness of that matching in the past should carry some inevitability about her connection with Victor in the present. I'll say it again: I don't see it.)

Henry Gordon radiates a sadness that Victor does not. Henry seems dried out and given up. Victor has a comparatively throbbing vitality of sorts, and a pretty hard shell. But Anne's virtual obsession with her father has never seemed to me to be based on the real Henry Gordon so much as on some fantasy of a man who never was. Or hasn't been in a long time. Since I've known Anne, when she talks about her father, it often sounds to me as though she's talking about a father she should have had, the Henry who would have been, had Anne's mother lived.

Have I told you how she died? It's almost like a joke, some cosmic practical joke on Henry. The Gordon family was living in Hastings-on-Hudson then. I've seen the house; Anne and I drove up there once. It's a pleasant, three-story frame house with a porch, pale blue, though Anne says it used to be white, in the sort of neighborhood that's perfect for trick or treat. You know: The houses are close together on narrow lots, there are swing sets in the backyards. Everybody barbecues; kids play ball in the streets.

Anne has lost touch with everyone she knew then and seemed puzzled at my suggestion that it was possible some of the people who lived there fifteen years ago might still live there. She didn't want to see inside the house, though I was hoping that we would. I offered to be the brave one to ring the bell, but she just shook her head no.

We sat in the car and looked at the house and the street for a while, and then Anne said she wanted to leave, so we did, though we had borrowed the gallery van solely for this trip. We spent the rest of the afternoon at the Cloisters, and the house was never mentioned.

You've seen the portrait I took of Anne that day: you know, the one where she's sitting in a car, leaning her head against the window, with her eyes closed? The house is just behind her, but you don't see it because the glass reflects the far side of her face instead.

One hot June afternoon, when Anne was in the final week of seventh grade at Fieldston, Anne's mother played tennis with three friends, went shopping, came home, put away her groceries, and decided to take a shower. In the shower, Elizabeth Byers Gordon stepped on a sliver of soap and lost her balance. Her head hit the grab bar and she was knocked unconscious. Her body blocked the drain. She never regained consciousness, and she drowned in the few inches of water that collected in the shower stall.

Anne came in from school and heard the water running, but thought nothing of it. It was not unusual for Anne's mother to shower after gardening or tennis. Anne helped herself to a snack and sat at the kitchen table doing homework.

A tapping sound in the front hallway caught Anne's attention, and she went to see what it was. Water was dripping from the ceiling. Anne ran upstairs, calling to her mother to turn off the shower because they had a leak. When she got to the bathroom door, water was beginning to flow out onto the bedroom carpet. It was too late. Anne will never know if her mother was still alive while she sat at the kitchen table eating cookies.

So that was that. It was the following year that Anne was sent off to the fancy Swiss boarding school and Henry fled to his lifeless little house in Jersey City.

So I don't see it, Anne's insistence that Henry and Victor have so many bonds. And Anne thinks that she herself is just like Henry. There's an intense link there, though not a classic Electra deal at all—Henry's not the least bit seductive, and Anne doesn't so much want Henry as she seems to want to *be* Henry. So how does that add up? Does that mean she thinks she's just like Victor?

And there's something in the air. I mean, it's their chemistry when they're together, Anne and Victor. When we're all together. It's creepy. I feel as though my presence completes a current that runs through everything, but I can't identify what that is. I feel as though *I'm* being used, as though I'm the mirror they need in order to watch themselves.

So I see I've begun to write something: I'm not sure what. It's not quite a journal. I'm using you, O Benedict Mine: you are my You. By the end of the month here, one way or another, I will either have written an accounting, of sorts, of these days in Geneva and what goes on here and what mental rummagings I've managed, or I will have chucked it completely in a fit of frustration. So maybe when you meet my flight on the first of August I will shyly offer you this dog-eared notebook that contains the secrets of my universe. Or maybe not. I'm not sure at this moment which would be preferable.

Noon. That's my cue. L.y. & l.y.

July 9

Well, Benedict,

A trout with its tail in its mouth. On a plate. Before me. It's called *truite au bleu,* and Victor insisted that I must have it, that it was my obligation as a visitor to Geneva to have it, and so I did, but disconcerting as that was—do you know they boil them alive?—it paled beside the disconcertingness of attempting to dine in public with Anne and Victor.

Since I got here, I keep having the feeling that I must have missed the first act. I still can't get used to Anne's transformation from my slobby, lovable roommate to this unknowable, chic, jaded woman: someone I would see in a restaurant and never know personally.

To get to dinner, Anne and I took a bus to the outskirts of Geneva, then walked for nearly a mile along a somewhat barren avenue where, believe me, nobody ordinarily walks. Anne had to walk in front of me because the traffic was so alarmingly close that walking together would have been dangerous. As it was, I thought that it was dangerous. We picked our way along the shoulder of this road that was like a suburban Riverside Drive. Cars would rush past us, and I would feel the force of air pushing me, pulling me. Anne's skirt would swirl up. She has great legs. Walking a few paces behind her afforded me the same view that strangers in passing cars were getting.

There was something oddly seductive about her; she has a new walk that somehow exaggerates her femaleness in an almost cartoonish way. Is this how a mistress walks? She has very high-heeled strappy sandals. (You'd call them "catch-me-fuck-me shoes.") She walks very fast. I felt as though, compared to her, I was a sexless companion, like a dog or an old nanny, lumbering along faithfully behind her, steady as she goes. And I was wearing the blue sundress you like, which you always point out looks so good with a bit of a tan. And let me tell you, I have quite a lot more tan than I meant to, because of yesterday's bizarre lake adventure.

Yesterday: Victor turned up unexpectedly, as Sundays are usually his family day when Anne does things like bleach her mustache and (very painfully) wax her thighs. Anne had, in fact, spoken of such activities, but was, luckily, languishing over a piece of toast instead of engaging in either pursuit when the downstairs buzzer sounded with Victor's specially coded three shorts and one long. (Mrs. Beethoven: "What, Ludwig, me inspire you? Ha ha ha haaa!")

Victor had been set free, he explained after an awfully long, silent greeting at the door, from which I kept my gaze tactfully averted while he and Anne did whatever it is that they do, with more passion than anyone else has ever experienced in the history of humankind. Annamarie had taken the children—let's not forget Lucien, Otto, and Minerva—to the beach. As everyone apparently knows, Victor does not like going to the beach, for reasons that will be revealed presently.

Anne, who can be maddeningly passive in her dealings with Victor (how can this be Anne, the least accommodating person I have ever known; just try to argue with her about the pronunciation of *forte* or *banal,* just try to get her to go in the main entrance of the Metropolitan instead of her beloved Eighty-first Street side entrance for the cognoscenti), surprised me when she began to pout about how *she* never gets to go to the beach, how she should have rung up Annamarie (she has dinner there from time to time and has baby-sat for them on three occasions) and finagled an invitation to join them if she had only known. (What beach, you might well ask. Some lakeside resort or other, with sandy beaches.)

I think she surprised Victor, too. He thought, perhaps, that he was calling her bluff when he said, "Oh, very well then, we go to the beach. Get your things. A towel. I cannot swim, though, because I have no swimming costume."

He sat at Anne's table with his hands placed palms up before him, as though he were old and weary and unable to do anything but acquiesce.

"We can buy you a suit at the chemist's on the corner—I've seen them there," Anne said. Victor looked helplessly at me. I didn't know what he wanted me to say.

"You two should go," I began.

"No!" They chorused together.

"I take so much of Anne's time from you, and you are her closest friend—it wouldn't be right to keep her for the whole Sunday," Victor said.

"There isn't much privacy at a beach anyway," Anne pointed out, as if this were a practical observation. (They weren't going to fuck anyway? Something about this remark highlighted the illicit point of this whole alliance. It felt loaded with some sort of beyond-obvious sexual je ne sais quoi I haven't grasped yet.)

So, Victor's swim togs were acquired, and we were all heading off in his white Citroën toward some beach. What if we were to run into Victor's family, I inquired mildly from the backseat. I never know if it's okay to bring them up or not.

"We go to France," Victor says over his shoulder as he drives too fast down an access ramp and onto a highway without pausing, which causes the BMW closing in behind us in the near lane to swerve around the Citroën with a blaring horn and an obscene gesture from the driver.

"Nazi!" hisses Victor, who speeds up.

Anne puts her hand on his arm and we drop back. "He had

Stuttgart plates," she explains to me, turning her head so she can see me. I feel as though I'm out with somebody's parents.

I didn't have my passport with me, but Victor assured me that no one would check at the border, and he was right; we were waved through, Victor's white Citroën looking like an ambulance racing toward the scene of an accident. I'm in another country, I thought. I'm in France.

The lake was near the border, and we were there in minutes. For someone who doesn't swim, Victor seemed surprisingly well-informed about the whereabouts of this beach, where the parking lot was located, where to change, where the cold-drinks stand was. Curious.

We changed in a wooden shack. Victor went in after we came out (I feeling particularly thigh-conscious in my old black bathing suit; Anne looking terrific in a black bikini I would never have known her to wear in her former life) and emerged wearing his new swim trunks, his office-y white, button-down shirt open. The swim trunks were an imitation Hawaiian print that was like canned laughter. He was wearing his dark socks and thick-soled leather shoes. His legs were somehow pathetic and birdlike. The rest of him seems more commanding and intense. I felt embarrassed for him when I glanced at his hairless shins.

We aligned ourselves on the sand with Anne between us. Victor took off his shoes and socks, and his shirt, which he folded into a fussy square for a pillow. Victor and Anne lay facedown on their towels, with fingers linked. They both faced away from me. I think their eyes were closed. I had the feeling that all the other people there knew what they wanted to do. I felt alone. I missed you, I wanted to have someone with me, too, so I wouldn't be the third wheel, and I hadn't brought a book. Damn. I sat up on my towel.

Nobody was swimming. It wasn't very hot. Only a few other people were around; no children at all. A woman several yards from us was sunbathing with the top of her suit pulled down to her waist. The woman sat very upright, partially facing in our direction in order to sun herself, with her legs straight out in front of her. I imagined her turning, like a plant, as the sun moved in the sky; isn't that called tropism? (You would say my obsessive need to know just the right word is *de trop*-ism.) She was not a bad-looking woman, maybe midforties, and in clothes she might have been rather chic. The posture emphasized her potbelly, and her nipples looked like a second pair of eyes staring at me. I regretted the decision to leave my camera in the flat. I felt her glaring at me and realized I had been staring. I was glad I had left my camera in the flat. There were no reflections here; even the lake surface was scumbled by a constant wind. I turned my head away.

I began to dig in the dry sand with one hand. I scrabbled out a rather large ditch that described the arc my arm could swing through freely without my changing position. I felt something under my fingers. It was a white plastic tampon applicator.

"A beach whistle," I observed to Anne, who had turned her head my way. She wrinkled her nose in distaste. I buried it near my feet, where I wouldn't disturb it again. Victor, who every now and then says something unexpectedly pleasant or ordinary (perhaps these remarks are indicative of the way he must behave in his other life), had announced in the parking lot, the way he might alert his children to an interesting aspect of their environment, that the fine, white sand here is renewed periodically with truckloads from the south coast of France.

I wondered now if they strained it for impurities. Either these beachgoers were unusually tidy or the French comb this beach regularly, because there was very little interesting detritus. I would have expected to find Gauloise butts galore. I felt the edge of a shell as I was reinserting the tampon applicator in the sand. I examined the shell. It was nearly flat, somewhat oval, a thin, yellow bit of translucency. It reminded me of the sort I used to find on the beach that summer I was six, the first summer after my brother died, when I spent two months with my mother and grandmother in Cornwall; it's a kind of shell I hadn't seen since.

"Toenail, anyone?" I said, offering my find to Anne.

"Shut *up,* will you?" she said to me with surprising intensity. Was this a No Talking beach? I had no idea what the problem was.

"Yes, please, I would like a toenail," came Victor's voice. I had thought he was asleep. His head was still turned away. "Hello. I ordered the toenail. Make that ten. Could you deliver them right away?" This wasn't Victor's style, that I knew of. Maybe he kidded around much more with Anne when I wasn't there. I was momentarily confused.

"Here's one," I said, holding the shell out to him over Anne's head. She had lain back down on her towel and was squeezing her eyes tight shut. Nobody moved. My arm was still extended over Anne. Her back heaved, and I realized she was suppressing sobs. Victor's head was still turned away. His voice was weirdly disembodied.

"Don't you have them ready for me?" he said languidly. I still didn't get it.

He rolled over and sat up.

"Anne is now upset with both of us," he announced. "She is upset with you for bringing up a bad subject. You did not know. She is upset with me for playing my little game with you. Isn't that right?"

Victor patted the top of Anne's head and stroked her shoulders. Something about her tears obviously pleased him. He was now sitting up in the same doll-like position as the topless woman on my right. I saw his feet.

Benedict, I know human flesh cannot melt, but what I saw looked like melted stubs. Victor has no toes. They froze off at Auschwitz. The Allied doctors wanted to amputate his feet, but he wouldn't let them. (Anne told me this when Victor went to get us cold drinks a little while later.)

The Pobble grinned at me. He saw me seeing his feet. I did not like his delight in my discomfort, in Anne's anguish.

"I'm sorry," I said, meeting his gaze.

"Of course you are," he said, rather nastily, I thought.

"Of course you wouldn't like to swim," sobbed Anne. "I didn't think."

"Of course you didn't, my pet," said Victor, smiling a cold smile.

We had been at the lake for about an hour, and we stayed there, more or less in silence, for another hour. It felt necessary to sit there so that it wouldn't have been the upsetting discussion that made us leave, even though I doubt that I was the only one who felt like bolting for the Citroën. While Victor fetched Perriers with straws, and the Belgian mocha biscuits that he considers superior to all other forms of cookie life, Anne told me the story of Victor's toes, gazing out at the lake the whole time. I found myself imagining their sex life being somehow profoundly affected by this absence. What does he have her do to make up for it? As Victor struggled across the sand carrying the mineral water and the biscuits, I had to avoid studying his gait. He had put on his shoes and socks for the short walk. I wondered if his shoes had special toe-weights that helped him walk. The sight of his fingers gripping the necks of the Perrier bottles was mildly surprising. I wondered if his toes had looked like his fingers. I curled and uncurled my own toes uncontrollably.

The drive back to Geneva was mostly silent. We all three of us had terrible sunburns.

"*Merde,*" muttered Anne when she was through studying herself in Victor's rearview mirror. (I was relieved when she was finished, as I thought he might want to have the use of it on the highway.) "In the office tomorrow, how do we explain matching sunburns?"

"I went to the beach with my family, and you went to a

different beach with your visiting friend," Victor answered. "Thousands of people went to the beach today. Why worry about the coincidence of it?"

What a shit, I thought. A charming shit. With a sunburn. And no toes.

I'm sorry, Benedict, how did we get here? Right: Anne and I were walking along the side of the road on our way to the trout restaurant, she with her skirt flying and her sexy legs, I with my sunburn and in the blue dress you like. Anne had just reported over her shoulder that we were nearly there when a car skidded onto the gravel in front of us, giving me a serious scare. It was Victor's white Citroën.

"Would you like a ride?"

Anne played it as if he were a stranger. "No, thanks anyway. *Merci, non.*"

Victor waggled his eyebrows at me. I shrugged.

"Very well, ladies. Ciao." He drove off. I could see his taillight flash about a quarter mile up the road, and then the Citroën turned right and was lost from sight.

"It's better to arrive separately, in case anyone's there," she said over her shoulder.

"Anyone?"

"Any friend of Annamarie's. Any friend of the family."

"You're a friend of the family."

"Don't be dense," she said reprovingly. "It would be a disaster." She lingered over the word *disaster* the way some people savor the words *foie gras*.

Although the Citroën had been in the parking lot for ten minutes by the time we approached the maître d's pulpit, Victor was nowhere in evidence.

"We have a reservation for three?" Anne said in French. "The name is Goldfarb."

We were shown to a table in an elegant garden courtyard. It was early by Swiss standards, and we were the first customers of the evening. There were only five or six tables, all covered to the ground with snowy tablecloths, and very widely spaced across the white gravel courtyard. The tables were all big enough to seat eight or ten people. Ours had three place settings at noon, four, and eight.

Anne and I picked up two wineglasses and moved together in the direction of the third. We sat down, leaving a place for Victor between us. This might seem like a small thing, but moments like that are what our friendship thrives on, has thriven on, that in-synch, "two thoughts with but a single mind" kind of instant: commonplace when we were roommates in New York, but so rare since I've been here that I made a mental note of it.

A flurry of Bemelmans waiters rushed to rearrange the place settings. (What we had done was very naughty.) There was a stream running by, only a few feet from us, and the noise of it meant that we had to raise our voices slightly to converse, even after our rearrangement.

"So typical," said Anne. "So Swiss to seat us that way—so we use the table completely—with no thought to conversational distances."

"Or something. Maybe they don't like the idea of private conversations," I suggested. "And who is Goldfarb?"

"I thought you knew."

"Do I?" Did I?

"It was my father's father's name. Daddy changed it."

"Why?" I never knew this before.

"Anti-Semitism, I suppose."

I thought of an imperious dowager of Scottish ancestry (and proud of it) called Peggy Gordon. I once heard her say to Gay that she thought half the Gordons in New York were Jews who had changed their names from Goldfarb, Goldstein, and so on. "Why can't they just change it to Gold?" she had asked plaintively. "It's shorter and neater, but you can still tell. I would rather expect them to like a nice glittering name like Gold."

Gay had laughed and offered her more to drink. I thought, from my vantage point in Gay's bedroom, where I was sorting out all her jewelry on her bedspread—I must have been about ten—that her laugh was not so much with Peggy as at her. There was also my own parentage to consider. I was not only Gay Gibson's granddaughter, I was Simon Rose's daughter. I wonder now whether Peggy Gordon ever considered for one second that her words could hurt me, could hurt my feelings. Doubtful. It probably didn't occur to her that I thought of myself as Jewish. She always fussed over me because I looked so much like a Gibson. I had "the Gibson upper lip."

Gay was fond of her because they went back a long way and had traveled to Reno together for their first divorces. By the time I was six I knew that the Truckee River ran through Reno, where you went for a divorce. You stood on a bridge and threw your now meaningless wedding ring into that river.

Once, when I was little, the people next door, the Antlers, had a terrible argument, and Mrs. Antler ran out the front door and threw her wedding ring into the bushes in front of their house. I saw her do it. That night I watched from my bedroom window as Mr. and Mrs. Antler together hunted through those bushes, on their knees, with flashlights, for hours.

So Benedict, where I come from there were a lot of wedding rings tossed around. Me, when I have a wedding ring, I don't intend to take it off. Ever. Just so you know.

Victor sidled into the courtyard just when the waiter was presenting us with menus as big as the bonnet of a small car. Victor joined us, and the waiter nearly knocked off Victor's reading glasses as he flourished another menu under his nose. We were each hidden from sight behind this menu flotilla. Everything about this place was slightly oversized. Perhaps that signifies luxury. I imagine that we looked, from above, like three giant moths poised for flight.

★   ★   ★

The voice of Victor insisted that I order the *truite au bleu,* the specialty of the place. Perversely, he spoke English with the waiter, perhaps to deprive the waiter of the home advantage of his native tongue. He ordered gray sole for Anne, who contributed no audible thoughts of her own about what she would like to eat.

"I will take the steak," Victor said to the waiter—rather imperiously, I thought. Why did it bother me so? *I will take the steak.* I have no toes, so I will not merely have, as others do, but I will take. I survived Auschwitz, so I can cheat on my wife and I will take the steak.

The waiter plucked away the menus. I cannot begin to enumerate all the ways that I do not like this man. I do not like what Anne has become, is becoming, will become. A spinster with a special feeling for a certain flower stall. A childless woman alone on holidays. A woman with a gray soul.

Why did I expect that Anne would pay for this meal? In fact, she did end up picking up the check, but not because Victor managed the simple maneuver of looking the other way. No, by the time the check came it was much more complicated than that.

Our starters had been served, consumed, and cleared (duck-liver pâté and vegetable terrine, quite good, actually, though Victor had been unpleasant with the waiter's suggestion that he might like soup—thoughtless of the waiter not to realize that, having lived on ghastly soup in a concentration camp, Victor is greatly pained when soup possibilities arise in his present life) when another group was seated across from us.

At this point Anne was seated between Victor and me; when Victor was shown to our table, Anne had moved over nearer to me, either despite or in response to Victor's murmured, "Ah, I shall be a thorn between two roses." So we had got ourselves into the same configuration as at the beach. I thought I saw Victor looking uncomfortable, but I didn't think it was in response to anything said (and assumed that a bulletin concerning his fascinatingly sensitive digestive system was soon forthcoming), as our conversation at that juncture was pointless and desultory, mostly about the food. The next time I turned my head, Victor had disappeared.

He had simply vanished. Anne looked quite disturbed.

"What happened to Victor?" I felt, for a brief moment, on the edge of hysteria, like Ingrid Bergman in *Gaslight*. I also had an absurd sense that Anne was about to launch into a complete summary of What Happened to Victor, up to and including the Allied doctors' wanting to amputate those hideous feet. Was Victor a demon? A golem? I wished I had taken his picture.

"Victor is right here—he's under the table," Anne murmured, looking straight ahead, her lips barely moving. Her tension was almost comical. I half expected her to say, "Just act natural."

"May I ask why?"

"A woman who plays tennis with Annamarie is at that table."

"Ah. An F of the F."

"Don't—this is serious," Anne ground out at me through clenched teeth. There was a muffled gasp from under our table. In an attempt to kick me, she had kicked Victor.

Our main courses arrived, borne out to the courtyard by three waiters in a procession. Each carried a tray on which was a plate under a silver dome. The domed plates were placed before us. Victor's was set down at his place. The three waiters looked confused.

"Monsieur?" one murmured.

"Monsieur had to leave," Anne replied, in English, so indistinctly that the waiter almost couldn't hear her over the rushing of the stream. He cupped his hand behind one ear and bent down over her shoulder.

"Is everything all right, mademoiselle?" he asked, also switching to English.

"Oui," she answered, cutting off any further discussion.

"You can leave the steak," I said, figuring that Victor might still want to eat it, somehow. Also, we were going to have to pay for it. Hell, I would take it home and eat it.

The waiters glumly went through their ritual of simultaneous revelation, whisking all three silver domes high into the air after a wordless count to three. Victor's absence had spoiled it for them.

Now what?

Anne and I ate dinner in total silence. One of her hands was in her lap all through the meal; I realized that she was stroking Victor's head, or something.

"Look, does this happen a lot?"

She shook her head, giving me reason to believe that it did and that discussion about it was unwelcome at this time. I didn't know whether to hurry or linger over the food. How were we going to get Victor out of there unseen? I poked at my trout, which stared me down. I ate my potatoes and my courgette matchsticks done up in a bundle and tied with a string of chive.

My few days in Geneva with Anne had seemed beyond ordinary experience from the start, but this evening was now taking on aspects of a Delvaux. The waiters, the artificial outdoor setting, the imitation of gracious service, the contrived arrangements of food, the deception of Anne's true love lurking under the tablecloth—nothing seemed real. The food had no taste in my mouth. The wine, a Gewürz, tasted like glass.

Across from us, the waiter was erecting menus in front of the people at the table with Annamarie's tennis friend, and when he had worked his way around, their view in our direction was completely obscured. Victor must have been on the lookout for this opportunity; he flung the tablecloth up and bolted straight out like a sprinter crouched at the starting block when the gun goes off.

Anne and I sat very still, as if we had agreed in advance to ignore this moment. Without turning my head I saw the edge of

Victor's jacket go by, and I could hear for an instant the crunching of Victor's shoes on gravel; perhaps I only thought I could hear the Citroën engine turn over. The escape from Stalag 17 was a complete success.

The people at the next table ordered fussily and precisely, with much mutual consulting, and their menus were folded away one by one until the waiter bustled off with news of their choices for the kitchen.

I asked our waiter for Victor's untouched steak to be wrapped so we could take it home. The waiter sneered and ordered a busboy to do it. Anne declined salad, cheese, a sweet, and coffee, and I didn't argue, although I would have liked coffee. The waiter shrugged and deposited the already totaled check on our table, showing that he had expected as much.

Anne paid. I had credit cards and cash, which I offered, but she didn't want to talk about it. The busboy returned with the steak wrapped in foil, which had been fashioned sarcastically into the shape of a swan, with the neck forming a sort of handle.

We got up to leave. I said, "What about—" and Anne shushed me so furiously that I felt slapped, humiliated. We left the courtyard. As we turned out of the restaurant entrance, and Anne stalked past the empty spot where the Citroën had been parked, I realized we were taking the bus back. Damn. I had been looking forward to the comfort of a car ride after dinner.

We filed along in uncompanionable silence, which was disturbed now and again by the rush of passing cars. It was even weirder to be traipsing along this road at night in near darkness. Cars sometimes slowed in an alarming way. I felt eyes appraising us. I was following Anne, as before, and could not decipher those shoulders, that stride. I felt like a child, with my party-favor swan.

I thought, too, of Victor, driving alone in his Citroën. I try to feel something like sympathy for him, but I don't. I try to see him through Anne's eyes—I want to, but I can't.

The bus stop was lit by a solitary streetlamp. It felt futile to wait there, long after any bus might come along, but Anne assured me that they ran hourly.

"What do you suppose Victor is going to do about dinner?" I finally asked, wanting to ask something, not that Victor's alimentary requirements were high on my list of concerns.

"That's his Axminster, don't you think?"

"Do you think the woman recognized you?"

"I don't see how she could have, as she's never seen me."

"Where do you suppose Annamarie thinks Victor is tonight?"

"I haven't the foggiest. I never think about that."

"Don't you think you ought to, from time to time?"

There was the longest, most uncomfortable silence. Like a mirage, our bus came into view.

Oh, Benedict.

Is this what love is, what love makes people do? On the one hand: would you hide under a table for me? On the other hand: why the hell would you need to? Maybe I'm just smug because I've got you, and, compared to this, ours is a simple life. Sometimes, for admittedly brief interludes, I persuade myself that it's all romantic, and European, and I'm a gauche American with naive ideas about how the world is.

But no. This is awful. I could leave before my stay is up, but Anne wants me here; she's made so many cryptic remarks about how important this visit is to her. Maybe I'm supposed to bear witness to this glorious erotic connection. Maybe I'm supposed to pass judgment. (Ignatz Mouse *wanted* to go to jail, remember. Am I here to see the flung brick and play Offissa Pup?)

And then there's you, whom I miss very much. How is life, I wonder at every other moment, at the most uncompetitive tennis camp in New England? (Sorry, I seem to be repeating myself again. Frog goes into a bank. Gay always said, "Once, a wit; twice, a half-wit.")

If you think I sound confused about Anne and Victor, you're right. I don't know which I fear more: feeling I might have to do something or feeling I can't do anything. And which would be worse? Do I just want to punish Victor? Could the unfathomable Annamarie possibly be grateful for a note, a telephone call, or would that be a betrayal of Anne, despite its being for the best? And would it be for the best?

I've got to go, but one more thing. I've been thinking about the dwarf. He was *so* angry. "Fuck you, lady," wasn't all he said. I had never heard the word *cunt* before. ("What a *nice* man," Gay had said, charmingly, while we had our coffee milk shakes.) But his fury was a reasonable response, I suppose, to being rescued when you don't need to be rescued at all. But maybe he was in danger. I've never thought of that possibility until right now. Maybe she did the right thing. What do you think?

I love you for sentimental reasons—

July 13

I haven't done a lick of work in days. I think about taking
pictures all the time. Isn't *taking pictures* an odd phrase? Such a
good one. I take my pictures as much as I make them. I seize
them. One never talks about taking a painting. I suppose this is
the endlessly rehashed argument about the relationship of photography to art, one that better minds than mine have attempted
to sort out. Sometimes I wish I could draw as well as I see, I
mean really see. In any event, I haven't been able to see at all.

I mean, there's something wrong with my Leica. My mirror
mechanism is jammed. It's supposed to flop up and down and
it's stuck in the up position, blocking light from the viewfinder.
Probably a piece of dirt in a strategic location. Anyway, I've
taken the camera to a place that seemed like the Mayo Clinic of
the camera world. That was yesterday's noontime diversion.

But I haven't been able to see in other ways as well. The
restaurant lunacy of a few days ago upset me in ways I don't
think I realized at the time. The sheer tension of it, the craziness
of it, is something that Anne seems to thrive on; the entire
romance, I think, gets its energy from moments like that. Where
would they be without the ducking and the separate elevator
rides and the skulking into restaurants where F of the F's might
be dining? And I hate my dawning sense that the excitement
provided by the chanciness of daily living is absolutely essential
for Victor, but in an inverted way. I mean to say: there's something sadistic there, some desire to see Anne squirm.

And I have begun to notice something else, or the absence of something else: Anne *really* doesn't seem to have any friends here. She doesn't want to get too close to the people at UGP because that would make for complications if they found out about Victor—but surely this is a pretty shopworn secret? People in offices invariably know about these things—and she doesn't have an opportunity to meet people anywhere else. Her life revolves completely around the office and Victor, and her evenings are spent all alone by the telephone.

And then there are those nights when Victor has gone out on the town with his wife, while Anne baby-sat the children. She has confessed to me that the moment Lucien, Otto, and Minerva were all tucked in, the first time, she prowled around and snooped maniacally. Apparently, Annamarie is a brilliant cook, plays the piano, and spoons culture into the children in large doses. Otto takes sackbut lessons. That first night, Victor tried to pay Anne, but she wouldn't take his money. Annamarie insisted, though, and finally stuffed the bills into Anne's jacket pocket.

So Anne's life revolves entirely around the people at UGP. There's a woman who works there called, fabulously, Sonya Trout, and Anne can be quite funny, in the old, familiar, and slightly wicked way, when she talks about her. Miss Trout is veddy, veddy British and sounds as though she could be played by Maggie Smith. She's a secretarial wonder, which is why Victor tolerates her. She's compulsive and wields a sharp Tipp-Ex brush, whiting-out offending errors wherever she goes. She has the annoying habit of applying it with extra care to Anne's correspondence.

Apparently, Miss Trout is the office snoop, and she has taken a blue-ribbon scunner to Anne, because our Miss Trout has carried a spinsterish smoldering torch for Victor over the years, and she knows perfectly well what goes on with those two at the luncheon hour. Apparently, I'm to blame, in part, because of an innocent mistake I made a couple of months ago, as follows:

When Anne left New York—did I ever tell you that she drew for me an elaborate and hilarious stock certificate that represented a 50% share in our household feline? Poor little Bask. Unlike his littermate, he was aptly named, the way he sits around. Doze was the manic one. He used to tear up and down the apartment in a frenzy for no apparent reason. Once I found him sitting on top of the Con Edison meter, which you may recall is mounted way up in the corner, near the ceiling, above the refrigerator. He was actually Anne's, and Bask was actually mine, but when Doze died, we agreed in a retroactive sort of unspoken contract that both kittens had belonged to both of us all along. I've never told you about what happened.

What a horrible day. It was about a year ago. It was a Friday, late afternoon, and Anne had gone directly from work to visit her father in New Jersey for the night. Having been out and about since the morning, I came into the apartment with the charming, unreliable, possibly sociopathic Jack Richardson—*that* was already quite a mess, but I must say he was sweet to me on this particular occasion, and I was glad of his company—and there was the window screen hanging crazily in the kitchen window, there was a crying Bask on the sill, there was Doze, nowhere, gone, gone, gone.

He must have hurled himself at the window screen, which was one of those cheap inserts you buy at a hardware store; maybe there had been a bird on the ledge. Could a cat intentionally commit suicide? When the screen gave way, he had fallen the three stories, had landed at the bottom of the air shaft, and had lain there for hours, mewing, his back broken. The odd, reclusive character who lives in the basement apartment in my building, whom Anne and I always called the Woman of a Certain Age, heard the crying and took him to a vet on Twelfth

Street, who at first refused to treat an anonymous cat with a broken back. The Woman of a Certain Age, whose name is actually Florence Tirone, didn't have any money, but in explaining all this, she described how, in desperation, she was able to barter two tickets to Radio City Music Hall in exchange for having Doze put to sleep. (It turns out she used to be a Rockette.)

It was the best she could do, not knowing who owned the cat, having no idea from which apartment window this pathetic scrap of bloody orange fur had plummeted. I know she meant to save him from his misery, and it was a brave and compassionate thing she did, getting him into a cardboard box and carrying him four blocks to the vet. But I have always wondered if Doze could have been mended, had I been there. (While Doze lay dying in the rubbish, what was I doing? Taking pictures in Tompkins Square. Buying film on Fourteenth Street. Throwing myself at an irresistible thirty-five-year-old cad. Eating a languorous lunch at Buffalo Roadhouse. Wasting time looking at Irish pottery on Bleecker Street.) If Florence Tirone had offered six tickets instead of two. If I had agreed with Anne about the other apartment we almost rented first on Gay Street, which was on the ground floor. Something.

I cried for hours that night. Jack tried to cheer me up by making waffles. I ate my waffle with tears dripping into the puddle of syrup. The waffles were overpowered by cardamom (Jack admitted to me that the top had fallen off the spice jar), a flavor I have despised ever since.

Where was I? Right: when Anne left New York. She gave me nine airmail envelopes, stamped and addressed to a "Mlle. S. Trout" at a Geneva address. The return address, I later realized, was fictitious: a Greek restaurant on Waverly Place. I was instructed to mail these from time to time over the following months, until they were gone. She offered no explanation, other than to say that it was a favor for a friend; the implication at the time was that it vaguely had something to do with somebody's child's interest in international postmarks, a stamp collection.

Over the next three months I did this, contributing my own variation on the theme by making a point of mailing them from diverse New York locations. One was even postmarked Staten Island—a commemoration of my last, sorrowful encounter with Jack Richardson. We rode the ferry back and forth, twice, while agreeing that it was Over. It had been too hot not to cool down. It had been over since the moment it began, but I'm a slow learner. When I got down to the final envelope, which I mailed from the mailbox on the corner of Eighth Street and Second Avenue, so it would have a different zip code from the one I had mailed at Waverly Place and Christopher Street, without giving it too much thought, I jotted on the back, "Last one!"

Well. The letters were a beard. Anne had been writing to Victor, in the months between their New York encounter and her move to Geneva, using the ever-helpful Miss Trout as a letter drop. The envelopes left with me had been designed to throw Miss Trout off the trail, as it would have been too obvious that Anne was Victor's New York correspondent if the flow of letters stopped the moment she arrived in Geneva. Pretty clever, those two. *Your* faithful correspondent, on the other hand, can be pretty naive, sometimes. Victor was not amused at what I had written on that final letter. Hardly the thing for the envelope containing a Dear John letter, which I suppose is what he would have indicated to Miss Trout. (And probably Victor had been all set to reap the secretarial benefits of her sympathy. Though whether La Trout noticed or commented on the words on the envelope isn't clear. Is anything clear?)

I have asked Anne if she has gotten to know other people at UGP, Miss Trout aside. Her reply, and I quote: "That's one of the reasons I came here: I like living where I don't know anybody."

★   ★   ★

A mysterious episode: This morning, around ten, the telephone rang. Anne was at work, and I was just back from a walk to the laundry place and the little grocery shop where I buy milk, the *International Herald Tribune,* delicious little crunchy breakfast rolls, herring, the world's most expensive Tampax, etc. I thought it would be Anne or a wrong number, but it was Victor. I thought he somehow thought Anne was still at home, but I was wrong, he wanted to speak to me. Would I be free in twenty minutes? Feeling confused and somehow disloyal to Anne, I said I would be. He said he was on his way.

I considered telephoning Anne at her office and mentioning that Victor was coming to see me, but I knew that it would be troublemaking. Maybe Victor wanted to talk to me about Anne, about their relationship. Why else would he want to see me? I gathered that Anne didn't know about the visit, but I had no way of knowing. God, these people make everything complicated. I tidied up the flat, and myself. I got nervous. I considered leaving the flat. Let Victor find it empty, let him be inconvenienced. Then I began to feel jumpy. Victor must have a key. Was he going to buzz me from the lobby, or would he let himself into the apartment? I locked the bathroom door when I went to pee, in case he showed up at that moment.

He must have used a key downstairs, but he did knock quietly on the door when he arrived, exactly fifteen minutes late. I backed away from him before there was any chance of a handshake or something worse.

"Am I interrupting you? I am sorry to keep you from your work," he said in a tone conveying doubt that I could possibly have work of any kind. He was wearing a seersucker suit, which made me think of the moment in *Sophie's Choice* when Sophie calls Stingo's suit a cocksucker. Victor's English is better than that, though almost too precise and very accented. (According to Anne, he doesn't think he has an accent at all and was irritated when she once referred to it.) But everything Victor says seems so weighted, so heavy, like certain kinds of terrible pastry.

He pulled out one of the chairs from the table and turned it so that it faced the bed. It looked like a practiced gesture. Next, he took off his jacket and draped it over the back of the chair. I stood there, meaning to make an insincere offer of coffee or tea, but found that I was able to make only a slight squeak as Victor slid the knot down his necktie and took that off, too, laying it carefully over a shoulder of his jacket.

It suddenly struck me that I was watching a routine, that this was how Victor undresses with Anne when they come here at lunchtime. I was in an absolute panic: I had no idea what to think. He unbuttoned the cuffs of his white shirt, then began to undo the front buttons, starting at the top, silent all the while. He worked his way down the placket, as deliberate and precise as if he were alone. I could only watch—and wish that his shirt had more buttons. When his shirt was fully unbuttoned, he took it off.

He turned toward me. We stood there then, facing each other. Victor had on a ribbed undershirt, which was stained by a faint intarsia of sweat. The sight of it tucked into his suit trousers made him look unexpectedly like an old man. There were wisps of gray hairs on his speckled shoulders. And of course, on his left forearm, there was the obscene embroidery of his number.

I imagined him as a brave, cocky, scared boy, standing not in an undershirt and suit pants and shiny black wing tips but naked, in a room with many other men, Anne's father among them, each waiting for his turn to be numbered. Now I was looking at the same skin.

He held out the shirt to me in a gesture I didn't understand. I stood facing him, my back to the doorless, ridiculous miniature kitchen. I took an involuntary step backward. Victor smiled. Our eyes were locked in a mutual gaze of enormous incomprehensi-

ble significance. Maybe he understood what was going on, I sure
didn't. What *were* we doing here? Behind Victor the sun was
splashing on the shuttered windows across the courtyard. Were
other people sleeping? Already at work? I felt as though Victor
and I were the only two living, breathing souls in the building. I
wondered if anyone would hear me if I screamed. I wondered
how loud I could scream. All of this took place in less time than
it has taken to tell it.

He held out the shirt again. I put out my hand as much to
ward him off as to take the shirt.

"Do you know how to sew?" he asked.

After a moment's pause, I began to blither. "Not really. I've
never been very good at sewing. Or very interested in it, either."
I was unfreezing, picking up momentum. "I've always been a
failure at things involving thread and string. I hated macramé at
camp. I was terrible at cat's cradle. I couldn't braid those lanyard
things to save myself. I would make a terrible sailor."

Victor eyed me with the unblinking scrutiny of a lizard. He
couldn't have understood half of what I was talking about. "I
have lost a button," he said.

So, Benedict. I got out Anne's sewing box—a round Mexican
tin box I gave her last year for Valentine's Day with heart-shaped
cookies inside—and handed him a spool of white thread and a
needle and, taking a leaf from his book, said nothing. Consequently, I had the slight satisfaction of watching him sew on his
own damned button. He sat in a chair, turned now to catch the
light from the window, and he quietly bit the thread and tied the
knot, and in the most civilized, Gandhi-like way, he humbly
sewed the button back onto the shirt.

It was one of the smaller collar buttons. Was this really why
he had come? Maybe it had dropped off when he was removing
his necktie, and he had caught it in his hand. Maybe he pulled it
off to save face when he saw the look on mine. I do not know.

Victor never did explain why he had shown up. Surely he

didn't expect me to think it was to see if I could sew his button. I forgot to offer him anything to eat or drink. We never spoke of Anne. When he was finished with his task, he bit the end of the thread, handed me the needle with a wisp of thread trailing from it, put his clothes back on, and left.

I looked at the clock and realized that it was half-past eleven. I wondered if Victor would go all the way back across town to the office to meet Anne, or if he had other things to do, or if perhaps he wasn't meeting Anne in the flat today. I was in a sudden panic to get out of there.

The air was surprisingly hotter than it had been until now, and still. The sky was a washed-out blue. People on the street looked tired. I bought a newspaper at one of those curious newsstands whereon the newspapers just sit, unguarded, and people pay for them on the honor system. In New York, a newsstand like that would be picked clean in ten minutes, don't you think? I aimed for one of my most recent discoveries in sidewalk cafés. The cafés in the Vieille Ville each have a distinct personality, though I can't say I could characterize them, exactly. This one is situated alongside a park with big shady trees, and the air seems to move and the waiters don't mind when people don't.

Victor was there. He was sipping an espresso and staring at women who passed by. He was frankly eyeing them, even nannies pushing prams. There was something faintly ridiculous about the sight of him. I stopped to lurk in the aisle of a fruit stall, not wanting him to see me but somehow finding that I wanted to watch him, see what he was up to. The air was fragrant with ripe fruit. Tiny little wasps hovered, drunk on it. My hands felt empty: camera-less.

Victor signaled the waiter with a writing gesture in the air. He paid, stood up very suddenly, drained his little cup as he stood there by the table, then strode off in the direction of Anne's flat —passing close by the fruit stall—as if on his way to an urgent appointment. Which I guess he was. For some perverse reason, I

sat down at his table. The seat was warm from him. Or from
the sun. I drank two double espressos—espressi?—and had an
overpriced sandwich and moved my chair to keep up with the
sun, and sat with my eyes closed for a dozey twenty minutes and
intermittently wrote you all this. Now it's close to two and I'm
suddenly exhausted. I think I'll go back to the flat and take a real
nap. Maybe, now that I think about it, I will nap on the floor.

I must try and have a real conversation with Anne this evening. We're supposed to go hear jazz. (I begin to think Victor
knows only waltz music.) I want to write you a real letter in an
envelope that goes in the mail. I'm all at sea; can this be love?

Now it's later, and I'm waiting for Anne to finish organizing
her face so we can go to dinner—this evening, I am instructed
by the absent Victor, who has conveyed his suggestion through
Anne, I must eat *filet de perche,* another fishy specialty of the city,
before we go to the jazz place.

On the walk back to the apartment this afternoon—I did
actually nap—I found a present for you: three scruffy old issues
of *Derrière le Miroir,* which have languished and got sun bleached
in the window of a secondhand bookshop that I pass each day.

I woke up from my nap and realized I had dreamed about the
summer in Cornwall with Gay and my mother, where Gay insisted that we go, after Adam died and then my father left us. It's
the only time we were ever together, just the three of us, for any
extended period of time, and I loved the connected way it felt,
the way I could feel people smile at us when we came into the
hotel dining room: three generations of Gibson women.

I dreamed about the box-hedge maze in the hotel garden,
which in actuality I had adored. I was lost inside it, unable to
find my way out, and as I ran down one blind alley after another,
the hedge seemed to close in on me, each space I tried seemed
to grow narrower, seemed to come to a hopeless point. I woke
up in total despair. It's been hard to shake the mood, it seemed

so real, and I felt so unalterably alone. Well, I have to keep reminding myself that I once was lost, but now I'm found.

I need to talk to you. I wish there were a telephone for less than emergencies at Highland Lake. Don't any of those rich kids have cellular phones? Don't they have to stay in touch with their therapists? Anne is waiting for me by the door, jingling her keys and humming the signature tune from *Peter and the Wolf.* We who are about to dine salute you—

July 17

Oh, Dear, Benedict,

Laps of luxury, lapse of judgment, laps in a Swiss swimming pool, thirty-six of them to a mile. (I worked it out from the meter measurements painted on the side of the pool; I needed to know because I can't think in meters.) I've become obsessed with swimming laps. I have my own lane and no one is going to cross my path, and I can just *go,* with none of the usual looking out for the other guy.

Swimming, my mind races. I think all sorts of chlorinated thoughts and wonder if it would be possible to achieve with a camera the effect of looking up through water to the surface. I don't mean that literally; I know that with the right equipment it is entirely possible to make underwater pictures. What I mean is that I want to figure out how to make pictures that have that sense of looking from the other side, from the other world. How do I generate that removed but not distant sense of being on the other side of the picture? Behind the mirror? How do I bring objects closer than they appear?

I do the breaststroke and pass between the two worlds in synchrony with my breathing, and I think about Swiss nose clips on the bottom of the pool, and Swiss Band-Aids trapped in the filter trough at one end, and when I stop to wipe my fogged-over goggles, I hear a woman calling her child in a sharp Swiss way that I shut out by going under, pushing off from the side with my hands straight out in front and gliding away, coming up through that mirrory surface and beginning my breaststroke again.

I've discovered training paddles here, although they're an American product. Yesterday, when I first glimpsed them, I thought I was seeing a man wearing Japanese sandals on his hands. You strap them on to your palms and it looks as though you're holding giant blue plastic playing cards. When I put them on—I bought a pair this morning from the crosspatch woman who takes my three francs admission each day I come to the public pool—I wanted to wave my arms in big, exaggerated motions. I felt as though I could use them to signal a plane coming in for a landing. Swimming with them is wonderful; they're fins for your hands and you can grab the water and push yourself along with a smug sense of efficiency.

Anne took me here a few days ago, and I've been taking myself here every day since. It's an easy tram ride or an energetic walk from the Vieille Ville down to the lake and on a bit, and I can get a sandwich lunch here, and I can take a shower, which is necessary because of the chlorine in the pool, and also a welcome opportunity because Anne has no shower, only a tublet with one of those telephone handheld showerheads, and she's only got about five gallons of hot water at a time anyway. I'm beginning to think the Swiss are not as clean as they look.

I lie on a chaise with my towel and book (I'm reading Anne's copy of *Rebecca*—I keep wanting to sing "On the Road to Manderley") and sunglasses, and when I get too hot, I swim, and then I come back and lie here some more. I've never spent time like this before. I'm alone so much, and my thoughts bounce around in my head, and I wonder if I look as though I'm thinking in English, and I imagine French thought balloons for everyone around me.

I brought the Leica with me today, now that it has been satisfactorily and expensively repaired, though I'm worried about it disappearing when I swim, and about getting it wet. I have the camera stuffed into my bag, under a pile of things. I've taken one picture, of a woman looking at herself in a handheld mirror while she applied white ointment to her not unlarge nose. I don't know why I'm so convinced that she was extremely satisfied by what she saw. As an American, I am perpetually fascinated by the sense of themselves that Swiss women have. Maybe I should include most of Europe; in my experience, women from most Western European countries walk, talk, and look at themselves in the mirror with an enormous amount of confidence that American women lack. Even the tiniest schoolgirls wear their little blue coats with a kind of authority and natural grace that's breathtaking.

Yesterday, I stopped in a boutique in the Vieille Ville, mostly because of a green-and-white-striped dress in the window that I thought I liked until I got up close to it and discovered that the green stripes were actually intertwined riding crops or something. Too embarrassed to rush out of the shop once I had made this discovery, I was tentatively poking at a few things on the rack when a Swiss woman walked in, strode over to the same rack, and began riffling through the dresses with an incredibly determined and practiced style. (At this point I had become invisible.) No, no, no, no, as each dress was thrust down the rail until one, two were maybes, then, no, no, no again until she was done. I left while she was still in the dressing room; I was utterly vanquished, utterly humbled, well beyond contemplating buying anything for myself ever again.

When I was swimming this morning, I had a minor apocalypse. Or was it an epiphany? Did you know this: when you swim laps, you are supposed to swim over the painted lines, not between them? I always thought the painted lines were like the lines on a highway, that they were dividers. Now I discover that they mark the path of the swimmer, and I am thrown into a deep pool of doubt. What else in my twenty-six years have I got slightly wrong? About what else have I missed the finer points, gotten details a little bit off?

For instance: I have some photographs with me. They're not mine; that is, I own them, but I didn't take them. Well, I *did* take them, but only in the sense that I took possession of them. What I mean to say is that these photographs are snapshots taken before I was born; they're of a man and a woman and a little girl. I found the pictures in the attic, when I was little.

For about five years I had terrible insomnia, though I kept it a secret. Like a restless ghost, every night I wandered through the house. That was a bleak time, beginning with Adam's death, when I was six, and lasting for five or six years, with my father's disappearance, right up to my mother's hospitalization. That year she was at Payne Whitney, that year I lived with Gay on Sutton Place; it was a turning point, though I didn't know it at the time.

No one ever came out and said that I was living with Gay. I just sort of stayed with her for a year. And in that time, I forgot to not sleep. One day I realized it—the sleeplessness was simply gone.

I had a strange time of it, sort of roosting in her frilly guest room, trying to do my homework (it was the entire year I was in seventh grade) on a tiny little makeup table without a good light, lurking helpfully at dozens of cocktail parties, seeing just about every Broadway show. Thinking back on it, I would have to admit that Gay probably had too much to drink on most nights, that it wasn't very suitable for a kid to live that way. I probably had a glass of milk about twice in that entire time.

Meanwhile, with one foot in this very grown-up world, I was commuting every morning on the subway back to Oxbridge Gardens to get to class at my junior high. The other people on the train who got off at my stop were mostly maids. No one at school ever knew that I wasn't living at my home address, or there might have been "trouble." At least that's what I was told. It was a temporary thing, no one knew how long it would go on. Maybe we were all waiting for my father, waiting for Simon Rose to show up. Most likely, Gay didn't have any intention of

discussing her daughter's suicidal depression with anyone, especially not poorly dressed public school teachers in Queens, on
the grounds that it wasn't their business and might reflect badly
on her.

Why do you suppose I colluded in that? I told no one. I had
few friends in those years. I was painfully shy. If you were in my
class, you probably wouldn't remember me. Really. From time
to time I did go by the house, in order to get a book or some
clothes, and to sort through the mail for bills Gay would have to
pay. Always, I looked for a letter from my father. Otherwise, the
house just sat there in its dust. My old cat, Tobermorey, had died
by then, and we never did have any houseplants, so there wasn't
anything else left that could die. (I came home from school one
day, in fifth grade, and my mother had left a note for me on the
kitchen table, saying she had gone to the store and that Tobe had
died.)

So, the pictures. I removed them at some point in that year,
so I could have them to look at back on Sutton Place. I had
discovered them long before that, in my nocturnal wanderings. I
used to go up to the attic in the middle of the night and visit
those pictures; they were a family that I felt I knew. I would
leave them as I had found them and discover them all over again
each time. The man in the pictures was my father. Was Simon
Rose. Truly. I recognized him in this other life. He had another
wife, another little girl. This is for real, Benedict, stay with me. I
know it seems wild; I worried, sometimes, up there in the attic
in the middle of the night, with all those old photographs spread
out on a blanket, that I was going crazy.

I know these things because the night we had the call from
the hospital in Paris telling us that my father had died, which was
just a few weeks into my first semester at Cooper Union, I asked
my mother if he had ever been married before. I had never raised
the question before that moment, though I guess I already did
know the answer, in a way. (When I think about it, the question

was as much a test to see if *she* knew as it was a quest for solid information.)

At first she automatically said no, but then she hesitantly told me the story, in fits and starts. He had made her promise she would never tell me, or anyone, but given the circumstances of his death—in a hospital in Paris, where we didn't even know he was living, mysteriously and with typical obscureness registered under the name Leon Rose—maybe she felt obligated to offer me some little explanation of the unknowable man who was my father.

He was married, at a young age, to a fellow radical he met on a picket line. Her name was Audrey Friedman, and she worked for a union. They had a little girl. Her name was Ellen. Ellen Rose. They lived in Larchmont. Audrey was pregnant with a second child when she and Ellen were both killed in a car accident. They were on their way to the birthday party of a child who was in Ellen's second-grade class.

I don't know where my father was that day. I don't know what happened next, what happened to the house in Larchmont. I don't know anything about the Friedmans, where they came from, if any of them were ever in touch with Simon later on (doubtful, as he told my mother he always felt that they blamed him for Audrey's death). All traces of this first family in my father's life were carefully eliminated—according to my mother, he only told *her* about it when they were already married, and she was pregnant with Adam, and he had become irrational about her driving in the car alone.

But there was another reminder of the existence of Audrey and Ellen (who would, I guess, be in her thirties if she had lived, while I wouldn't exist at all): the money. Simon apparently received a substantial insurance settlement because the driver of the other car had been to blame for the accident. Which explains why, despite the vagaries of the Christmas-light business, there was always money. And I don't mean from Gay. We were, as they say, comfortable. (An elderly man collapses while walking along the beach in Miami. As he's being loaded into an ambulance, one of the attendants hovering over him asks, "Sir? Sir? Are you comfortable?" He sits up on the stretcher and says, "Well, I don't make a bad living.")

Our house, my mother told me that day, as we packed Simon's old suits into boxes for the Salvation Army, had been paid for with that money. Blood money. Interestingly, my mother had never seen their faces, knew nothing of the existence of those attic snapshots. She didn't want to see them then, either, and still hasn't.

Why do you suppose I never asked anyone about those pictures? I was only ten or so when I found them. I sensed forbiddenness, perhaps. I knew they had been hidden. And I wanted to keep them a secret, keep them for myself. And why do you suppose I've kept them a secret from you? Maybe I was afraid of scaring you away with all the weirdness, the history I drag around with me by the sackful.

So. How did I get here? Right: about being a little bit off. Which I was: it never occurred to me that the people in the pictures didn't exist somewhere, living their lives. Not only did I imagine their existence, I assumed my father preferred them to us, that they were his real family and we weren't.

I look at those pictures all the time here. I want to show them to you. I'm using them in some of my new work, too. Oh, the past is always present.

Later. Too much sun, again. Anne seems distinctly bothered about something that has to do with Victor (not that there is anything that does not have to do with Victor), but I can't tell if it's very large or very small, or like a biscuit box. I've written so much in my enormous Journal/Letter to You about all this, and I wonder if any of it is coherent. I begin to wonder if my being here has strained things between them. I don't think Victor likes me. Why should he? I can hardly abide him.

Oh, it's so hard to think. For some reason I keep returning to Gay. I wish she were alive. Not alive the way she was at the end, but really alive. I wish you had known her. Anne just barely got in the door—I took her to Sutton Place for a couple of not entirely relaxed or successful audiences—before "the dwindles," as Gay called them, got the better of her. (At the end of that first visit, Gay took me aside and said, "Your friend Anne has hair-colored hair and a face-colored face. She needs to go see Mr. Edward. Make an appointment for her.")

If only she could see Anne now. Anne and Gay together would be lamenting *my* unglamorousness. Where the hell is Gay? It's not possible that she doesn't exist anywhere.

Her slide into senility was actually quite swift, a matter of months. I had hoped that her death would allow me to forget the way she had become at the end, like some great mad baby. But I keep going over in my mind those last days, the moment I told the doctor I wanted her to have a good death and that she wasn't to have intravenous hydration or tube feeding or anything. She was suddenly completely senile, and ninety-five, and her refusal to eat or drink anything at all seemed like a kind of declaration of intention that should be honored. My overwhelmed-by-life mother, with no one else to lean on as an only child (she was squeezed in somehow between more amusing diversions and marriages), couldn't bear to see Gay so diminished, couldn't deal with the details, and turned to me to organize it all in the end.

Now, my mother can just manage to navigate through her days and weeks and months, but there are no margins, there isn't any leeway, if you follow me. Ruth Rose has made a success of simulating a real person having a real life, but only to a point. When you're a Payne Whitney retread, any first straw always has the potential to be a last straw. Don't get me wrong—I let myself be put in charge of Gay at the end; I wanted to do it. My mother needed to stay away; I couldn't stay away.

So why do I feel responsible for allowing Gay to die? All I did was arrange to do nothing; fail, by design, to do something. The poor soul had no past, and no future, and I told the doctor that as her present moments were all she had left, they shouldn't feature a needle in the wrist or a tube in the nose or any other discomforts. And the doc was very neutral about it and ordered the nurses to offer her frequent opportunities to drink something and otherwise let her be. So she died in her own bed in that elegant apartment on Sutton Place.

You've heard the funny stories about the funeral (though I haven't told you about Peggy Gordon getting drunk and trying to tell me that my father had once been a lover of Gay's), and about Gay's old friends having a party in her honor at the Cosmo Club, and all the rest.

But there's a part I've left out. I'm always leaving things out. Sometimes I feel that no matter how hard I try, whether it's describing something with words or making a photograph, I'm always leaving things out.

The last time I saw my grandmother, when I was sitting at her bedside, Maggie, the Irish nurse who had been with her during the days for the last couple of months, was on duty. Gay was clearly dying. (It was Maggie who had solemnly reported to me, near the beginning of her tour of duty, when Gay was still capable of some madcap scenes, that all the place mats from the dining room had mysteriously begun to disappear, and she had finally caught Gay in the act of hiding the last place mat under her mattress. "She's got an asphyxiation on them place mats, the old sweetheart has," Maggie told me.) Maggie was, on this last occasion, trying to get her to drink something.

"Gay, will you take some water?"

No response, as had been the case for the previous five days. Gay mostly just stared off, and her eyes were at this point rolling around in some sort of neurological twitch, owing to the total deterioration of every system in her body, caused by this benevolent starvation. She was beyond thirst.

Maggie held a smeary Waterford tumbler of water to my grandmother's lips and tipped some into her mouth. Gay reacted violently, spitting, pushing Maggie away with surprising strength, and she croaked out, "No."

Making what I meant as a mild joke, for my own amusement and to calm Maggie, who was desperate to do something for Gay, of whom she had grown quite fond, I interjected, "Well, then, how about a vodka and tonic?"

Gay seemed to focus for a moment. "Yes!" she said clearly, a flicker of recognition sparking the old animation, before dropping back on the pillow and closing her eyes. (That was, in fact, her last word.) I went to her bar and found what I needed to mix up one last stiff vodka and tonic. I brought it back to her bedside and tried to get her attention.

"I apologize for the lack of lime," I said, mostly to myself, and held the glass to her caked mouth. When I tipped a little bit in, she seemed to smile, and she swallowed a sip. It was the last thing to pass her lips. A moment later, though, as if to say, Okay, Harriet, you've had your fun, and now let's get this show on the road, she screwed up her face and folded up her mouth like nothing I have ever seen and refused anything more.

Maggie whispered to me, "Somebody's going to D-Y-E, you know. I think it's today." I left perhaps a half hour later, and she died a few hours after that.

I know that everything I have just described might seem wonderful and just right to you, and I thank you for that, but I cannot help wondering if I helped push her along with that drink, just as I cannot help but wonder if I had approved some sort of tube feeding, whether she would have pulled out of that final slide, elected to stick around awhile longer.

Senility is a cruel thing. When did she actually die? When was she gone? Was she still intact in some hidden way, and did I deprive her of the last bits of her life to which she was entitled? How do we know when a person has had enough, under those circumstances? In other words, did I assist, or did I merely interfere? I will never know.

So, Benedict. That's who you're dealing with: Harriet Rose, faulty to a fault. And while we're on the subject of assistance that turns out to be interference, or vice versa, there's another olive in this jar: the family next door, on Rutland Close, the Antlers. I did something that I will try to tell you about someday; I will never know if I rescued them or destroyed them. Maybe it was both.

Sometimes it's all laughable and unphotographable. Sometimes I can hardly bear it.

July 19

Oh, Benedict:

Walking on the streets in the Vieille Ville I find myself hearing
the tones and structures of conversations between people, minus
the content, because I don't know the languages spoken all
around me. I don't always even recognize the language. So I am
free to make up what they might be talking about. Two old men
in impeccable gray banker's suits, walking slowly ahead of me
down the Rue de la Cité, speaking Swiss German (I think),
were, perhaps, discussing investments. Maybe they were art deal-
ers. But maybe they were in real estate. Or watches. Maybe they
were very elegant criminals, on their way to lunch with Claus
von Bulöw.

I found myself thinking about a moment with my father when
I was about five years old. When I was little, my father took me
with him, probably three or four times, on Saturday mornings
when he had work to do at his office during the Christmas rush.
(The irony of Simon Rose being in the Christmas-light business
didn't dawn on me until an incredulous high-school teacher
pointed it out.) On this occasion, when we were walking along
the side street to the parking lot—this was in Long Island City,
near enough to the Chiclets factory to smell the peppermint
fumes—he began talking to me in a way I didn't understand. I
was holding his hand, and ahead of us on the sidewalk were two
old men in dark coats and round, broad-brimmed hats, and my
father began to speak to me in an insanely repetitive sort of
question-and-answer dialogue in a tone I couldn't comprehend.

It took me a few panicked moments to understand that my father wasn't quoting something I was supposed to recognize, and he hadn't gone mad and begun speaking two-part nonsense to me; he was parroting the Yiddish conversation taking place a few paces ahead of us. This Talmudic enlightenment/mockery was a typical communication from my father, mine to do with as I would and could. A little Simon Rose *Jew d'esprit.*

Last night, early evening, though still daylight, Anne and I were walking down by the lake, eating ice cream yet again, and ostensibly seeing the *Jet d'eau,* an enormous, pointless fountain. This has always been a difference between us, my ability to wander aimlessly in contrast to Anne's need for systematic sight-seeing goals. In New York, it was bad enough. We would be walking in the Village and she would start haring about, trying to find the house where Washington Irving spent the weekend, or Edith Wharton first menstruated. But in Geneva, she's gone wild and insists on visitations to places where empresses were assassinated in the nineteenth century and so forth. Voltaire seems to have done something on every street corner. (It was Voltaire who said of Geneva, "There, one calculates, but never laughs.")

So we were walking along the lake, enjoying being two people in Geneva eating ice cream cones on a summer evening. Anne was telling funny stories about the secretary at UGP, the demonic Miss Trout. (Do you remember the old sanitary-napkin advertisements? Anne has a fantasy advertisement starring Miss Trout, who stands in her slip gazing dreamily into a glowing copying machine. The caption reads, "Tipp-Ex . . . because.")

Though funny, I've heard it all before, and I wasn't paying strict attention. I missed completely the shift to a somewhat nervous undertone with which she started to describe aspects of her sex life with Victor. For Anne to talk about sex in an intimate way is so out of character that I hardly realized it was happening, and I missed the beginning of it.

I had been thinking about the way conversation sounds, and about the way people communicate, if that doesn't sound pretentious, when I caught a glimpse of a little dark-haired girl walking alone almost alongside us. She couldn't have been more than eight. I couldn't get over how much she looked like me, like pictures taken when I was little, I mean. Her hair was bobbed in a pixieish style that was subtley European, though I couldn't tell you why, but something about her struck me—I just couldn't get over her resemblance to my eight-year-old self.

I began to wonder, crazily, if she were possibly related to me in some way. She looked like a cross between the child in those snapshots, Ellen—my half sister, though it feels strange and false to write the words—and me. I was imagining that she was listening to our conversation in English, a language she probably didn't know, and perhaps might not even recognize, and I was just about to point her out to Anne when I tuned back in and caught the tail end of Anne's confession.

So the first thing I heard her say was, "Sometimes I don't come." Having missed the preamble, I tried to scroll backward for the sounds of her words, the way you can tell the time by counting up the number of bell tolls you've heard but to which you've not paid close attention from the start. But Anne, who ordinarily transmits so elegantly with her BBC–Tammy Grimes enunciation, was here talking in such a soft, mumbly rush, I just hadn't heard it all. And I could hardly say, "Sorry, I was just indulging myself in fantasies that the little girl over there might by some preposterous twist of fate be a long-lost relative. What was that you were saying about being nonorgasmic?"

"Victor says it's because I worry about it too much," she concluded.

"Do you?" I tried to sound as though I knew for sure what we were talking about. I guess I did.

"I worry that it hurts Victor's feelings—it makes him feel that he's not attractive enough to me." Anne eyed me for a moment while she crunched the end of her cone. She pushed a straggle of hair out of her face. She suddenly looked not so much beautiful as pathetic to me. She looked very young and at the same time haggard, and I was overwhelmed by how hard she works at all this. "He thinks you're very attractive, I think," she added, as if this were significant to the discussion. She looked away. She looked embarrassed.

I looked around, hoping the right answers might be nailed to a tree. The streetlamps had come on, though the evening was still bright. It was getting chilly, and the little girl had disappeared. The park was filling up with a different kind of people, and some sort of brass band had begun to play in a pavilion we had passed. Whose idea was this relentless and everlasting Scott Joplin craze, anyway?

"You don't seem very happy," I observed, feeling silly for being so American and direct with Anne, she who had become so European and complicated.

"What I require is the proper squire?" she said scornfully. But then she burst into tears.

I put my arms around her, tentatively, what with all the chains and scarves and makeup. We used to hug all the time in Eighth Street days, we even held hands walking around the streets, though it always seemed to me that Anne rather liked the effect —that she rather liked imagining the assumption on the part of passersby that we were a couple.

In any case, here we rarely touch at all; it's been as if she were reserved for Victor in all ways. And sleeping in the same bed as we do has led to a kind of exaggerated respect for personal space. My God, she's become thin and bony. She felt incredibly insubstantial as we stood there by the lake and she sobbed on my shoulder.

"Sorry, sorry, sorry," she murmured in my ear. I could feel her tears trickling down my neck.

"Look," I began. How to begin? "Is this what you want? This whole life? Being somebody's mistress? Or is this only a mood, a brief interlude?"

"Yes. No. Oh, I don't know." She straightened up and peeled herself away from me. I gave her a crumpled Kleenex from the pocket of my cardigan, and she snuffled into it.

"For someone who claims to be doing what she wants, you seem tortured," I said, feeling unkind in my directness.

"It's simple for you, you've got this Benedict."

(Well, true.)

"Anne, do you love him?"

"It's got to be love," she began, and then our eyes met and we both laughed. Us again.

"Feels like tonsillitis," she whispered a little sadly. (Oh, A for effort! This touched me. When we met, Anne thought Rodgers and Hart were the guys who did the six-o'clock news.)

"Well, you're not going to meet a nice, unmarried member of your own peer group this way," I blundered, killing the moment. Worse, I continued, in a terrible mock Freudian accent, "Und vy do you suppose you are attracted to a man who so closely resembles your fadder, Miss Gordon?"

"Incest is relative, is that your point? Thank you very much for the profound insights," she snapped.

I felt myself becoming impatient back: "Look, you're telling me that you don't get much pleasure out of all this 'luncheon' sex with him, you seem agonized, and I really don't understand what goes on here. Do you?"

"I know we love each other, in a way. We need each other."

"Tell me his wife doesn't understand him, Anne."

"She doesn't! You're so cynical! He never meant to marry anyone. He was trapped into marrying Annamarie in order to get her a visa. He felt sorry for her."

(Right. He thought three children and twenty years of marriage might cheer her up. Very considerate.)

"You're missing my point, Anne. I'm asking how you feel, not about the rationale." By now, I felt as though Anne was responding to me with the warmth she would have for her incompetent lawyer, visiting her on death row.

She looked out at the breeze-pleated lake. It was darker and colder, and she shivered and hugged herself. Most of her new getups are witchy outfits of sheer black God knows what, and they don't look warm. She was wearing a skirt thing and a blouse thing, but words fail to capture the complication of layers arranged on those bones. She had a shawl thing, too, that was mostly open-work knots of I don't know what—horsehair.

I put my arm around her shoulder and squeezed her, probably a little too heartily. We stood together for a moment looking out at *Jet d'eau* spray blowing in a Disney-esque illuminated sheet. I was about to ask her if she would seriously consider coming back to the States with me at the end of the month when a hand clapped down hard on my shoulder and startled the life out of me; it was Victor.

"Am I intruding on an intimate moment between old friends?" He insinuated himself between us and in doing so levered my arm up and away from Anne.

Neither of us answered him for a moment too long.

"So. Maybe a *very* intimate moment between old friends." He dropped his hand from my shoulder and in doing so gave me an almost imperceptible push away. "Yes, it's clearly quite a friendship. I hadn't realized. This is very interesting, my darling." He stood close behind Anne with his arms circling her, and with his eyes on me, he began to nibble along the side of her neck. She looked at me with imploring eyes I couldn't read.

They give me the creeps, Benedict.

After another long, awkward silence, with nothing else to do, the three of us began to walk back toward the Vieille Ville. Nobody talked. The two of them were in a close lockstep, while I kept feeling as though I were constantly moving either too fast or too slow; however I paced myself, I kept having to pause and drop back or skip along to keep up. At one point, when I stopped to adjust my sandal strap, they got so far ahead of me that I had to run to catch up. And afraid of a disaster, Miss Clavel ran fast and faster.

We were going at a brisk pace up a steepish street lined with galleries and antique shops only a couple of blocks from the flat when Victor stopped—we all stopped—and said, "So, what is the plan?"

I wasn't sure whom he was addressing at first. Anne said nothing and seemed suddenly transfixed by the very bad imitation Nicolas De Staël painting of boats that was ostentatiously displayed on an easel in the window of a gallery.

"The plan for the night, the plan for tomorrow, the plan for the rest of our lives?" I realized as I spoke that Victor was so agitated and humorless that he probably thought I was mocking him.

"Let's start with tonight," he said, smiling/glaring at me. (Just watch those icicles form.)

"Don't. Please don't," Anne whispered.

"Look," Victor said to me, taking me by the sleeve and walking us a few feet beyond Anne, who remained transfixed by the gallery window.

"What is your agenda for Anne?" He spoke to me as though these were his opening remarks at a business meeting.

"I'm not sure I know what you mean. I don't have an agenda for Anne. I don't have an agenda."

"Everyone has an agenda," Victor explained wearily to me. "Of course you do. We all want to make other people agree with us, we want others to be more like ourselves. That's perfectly natural. What do you want for Anne? What is your plan?"

"If I have what you call an agenda for Anne, I suppose it would be to see her be her best self. How's that?"

"Then we have the same agenda for Anne. But we do not agree about the things her life should consist of. For instance, you do not approve of me, do you?" He didn't wait for an answer to this and went on, "I, on the other hand, approve very much of you, both as a friend for Anne and because you interest me very much." His grip tightened on my arm. I didn't like it.

"Victor, what would happen if your wife, or a friend of Annamarie's, were to come along right now? How would you explain being here with Anne, with me?"

"That would actually be useful," he said, intrigued by the possibilities. "You see, I would then do this"—at which he seized me in a parody of a romantic embrace and kissed me on the mouth.

He had the foul breath (with a veneer of peppermint) that I guess I always assumed would go with his yellow teeth. I had unkind thoughts about the absence of flossing materials at Auschwitz. The skin of his face was strangely cold. I shoved him away, harder than necessary. Anne, looking terrified, stood frozen and murmured, "His back."

Victor snickered and said, "My back has survived worse." He turned from me and took Anne's arm, and they began to walk again in the direction of her flat. I followed them, feeling as disoriented as one does when walking away from some nauseating ride at a carnival.

Over his shoulder, he said to me, "It would be a diversion, you see? Then she could not suspect Anne."

I ran a few steps to draw even with their procession of two. Victor had Anne's left arm twined through his right, with his left hand locked on her wrist.

"So, you mean, she knows you have affairs, but she doesn't know with whom?" I don't know why it seemed so important to me to pin this down.

"Something like that," he said dismissively, now bored.

"You're a very selfish man," I heard myself saying.

"Don't," I heard Anne saying. I dropped back a few paces behind them again. I stalked along behind them, but my outrage grew, and after a moment I shouted after them, "Victor, don't you have a conscience?"

"Perhaps my conscience isn't cut of material that suits you," he replied over his shoulder.

"Items from the Lillian Hellman Catalog," murmured Anne, a reference to an old joke between us that was an interesting and unexpected signal that this was still Anne, in there somewhere. It made me think of the way one of the Iranian hostages would make cryptic references to Evelyn Waugh characters as if they were relatives, on his videotaped statements, knowing it would go right over his captors' heads.

We were almost at the apartment. The empty streets were shiny and wet, though it hadn't rained. A taxi roared up the hill in a low gear and passed us; its exhaust stink hung in the air, smelling of European cities. I wanted to go home.

We reached the entrance to Anne's courtyard, and they paused beside the arched entrance passage so I could catch up with them.

"We're going to walk awhile longer—why don't you go on up?" This, from Victor, was more of an instruction than a suggestion. Anne looked into some unknown middle distance. I stood still, wanting to catch her eye, but Victor turned her away and together they glided into the evening; I was alone.

Benedict, maybe I should have followed them. As it was, I paced frantically for more than an hour, made a cup of tea, forgot it until it was tepid, made another on which I burned my mouth, wrote some of this to you, and wondered if I should check out some of the nearest cafés and bistros. I didn't want to leave, though, in case Anne came back.

I kept looking at the telephone but had no idea whom to call. The police? (Hello? I'd like to report a suspicion of sadomasochistic activity somewhere under cover of darkness?) Anne's father in New Jersey? (Hello? Henry Goldfarb, I mean, Gordon? It's about your daughter and your oldest, closest friend whose life you saved, or was it the other way around?) Annamarie? (Hello, Mrs. Marks? We haven't met but I've been wondering: How did your husband explain his sunburn to you that day you took the children to the beach? We have a lot to talk about.)

I heard Anne's key in the door and suddenly worried that Victor was with her, but she was alone. She came in, shut the door, put down her bag, sank into one of the wooden chairs, and dropped her horsehair wrap slowly onto the floor, as if she had forgotten that I would be here, as if she didn't realize that I was here.

"So?"

She looked up at me then. Her face was terribly blotched and almost pulpy looking; her mouth looked bruised.

"What?" As I asked, I realized I knew. I went to stand behind her chair. She began to cry, harsh, racking sobs.

"Where did he take you?"

"The park." Anne continued to cry, silently now, to shake with sobs. Her jaw was clenched. She hunched over, her head down, and gripped her hair with both hands, her elbows on the table; I felt that I ought to put my arms around her or at least pat her shoulder, but I couldn't bring myself to touch her. Images of Victor's spurting penis in her mouth sprang, unbidden, to mind. The doctors should have amputated

Now it's the next morning. Anne emerged from the bathroom last night, got into bed, and either went straight to sleep or fell into a catatonic stupor; in any case, she was clearly unprepared to talk to me about it. I lay there most of the night thinking and listening to her breathe.

Early, birds were chirping and gray Swiss light was filtering into the room. Her hateful clock that sounds like a car alarm went off at seven, Anne walked around the flat muttering *Merde,* got dressed in a black-and-white-miniskirt suit, ate a banana (I know, I could hardly believe my eyes), applied makeup, and left for work, all as per usual. I stayed in bed and slept again for a couple of hours, still exhausted after those two or three hours of freeze-dried sleep substitute.

I had a dream about my father this morning, after I went back to sleep. It was in the living room of our house, the way it used to be, when Adam was still alive. My father is crawling around underneath our Christmas tree (the Christmas tree for which, as an annual ritual, he would always bargain, in Yiddish, in his old neighborhood in Brooklyn), and as he goes to plug in the lights, there is a short circuit, which I can somehow anticipate, a sizzling pop, and then he is lying still, under the tree, electrocuted. I reach for his hand, knowing that I risk electrocution as well, and then there's a dazzling shock, as our hands touch, and then I have a feeling I'm falling, and then the dream ended. My first waking thought was this: how lucky I am to have fallen into Anne's bed.

My second waking thought was this: actually, it hasn't been lucky at all.

Geneva

July 21

Dear Benedict,

So how the hell are you? It's incredibly complicated here. And the oddest thing. I can't find the letter journal I've been keeping since I got here. It's just a spiral notebook. I didn't think I took it with me when I went to the park yesterday, but it wasn't in the flat when I got back in the afternoon, and Anne says it wasn't there when she and Victor came in during the middle of the day.

Maybe I've left it on some park bench or in some café. Or at the pool. I could swear it was either in my tote bag or on the table in the flat, and now it's gone. Pages and pages and pages. I just can't believe it. I hate losing things; I still pine for my grandmother's Movado watch with lapis lazuli around the dial. She gave it to me for my twenty-first birthday, as my grandfather had given it to her for her twenty-first birthday, and I loved everything about it, can picture it still. It disappeared last year—I don't even know quite when—and I searched through my apartment over and over. Perhaps it was swept into the trash by mistake. Perhaps it was stolen. Perhaps it fell off my wrist on the crosstown bus. I will never know. I want it back.

Where is my journal? The most obvious thought is that Anne has it, or has destroyed it, but though I suppose she would be capable of reading it, of taking it, even if she did do that, even if she tore it up page by page—which response she would certainly consider, if she read it, as I've been pretty blunt about all sorts of things—I can't believe she would lie to me about it when I asked her.

I don't trust Victor, for a variety of reasons, but his style would be different, somehow, I don't know; maybe he would invite Anne and me out to a nice restaurant and then read it aloud at the table, in order to create a maximally uncomfortable atmosphere. Devious as he is, I can't imagine him bothering with something like a notebook, actually.

I even find myself suspecting the old woman in the black dress who is perpetually scrubbing the hallway. She glares at me politely when I come in and out. I feel like pointing out to her that I'm not the one meeting my elderly married lover at lunchtime for a quickie. (The situation here is all in a kerfuffle, as I have said. Much to explain.) But seriously, even if she does have a key, what would she, or anyone else, want with my writing? My camera equipment has seemed more of a risk, and that's untouched.

Well. I'm frustrated. Apologies for breaking the embargo. What you may have experienced as our agreed-upon thoughtful silence all month was in fact a din, a conflagration of words and thoughts, and even that rarest of commodities, feelings. I've been trying so hard to think and feel instead of act, for once. Nothing is really lost, I suppose. What's gone missing is a marathon Harriet Rose arrogant commentary on the very odd situation here. It's a mixture of blather and reflection, and though it was addressed to you, it's really been a way of talking to myself. I've been using you as my You, Benedict; Anne Frank had her Dear Kitty. Have I been feeling that imprisoned here, I wonder?

I was writing about my work. And some stray thoughts about Us. And I had put into words some stories that might begin to explain me to you, a little. I have also expressed myself freely on the subject of Anne and Victor; I was wildly careless to leave the notebook around. Did I want them to find it, to read what I wrote? (But I have to trust Anne.) Paging Doctor Freud. (The man who put the Id in Yid, as my father used to say after every meeting with the school psychologist, who tried to talk to them about Adam.)

Things here are enormously complicated. I know I keep saying that. The famous Victor turns out to be a married cad. (Also a lot of other, more complicated things.) Anne is miserable, not herself. I'm in the middle of it all and have begun to feel quite desperate. My work is spotty. This is not the July it was supposed to be. How to begin? Certainly not at the beginning. And not now. Oh, Benedict.

With the promise of a better letter later—
And much, much love

HARRIET

P a r t   I I

Next Door

Even before the Antlers moved in, the house next door fascinated Harriet. Looking at it was like looking into your bedroom mirror and seeing everything in the room but yourself, it was that identical to the Roses' house.

Because the houses on Rutland Close fronted onto a circle, the faces of the houses were slightly tilted together. Every house on the Close was like a reverse image of the house beside it, because all eight houses shared the same somewhat Georgian plan, flip-flopped around the circle. The neighborhood was designed to mimic a certain London suburb, and it was situated, extraordinarily enough, in the middle of Queens. The architecture of the entire cloister ran to large, top-heavy houses on small parcels of pruned lawn and garden. The effect was not unlike that of a fat lady making the best of a narrow theater seat.

This carefully planned mixture of about two hundred houses erected in the 1920s in styles resembling Georgian, Tudor, and the occasional Mediterranean was known as Oxbridge Gardens. Each house was a part of the whole; it was like an elaborate board game with many pieces. The quaintly named narrow, winding streets, graceful closes, and enclosed parks were alleged to have been laid out by Frederick Law Olmsted, and had been named after Uxbridge, or perhaps after Oxford and Cambridge.

Harriet could remember moving into the house on Rutland Close when she was two. On moving day, a man in dirty overalls was laying the last of the black-and-white linoleum tiles in the front hall, and Harriet had walked across the sticky goo he had troweled down. She remembered clearly the awful feeling of being unable to lift her feet from the floor, and Harriet's screams had not been because she was worried that the tile man was angry because she had done something wrong, as all the grown-ups assumed. She had screamed and screamed because she thought something was wrong with her legs and she couldn't walk anymore.

Harriet's brother Adam's room was down the hall from hers, and it was painted a gloomy, darkish blue. She didn't like his room and never went past the threshold if she could help it. She held her breath sometimes when she went by his room on her way to the bathroom they shared. His room smelled because he wet the bed, and there were always unpleasant gritty things in the carpet, things that stuck to the bottom of Harriet's bare feet. He usually peed all over the toilet seat, too, and Harriet had developed the habit of squatting over the toilet the way her mother had taught her to pee in public bathrooms in department stores.

Although Adam was almost three years older than Harriet, he wasn't really her big brother, or at least he was different from the other big brothers in the neighborhood, because he had something wrong with him. No one ever actually said this to Harriet, but she could remember only one instant of her life when she didn't know it. She could recall being pushed in a swing by Adam when she was just a baby, and he had laughed and run underneath the swing, and she had loved the feeling of his hands on her back and the sky tilting toward her.

Harriet's room was painted a shade of pink that was both too bright and too dark; Harriet hated the way it made her think of the plastic flesh of certain cheap dolls. In the house next door, the matching room that faced her bedroom windows was painted a beige color and belonged to an old lady who was always sick.

Harriet was perpetually reminded that she must be quiet when she played near Mrs. Marshall's bedroom window. Harriet never understood the point of these instructions, as she was a solitary and silent child who rarely made noise or trouble. It was true that some children did make noise, a great deal of noise, especially groups of little children, especially boys. But to admonish her was silly. It was as if these grown-ups were trying so hard to be considerate of Mrs. Marshall that they didn't even see Harriet when they said this. It was as if Harriet were just any child. So she would shrug and run outside to play one of her games and try to be as quiet as a large group of noisy children being quiet might somehow manage to be. "Shhh," she would urge herself from time to time.

Harriet saw the old lady only once, when she had looked up at the window that was the mirror of her own and had seen through the perfectly familiar mullioned panes of glass a ghostly face and a waving, clawlike hand. Harriet didn't wave back because she was scared of that eager, smiling face, those deformed fingers, and she felt somehow guilty about being caught looking.

For days after, Harriet avoided playing anywhere in sight of Mrs. Marshall's windows. And it was only a few weeks later, right after Harriet had begun kindergarten, that she came home for lunch one day to the shocking sight of an ambulance and a police car sprawled in the street in front of Mrs. Marshall's house. The poor old thing had "give up the ghost," Carrie, the Roses' housekeeper, explained gently as she poured Harriet's milk. Harriet pictured one of the claws grasping the edge of a ghost's trailing hem and letting go, like someone releasing a curtain that fluttered free in a breeze.

The house was put on the market by Mrs. Marshall's daughter, who lived in Connecticut and had rarely come to see her mother, a fact pointed out by Mrs. Marshall's housekeeper, one Lavinia Patterson, a middle-aged alcoholic (according to Harriet's mother, Ruth Rose, who sometimes called her Tabitha Twitchit and sometimes called her Mrs. Danvers) who had stuck around for years because Mrs. Marshall had always promised "to take care of her." It had been she who had done the taking care, for twenty-eight years, and now she was left with two weeks' severance pay and nothing else to show for it.

Harriet didn't like the sound of Mrs. Patterson's voice, and the way she began her sentences with expressions like "to tell you the God's own honest truth" and "believe you me." Mrs. Patterson, engaged by the estate to clean up the house and pack for the Goodwill people everything the daughter didn't want, kept coming by for coffee, and Carrie didn't know how to turn her away.

For several weeks, every day when Harriet came home from kindergarten, hungry for lunch and bursting with observations of her morning that she knew would intrigue or amuse Carrie, there would be Mrs. Patterson, drinking coffee and laying her hand across her heart for emphasis as she proclaimed the truth and injustice of it all.

When she denounced the indifferent daughter in Connecticut yet again, her voice would grow louder and higher, until Harriet, sitting at the table eating her lunch, would begin to count the number of words in each sentence she spoke. Sometimes Harriet counted other things, too, such as the number of times Mrs. Patterson used the word *I*.

Harriet's mother was not in the habit of joining her children or housekeeper for lunch. She preferred to have something on a tray in the bedroom where she spent most of the day reading. Sometimes it seemed to Harriet that her mother was afraid of doing something wrong around Adam. Maybe she was afraid that she could make him worse. Harriet had come to feel that even when her mother had just entered a room, she was always leaving. Carrie usually carried the tray up the stairs to her, and Harriet would listen for the familiar, worrisome sound of Carrie's bad knee cracking with each step.

Adam usually ate a sandwich on the floor in the living room in front of the television. He wasn't in school right now because the Roses were waiting until January when a space would open in a special school, and meanwhile the regular public school a few blocks away that Harriet attended didn't want him to come back. So instead of starting third grade like any other eight-year-old boy, Adam was at home every day that autumn.

Harriet loved her lunchtime conversations with Carrie, missed them, and was terribly relieved the day Mrs. Patterson announced that she was finished with her work next door and wouldn't be back.

"That poor lost soul," Carrie said to Harriet after Mrs. Patterson had bid her farewells and stalked off into the October afternoon for her last walk to the subway station, loaded down with four shopping bags filled with the last haul of "things Miss High and Mighty would never miss anyway."

"Why do you say lost?" Harriet wondered.

"She doesn't know what to do without Mrs. Marshall," Carrie explained. "She loved that old woman like they were family to each other, like Mrs. Marshall was her own little child, and now she's all alone. Those bits and pieces won't hardly comfort her. But it wasn't right, what they did, leaving her out that way. It wasn't right. You won't leave me out, will you, Rabbit?"

Harriet wasn't sure what Carrie meant, but she agreed. Would she someday be very old and wave a clawed hand to a little girl under her window while an ancient Carrie prepared soup down below? She couldn't imagine leaving Carrie out of anything.

Mrs. Marshall's house wasn't on the market for long. Ruth Rose heard from the mailman that a family had bought it and would move in right before Christmas. Soon after that, workmen began to appear regularly, as the house next door was readied with new bathrooms, a new kitchen, long, rolled carpets. When the only van left belonged to the painters, an odd-looking truck arrived one afternoon. Enormous sheets of smoky mirrored glass were mounted on both sides of the truck, and Harriet watched from her lawn in fascination as two men first undid straps and then slowly hoisted the first mirror high and turned to carry it up the front walk, each man supporting his end by a strap below and a grip that looked like a giant suction cup above.

Harriet looked into this momentary window and could see her house, and the winter lawn, patchy with snow that looked gray and swirled in the reflection. In the middle of the lawn she glimpsed herself, a little girl in a red plaid jacket. As the mirror moved by, with only the legs of the men showing underneath, it looked like an enormous snapshot. Then the mirror was tilted as they prepared to clear the steps, and it changed to a silvery sheet that dazzled her eyes for an instant.

Then the work was done and the house was ready for the new family. When Harriet came home from school now, trudging the shoveled sidewalks in the cold, her bare legs chapped because she couldn't, wouldn't wear tights, but didn't want to appear tomboyish in overalls either, she would automatically check the windows of the house next door for some sign of change.

Finally, she was rewarded one afternoon by the sight of Mr. Antler, and a moving van so high it had broken a big branch off the maple tree that arched across the entrance to Rutland Close. Mr. Antler spent most of the afternoon standing on the front lawn with a clipboard, which he consulted frequently while instructing the movers on destinations for boxes and items of Antler furnishings.

The movers were slowed by drifted snow on the front walk and brick stoop, which, unshoveled, had been worn to slush in a narrow path by their traffic. Emptying the truck took a long time.

The first time Mr. Antler spoke to Harriet, when he spotted her playing that afternoon behind a yew bush that grew beside the Roses' house, he doffed his old-fashioned black homburg and greeted her very formally, calling her Young Lady. He was enormously tall, and Harriet thought he was handsome, like the jack of diamonds.

Harriet's parents made no effort to meet him, although they were, she could tell, exceedingly curious. Moments after the moving van had pulled up in front of the house next door that morning, Simon Rose had decided that he didn't need to go to the office until the afternoon. When Harriet came in from school —Carrie was away that week and the next, visiting her sister down South for Christmas—her father and mother sat down together to have lunch with her, which was an extraordinary circumstance in itself.

While Ruth was pouring milk for Harriet and coffee for her husband and herself, Simon turned to Harriet as if she were an adult he was having lunch with in a restaurant and asked her how her morning had been. She said it was okay and stared into her soup, at a loss for what else to say. He said that he wasn't sure there was enough work on his desk to make it worth his while to go in to the office at all that day, seeing as how he was still home and here it was almost one o'clock. Harriet looked up at the teapot-shaped clock over the refrigerator to see what one o'clock looked like. It didn't look very different from noon.

Harriet had heard him complain about the Christmas rush only the previous night. Grown-ups were such liars sometimes, but the difference between grown-up lies and kid lies was that when the jig was up, kids would admit it. But you couldn't say, "Liar, liar, pants on fire," to a grown-up, or you could, but then you would be in trouble.

All during lunch, Simon and Ruth kept getting up from the table to peep out the kitchen window. Harriet slurped the to-mato soup as loud as she dared, louder and louder, but no repri-mand was forthcoming; the usually squeamish Simon was that distracted. He and Ruth kept up a running commentary on the Antlers' worldly goods as various pieces were removed from the van and carted into the house: "Matching highboy and lowboy. Reproductions." "Piano." "New bedroom set."

Later that afternoon, after the moving van had gone, Mr. Antler introduced himself. He rang their doorbell ("Like a sales-man," according to Simon) and stood smiling on their front steps with his hat in his hands. Simon and Ruth went to the front

door together, something Harriet had never seen them do before. (Simon often said, "Bells are for servants," and rarely re-
sponded personally to a doorbell or ringing telephone unless no
one else was at home.)

"Hello, neighbors! Albert Antler!"

Mr. Antler offered his hand to Harriet's father, who slowly
extended his own and introduced himself in a wincing way,
saying, "Simon Rose. I believe you have already made acquain-
tance with half of my offspring."

This was not entirely correct, as Mr. Antler did not yet know
Harriet's name, and she squirmed as Mr. Antler peered into the
dark hallway behind her parents and spotted her where she stood
on one foot, twiddling the coat-closet doorknob.

"Yes, indeed!" he boomed, too loud, as though he sensed that
something was wrong with the entire Rose family that could be
remedied by a jolly tone. "And who is this young fellow?"

Adam had been drawn to the sound of voices in the front hall
from his nest of pillows on the living room floor in front of the
television where he spent his days. He had dribbled tomato soup
down his chin, and it was all over his pale blue shirt. Carrie knew
better than to serve him soup by himself, Harriet thought.

All week, Ruth had left the crusts on Harriet's sandwiches,
and she hadn't known that Harriet liked a drop of vanilla extract
stirred into her milk. She hadn't even known there was vanilla
extract in the house, and Harriet had climbed up onto the
kitchen counter, stood, and opened the high cupboard where it
was kept to prove that there was. Now she had given Adam
soup.

Adam spoke, surprisingly, given the presence of a stranger. He
had speaking days and nonspeaking days, but could rarely be
persuaded to talk in front of someone he didn't know.

"I am Adam Jacob Rose. Although I am only eight, if you
want me to, I can name every movie Jerry Lewis has made." He

enunciated clearly, as if he were speaking into a microphone, which Harriet guessed he was, from his point of view. He often communicated with his family through a series of public announcements.

"Well, an expert," said Mr. Antler with a confused laugh, straightening up from his talking-to-a-child crouch and addressing Harriet's mother now, with whom he was face to face. She smiled tentatively at him and said, "Hi." There was a pause. As the silence lengthened and she said nothing more, Harriet's father footnoted, "Ruth Rose, mother of the expert."

Feeling left out of this introduction, Harriet wondered if Mr. Antler wasn't quite sure about who her own mother might be, then decided that if he thought she was adopted, that would be okay, too.

They all stood there that way for another moment, Mr. Antler on the front steps and the entire Rose family gathered at the open doorway as if grouped for a family photograph. Harriet wondered what someone passing by just then would make of her family. It was hard to believe that anyone would think they were a regular family, but you never know. Most people don't notice what they're looking at.

Mr. Antler, deducing that no invitation to enter the Rose household would be forthcoming at this time, put on his hat and then tipped it toward Harriet's mother.

"My family arrives from Philadelphia tomorrow, and I am sure my wife will be pleased to meet our new neighbors. I myself am blessed with two fair maidens for daughters, and we are expecting another wee one, perhaps an heir to my own modest little kingdom, in early spring." Mr. Antler sounded to Harriet like someone reciting lines from a school play. Or was he quoting something that grown-ups would recognize?

"He takes himself awfully seriously," her mother murmured after Mr. Antler had been "gotten rid of." They all stood at the door, still united by their common curiosity, and watched Mr. Antler as he inexpertly maneuvered his car away from the curved curb of Rutland Close. He signaled for a right turn at the corner, although there was nobody behind him, nobody to see his turn but the Roses.

Harriet's father had explained to her that it wasn't necessary to signal when leaving Rutland Close because there were never any cars behind you, and it was more like turning from a private driveway. Harriet's mother, on the other hand, always signaled, "just in case." (In the same discussion, she had also cautioned Harriet about the danger of turning off one's turn signal manually. It strained the signal stem, she said.)

Now that Mr. Antler was gone, the Roses were all self-conscious, standing there together. Harriet's father began sudden preparations to leave for his office after all, murmuring something about work piling up in this frantic season. "A pleasant stuffed shirt," he pronounced as he carefully wound a muffler around his neck and buttoned himself up for his walk to the subway station. Harriet's mother asked him if he would be home for dinner. He didn't answer, and she didn't ask again.

Harriet gathered up the Roses' old orange cat, Tobermorey, who lay sleeping in a patch of sunlight on the windowsill in the dining room. Clutching him like a bundle, she went upstairs to her room. She shut the door and dropped him onto the bed, where he obligingly stayed, a creaky rumble of a purr beginning to form somewhere deep inside him. As she lay down next to the cat, carefully curling herself to fit his contours, the purr surfaced and she began to stroke him in rhythm with it.

"I love you more than anything," she whispered into his broad, striped back.

Through the wall Harriet could hear Adam in his room. His favorite record of John Philip Sousa marches began to play. Under the thump of the familiar music, she could hear the sound of his voice, and she knew he was reciting titles of Jerry Lewis movies in time to the music. She looked out her window, and from her bed she could see the side of Mrs. Marshall's house. The Antlers' house, Harriet corrected herself. Two fair maidens. She got up and went over to the window. She raised her hand and moved it back and forth, tentatively at first and then with a more intentional motion, as she practiced waving.

Croup

The humidifier made the paint peel. Hot steam came out of the dark green glass cylinder in a constant gush. The noise made Harriet uneasy; it reminded her, especially when she was feverish, of people screaming far away. The mirror on her closet door clouded and ran with the medicated vapors that filled Harriet's room. When she was sick this way, a special night-light was left on; the shade revolved slowly on a pointed stand, from the heat of the bulb inside, and the sinister circus parade that went around and around was not soothing but additionally terrifying.

The barking cough that lodged in her throat was called croup. Just lying in her bed, Harriet could hear the rasp of her breathing, as if every breath had to pass through something she had swallowed that was stuck.

When she had croup, it was always night, and everything was wet; her blankets were beaded with moisture from the steamy vapor, and her sheets were damp and clammy from her fever sweat. Her mother would come in and give her sips of ginger ale, and then Harriet would doze with the taste of it souring in her mouth. Strange, rasping sounds would yank her awake through the night; the noise of her mother opening the door and shuffling in to check on her would rouse Harriet further from strangled half-dreams, and she would realize then that the sound was her own. Croup.

Tonight, for the first time Harriet could remember, Adam had it, too. Harriet's occasional cough, always much diminished after the first night (and this was her third night with it) would be answered by Adam's croupy bark, which she could hear through the wall between their rooms. Her room, though still slightly steamy, was silent for once, as her mother had come in to move the vaporizer into Adam's room an hour before. The circus-parade light twirled slowly: the cartwheeling clown, the ringmaster in a top hat, the lion behind bars, the elephant, the seal with the ball on his nose, the clown again. The steam was clearing, too; Harriet could see in the mirrored closet door a cloudy reflection of herself sitting up in bed.

Adam's cough repeated and repeated, like hammering, like a broken alarm. Harriet listened for her mother's steps, but heard only the wall-muffled coughing. She looked at the clock that hung next to her door; it was shaped like a cat, and the tail was supposed to swish back and forth, but that part was broken. She couldn't really tell time, but she knew that when both hands were bunched on the right side of the dial, it was the middle of the night. She got up and opened the door to the hall. Adam's coughing was louder. She walked toward his room and stood outside the door, listening.

The coughing continued, if it could be called coughing. It was like the rasp of a saw going through wood, though sharper, more urgent. Harriet turned the knob and eased the door open a crack. Through the mist of hissing steam that rose from the vaporizer in the middle of the rug, Harriet could see Adam's illuminated globe (a seventh-birthday present from Gay) glowing on its stand. In the bluish light of the world Harriet could see Adam lying under his covers in his bed on his back with his mouth open. He coughed again, and again, and she watched to see if he noticed her, but his eyes remained closed. A medicinal wetness was in the air. She began to breathe through her mouth, which made her taste the menthol in the mist. She coughed a nearly normal cough. Harriet made a mental note to report to her mother in the morning that her croup was over.

Adam started to cough again, a new whooping sound, and his hands went up to his throat, though he seemed to be asleep. Harriet tiptoed over to the side of his bed and stood over him. Sweat, or condensation, was beaded all over his face. Ordinarily, she wasn't allowed in his room, she wasn't supposed to bother him, there were rules about getting out of bed at night, but this was different. Where was their mother? Harriet couldn't remember if her father was home or away on one of his business trips. If he was home, he had come in after her bedtime. Adam's cough sounded again, louder, and then, in midwhoop, it stopped, as if cut off. Adam writhed in the bed, his face darkening with effort. His eyes flew open, and he looked at Harriet for an instant, and then he looked away and closed his eyes.

The hiss of the humidifier seemed suddenly loud. Then Adam started to cough again, and Harriet realized that he hadn't been breathing at all for that moment.

"Adam?" She poked his arm. "Adam? Are you okay? Do you want me to get Mommy?" His face looked less red; it was more bluish white. She could hear his breathing now because it was loud and fast. It stopped again for a long moment—Harriet held her breath too, until Adam's chest dropped and rose again; then she let her own lungs empty—and then Adam began to thrash under his covers as if something were holding him down, while emitting a new and frightening choking, gagging sound.

Harriet left him then and ran to her parents' room, where she found her parents cuddled together like spoons, asleep in their bed, a radio inexplicably playing scratchy jazz, faintly, on the bedside table: this moment was to become fixed, like a snapshot, in Harriet's earliest memories.

Everything after that happened very fast but in slow motion, like the circus light, like a fever dream. Her parents racing to Adam's room, from which now came no sounds of coughing or choking. Stinging like a slap were Ruth Rose's words: "Why didn't you come to us sooner, Harriet? What's the matter with you? How could you wait? *How could you?*" Harriet retreated to her room then and sat on her bed listening while her father yelled into the telephone about sending an ambulance and her mother kept saying, Adam, Adam, come on, Adam, but Harriet didn't hear an answer or even any more of that hideous coughing.

Then ambulance men seemed to fill the house, although there were only two of them. Harriet sat for a moment on the carpet in the hallway and pressed her face to the bannisters so she could see down through the slot next to the stairs. There were two policemen, and another policeman who was a doctor, and at one point Dr. Morris the pediatrician was sitting at the kitchen table with Harriet's parents, although Harriet didn't know when he arrived or who had called him. For some reason Mr. Antler was there, too.

The police doctor stood in the doorway of Harriet's room and asked Harriet to come downstairs into the living room, where he said he had some questions to ask her and would she help him? He let her go down the stairs first and stopped, two steps behind her, when she stopped to draw a circle with her fingertip in the dust on the molding that paralleled the staircase. Scrabbled in the dust were a series of hieroglyphic circles, squares, and triangles. What were these marks for? he asked Harriet, who didn't answer, too shy to explain the way she made promises to herself that were witnessed in the dust: By the time I draw another square it will be my birthday. By the time I draw another triangle I will be in first grade. By the time I draw another circle they will have told me about Adam.

The police doctor followed Harriet as she led the way to the living room, the room for important guests. She was how old, seven? Six. Her name was? Harriet Gibson Rose. He kept asking her about how much time had passed while she was in Adam's room, and what time she had last seen her mother, and did her parents drink a lot of whiskey or wine, and did they ever hit her, and what time was it when she first heard Adam coughing, and Harriet had to admit that she couldn't tell time. It made her feel like a baby.

"So, do you think you waited ten minutes before waking up your mommy and daddy?" he asked her, his pen poised to write down her answer on his clipboard that was like the one Mrs. DelVecchio the gym teacher carried out to the recess field.

Harriet nodded her head, hoping that was the right answer. She heard the ambulance men in the hallway talking about some other child in Oxbridge Gardens who had died of something called Rice syndrome, and she wondered if eating at Lucky Garden had poisoned her brother, although Adam didn't like rice and couldn't have eaten very much. Maybe Harriet should never eat rice again.

She knew Adam was dead, though nobody said it to her. Why didn't they say it? She didn't really have to know it, though, until she was told.

Harriet sat there in the big armchair in the living room, her bare feet tucked under her. She had put on her fuzzy blue bathrobe, but had forgotten her slippers. She shivered with cold. The police doctor asked her to describe how Adam was coughing, and when she imitated the sounds he had made, the doctor nodded his head up and down while he wrote more things on the clipboard. It didn't have a whistle on a string attached to it like Mrs. DelVecchio's.

Mr. Antler came into the living room and exchanged looks with the police doctor, who stood up and put the cap on his pen.

"I'm a friend of the family," Mr. Antler explained, and then he sat down beside Harriet in the chair and shifted her up onto his knees. She leaned back tentatively, and he put his arms around her. She settled into this unfamiliar lap.

The Antlers, especially the children, were a familiar part of her everyday life now, but she hadn't ever thought about how she would describe her connection to them. They were the family next door. People were friends with each other, but she had never thought of it that way, that a person could be friends with a whole family. While Mr. Antler patted her shoulder in a pleasant, soft way she had never seen him use with any of his own children, Harriet repeated the words *friend of the family* silently, over and over, until they made no sense. Mr. Antler usually wore dark suits with neckties, but he was wearing a soft, gray sweater and old, soft corduroy pants. The police doctor waved to her as he left the room, shrugging into his jacket.

"You stay in here with me for a little while, sweetheart," Mr. Antler said gently, now stroking her arm with one of his big hands. Harriet looked down at his hand and was fascinated by the clumps of hair growing out of his wrist; there were even a few little dark curls growing down his knuckles.

Harriet could hear a lot of footsteps slowly coming down the stairs, all together. They were carrying Adam out. She could feel Mr. Antler's arms tighten around her, though she had made no attempt to get up. They were not hurrying. There seemed to be no rush about anything now. Harriet could hear the sounds of the front door opening and shutting.

Simon had his hands on his wife's shoulders. They were both in bathrobes, and as he steered her into the living room, they seemed to sag together, like two lightning-struck trees. Harriet thought they looked astonished at the sight of her snuggled in Mr. Antler's lap, and she sat up, feeling that she had been caught doing something wrong, or that they had forgotten she was here.

Dr. Morris stood behind them, and he shouldered past them now and crouched down in front of Harriet. She liked Dr. Morris, though his accent made him hard to understand sometimes. When he said *this,* it came out *zees,* and when he spoke her mother's name to his nurse, he gargled the two *R*'s in a comical way that embarrassed Harriet.

He had a little blue row of numbers on his left arm, up near his elbow. Harriet knew he had escaped from a prison camp run by Nazis a long time ago, though she wasn't sure what that meant. She always felt ashamed when he asked her to describe symptoms of her own illnesses, considering the things her mother told her Dr. Morris had been through. How could the itch of chicken pox or the pain of a sore throat be bad enough to complain about to someone who had lain in the snow all night pretending to be one more dead body, not moving even when a guard walked on his hand?

The last time Harriet had seen Dr. Morris was a few weeks before when she had been rushed to his office because she had swallowed a twig. Harriet had been pretending to smoke it, like a cigarette, and Barbara Antler had probably only meant to knock the stick out from between Harriet's lips, but instead the stick had gone down her throat and lodged crosswise. Harriet had been unable to croak a sound and had run into the house and gestured frantically to her mother, who had rushed Harriet (with Adam humming beside her in the backseat) to Dr. Morris.

All the time the twig was in her throat and she could hardly breathe, Harriet had thought of Dr. Morris pretending to be dead and had tried to be as brave as he had been. While Dr. Morris rummaged in her throat in order to grip the twig with his frightening tongs, and blood filled her mouth, Harriet stayed quiet and still, so the soldiers wouldn't know she was alive; she had been praised for her good behavior.

Now Dr. Morris took her face in both of his hands and said to her, "It was a freakish thing, Harriet. His windpipe swelled and closed completely because of the croup. He did not have the usual defenses, I think." Harriet breathed in his warm coffee breath. He studied her face for another long moment, then added, "Your parents are lucky they have you. My brother died also when I was a child. We share that now, you and I."

Harriet didn't know what she was supposed to do. She looked toward her parents, who stared back at her. Mr. Antler cleared his throat and said, "Why don't I take her next door for the rest of the night?"

Harriet didn't want to go. She enjoyed playing at their house, but the Antler children slept in beds without top sheets, under blankets that were pilled and grubby, like old stuffed animals.

Dr. Morris smiled at her and tousled her head. "I'll call tomorrow, okay?" Harriet nodded, though she had no idea what they would talk about. Having dead brothers? She scrambled off Mr. Antler's lap and crossed the room to the sofa where her parents were sitting side by side, holding hands. They looked like tired strangers waiting all night for a bus that would never arrive. Harriet stood in front of them. She wanted to wriggle in and sit between them. She wanted to tell them that she was fine, all better, that they didn't have to worry about her. She wanted them to put their arms around her and tell her it wasn't her fault, that there wasn't anything she could have done.

At that moment, standing in front of her stunned, sealed-off parents, Harriet became aware that the room was tilting, and she was tilting with it. Her feet were growing out of the floor, the way a tree grows out of the ground. Yet, despite the difficulty of knowing where she left off and where the room began, she was separated from everything else in the world by a perfectly clear film. It was like looking up from the bottom of a pool, when you can see the surface from underneath. It looks silvery and substantial, but you put your hand through it and you can hardly feel when you've gone through the water and come up into the air. Your wet hand cannot feel the dry air. Everything is farther away than you think. You're floating alone in your suspended world, where solid water pressing in leaves no space for flimsy, airborne particles of rage or sound.

The Project

Harriet was to spend Friday night with Carrie. The only other time she had ever slept over somewhere was when Adam had had pneumonia two years earlier, when Harriet was four, and she had stayed with her grandmother in her apartment for three nights. Gay's chiming clock, a clock Gay called Ursula, as though it were an ancestor who had somehow been preserved in this form, had woken Harriet throughout each night. But Carrie wouldn't have a fancy clock like that.

Harriet had never gone anywhere with Carrie before, and she couldn't tell if Carrie really wanted her to go home with her. But after a rushed after-school snack of cookies and milk, which Harriet ate alone at the kitchen table while Carrie tidied things up, when it was time to leave the house and walk to the subway stop, Carrie held out her hand to Harriet and gave her a big smile, and Harriet suddenly looked forward to the adventure.

Carrie's apartment was in the depths of Brooklyn; it was a long subway ride from Oxbridge Gardens. If they were to ride in the front car, they would have to walk a block more at the other end, but Carrie agreed to it, making Harriet's pleasure complete. Carrie sat in the seat nearest the front door of the train, next to a Chinese man who had his eyes closed. She faced the engineer in the little booth behind a windowless door; he couldn't be seen from inside the train, but interested passengers could hear occasional bursts of squawky static on his radio, and his answering voice, and Harriet had seen him when the train had pulled into the station.

She stood with her nose pressed to the glass and swayed with the rhythm of the train, bracing herself against the door panel but not wanting to give the impression that she needed to hold on in order to keep her balance. The engineer made the train go slower or faster, but he didn't have to steer. Harriet thought it was much more thrilling than driving a car, this business of making the train just go. What freedom. Sometimes she dreamed about gliding on a perfectly smooth track. It would curve up, and up, until she would be sailing through the air. Every time Harriet woke from this dream she was struck anew with the terrible realization that she could not fly.

The rails glittered in two sweeping curves as they sped through the grottoes of subway tunnels that seemed both sinister—the shiver and thrill when Harriet glimpsed a rat lurking beside a puddle—and splendid with grandeur and what seemed to be ancient meaning. The familiar Piranesi print in Gay's foyer was, Harriet thought, a reasonable representation of the IND line.

Occasional lights of a local station flashed by as they plunged along importantly on the express track. A chain crossed the door on the outside, and the glass window was embedded with miniature chicken wire. There was no chance that a child was going to fall out of this door, especially a careful child who wouldn't dream of touching the door handle, a careful child who was unusually cooperative (they always said that, a praising expression that served as a reminder of this expectation above all others), a careful child who didn't have to be told things twice. She rocked on her heels and toes and peered at the hurtling gloom.

Carrie had her usual shopping bag between her feet, and her purse, along with Harriet's overnight bag, stowed on her lap. From time to time Harriet turned to see her; she was always looking back and smiling. The child was relieved that Carrie didn't think it was necessary to stand with her or for them to sit together. Harriet knew Carrie's feet hurt and would have given up her place at the front of the train rather than cause Carrie to stand for the long ride. Over Carrie's head was a sticker, illustrated with a cartoon drawing that reminded Harriet of an old book at Gay's, about Barnaby and Mr. O'Malley. It said, "Little Enough to Ride for Free? Little Enough to Ride Your Knee."

Harriet loved paying her own fare. On the three or four occasions she had gone "into the city" (which is what they called going to Manhattan, although Oxbridge Gardens was already part of New York City) with her mother since she had passed the age of ducking under the turnstile and riding for free, she would be given a dollar bill so she could buy her two tokens herself. In exchange for the dollar shoved under the window in the hollowed wooden scoop on the counter that Harriet could just reach, a hand, just a glimpse of brown knuckle, would shove back two dull brass tokens and some change.

Harriet would keep the two tokens and immediately drop one into the slot of the turnstile and lunge through, using all her strength to turn the paddle and process herself through to the other side, where she would arrive transformed into a passenger. The second token Harriet would keep in her glove for a while, feeling its engraved surface against her palm when she held tightly to a pole. Then she would give it to her mother to keep.

Carrie had produced two tokens from a change purse and had dropped them both into the turnstile slot; she didn't know that Harriet liked handling her own token, because they had never ridden the subway together before. Harriet had never seen Carrie away from the Roses' house, except once or twice when bad weather had made it necessary for Harriet's mother to pick Carrie up or drop her off at the subway station, and Harriet had gone along for the ride in the car. Now they were out among strangers together, both of them shy about it.

As the train raced on, with longer stretches between stations as they left Queens and headed into Brooklyn, Harriet realized that this was the ride Carrie took every morning when she came to work, and every evening when she went home.

Harriet turned around and looked down the subway car. There were fewer people now. At one point there had been so many people standing between them that Harriet had worried because she didn't have a clear sight of Carrie, just a glimpse of her hands folded on her lap in front of the bags. All the people looked tired. Carrie looked tired. Her head was tipped back and her eyes were closed. Now, feeling Harriet's gaze, she opened them, located the child, and smiled. She patted the seat beside her where the Chinese man had been. Harriet hadn't seen him get off. She would never see him again. She wondered if he had thought something equivalent when he had gotten off the train at his stop: "Look at that little girl in the red sweater. I wonder where she's going. I'll never see her again. Good luck, little girl."

The Chinese man who ran a little restaurant near Oxbridge Gardens always said "Good luck," and Harriet had come to think that it was a particularly Chinese thing to say. The way he said it sounded more like "Good ruck." His restaurant was called Lucky Garden, and when he answered the telephone, he said, "Rucky Godden."

Harriet asked him once if he got a fortune every day, and he told her that Chinese people don't eat fortune cookies. He had been eating behind the cash register, shoveling something from a rice bowl quickly into his mouth with shiny black chopsticks, different from the plain wooden ones that Harriet's father (and no one else) was using at their table.

"Only for people like you, missy," the Chinese man explained, waving with his chopsticks in the direction of the table where the Rose family sat with the Antlers, who had just moved in next door. Harriet was embarrassed, and unclear about what people like her were like, and she ran back to the table with the soy sauce her father had sent her to fetch. They were the only customers in the restaurant, and it was to be the only time the two families went out for dinner together.

Harriet described what Mr. Lucky Garden had been eating. Mr. Antler said that the real food Chinese people ate was never on the menu, and Mrs. Antler giggled and pretended to bark like a little dog. Harriet's father said, Oh, my God, and stood up suddenly, in order to fish his money out of his pocket so he could pay their share of the check. This would be another evening of early escape for him, when he would go back into the city to deal with the never ending postseason crises of Rose Lights, wholesale manufacturers and importers of Christmas-tree lights to the trade. It was the time of year that stores returned defective and unsold merchandise, and Simon Rose chewed Maalox tablets as if they were candy corn most of the month of January.

Harriet's mother turned to Adam and began wiping at the sides of his face with a napkin she moistened in his water glass. He continued to chew the food in his mouth and swing his foot against a table leg in identical rhythm, oblivious to her ministrations. Today was a no-talking day, though Adam would always be willing to break his silence in order to read something, anything, out loud. Ruth had told him in the car that he wasn't going to be permitted to read the menu to everyone—it was much too long—so he contented himself now with a brief reading from the words on the paper packet in which Simon Rose's chopsticks had been brought to the table.

"Please try your nice Chinese food with chopsticks, the traditional and typical of Chinese glorious history and cultural," Adam read, with great animation. His relatively cogent delivery when reading was one of those mysteries, like the way stammerers can sing flawlessly.

"Thank you, Adam, that was very good," Mr. Antler said graciously. Adam stared at him, then went on, "Product of China."

"Excellent, very well done," praised Mr. Antler.

"Packed for Well-Luck Co., Inc., Jersey City, N.J. 07139." Adam knew to say *company* for *Co.* and *incorporated* for *Inc.*

"Well done, you're a very good reader, young fellow," Mr. Antler tried again. Adam looked at him until he stopped talking, then looked down again at the strip of red paper in his hand.

"U.S.A." Now Adam really was finished.

The Antler children, Barbara and Debbie, began to squabble over the last sparerib. Mrs. Antler sighed and put both hands on her belly; she was very pregnant with another little Antler, who would turn out to be Rachel, the third girl.

Harriet's father stood beside the table and rested his hand on the top of Harriet's head, and she sat very still. She sensed that he hated being there with all of them, but his hand on her head was like a sign that she alone was not a source of shame, and for that moment Simon Rose seemed to be including his daughter in his state of separateness from and scorn for these neighbors (whom Simon Rose regarded as vulgar and tedious, two words whose meanings he had explained to Harriet during the drive to the restaurant in the Roses' beat-up old Cadillac that Simon Rose had accepted in lieu of payment from some down-and-out wholesaler; while listening to this vocabulary lesson, Harriet had angled herself in the backseat until she could see in her father's side mirror the Antlers, who looked as if they were singing, following behind them in their Dodge Dart), his wife ("Not a real woman," he had confided more than once to his daughter, who wasn't sure what he meant), and his son (whose strangeness left no evidence of early brilliance and felt to Simon Rose like a betrayal).

Harriet sat down next to Carrie in the Chinese man's seat, and the housekeeper put her arm around the child. Her hands smelled pleasantly of hand lotion, and Harriet liked the pink of her polished nails. They were so long and tapered. Carrie always took care of her hands, and she wore thick rubber gloves when she scrubbed the Roses' house.

"Are you tired, Rabbit?"

Harriet shrugged and gazed up at the advertising placards overhead.

"We get off at the next stop."

Harriet read about a secretarial school, a hemorrhoid ointment, and a pill for backaches. There were instructions in English
and Spanish about not getting out of the train if it stopped
between stations. She hoped the train would not stop between
stations. The brakes began screaming and a number of people
began gathering up their parcels and newspapers as they were all
first pressed forward with the motion of the train, and then,
when the train halted, all flung back. The doors opened, letting
in cooler air from the station. Harriet ran her hand over the hard
orange seat and thought that she would probably never sit on
that particular seat ever again, in her whole life. Carrie grabbed
her hand and they were off the train and up two flights of stairs
at a breathless trot, moving faster than most of the people around
them, who all seemed headed in the same direction.

Harriet couldn't have said what she had been expecting. In
countless kitchen conversations, Carrie talked about "the project" all the time, but Harriet hadn't ever realized exactly what
she meant. Harriet knew it had to do with where Carrie lived,
where other members of Carrie's family lived, and friends she
mentioned from time to time. Harriet thought it was something
like a school project, or a meeting of some kind, a club. It
seemed to be a community, she gathered that much, but she still
held a vague mental picture of a group of people gathered around
some sort of shared idea or activity.

Carrie's project was none of those things. It was a sea of tall
red-brick buildings. They were set on a flat plain of concrete,
punctuated here and there by chain-link fences and concrete
benches. She steered Harriet in the direction of her building, and
swinging their clasped hands between them, they went in
through a pair of heavy, scarred doors.

Harriet had anticipated an elevator, a fond association she
made with the few apartment buildings in her experience. But
no elevator was in evidence, and they began trudging up some
dimly lighted stairs. After the first two flights, Carrie told Harriet

it would be two more. Carrie was carrying Harriet's overnight bag, and the little girl worried as she heard Carrie's knee joints crack at every step.

The apartment was a relief, it was so clean and ordered. Harriet had been holding her breath intermittently all the way up the stairs, and now she let it out and took in a deep breath of safe apartment air. She followed Carrie through the living room to a bedroom, where Carrie laid her charge's overnight bag on a tightly made bed.

"This is where you'll sleep, Rabbit," Carrie said, smoothing the child's hair. "Do you like it?"

Harriet nodded politely. "Where will you sleep?" she asked as Carrie picked up a net from her dresser and did mysterious things to her hair with it.

"I'll sleep on the couch tonight. I want you to get a good night's sleep so your mama knows I took good care of you."

Carrie stationed Harriet at her little kitchen table with a glass of milk, poured from a new carton, while she fixed their supper of franks and beans. She put them all together in one pan to warm them up.

The two were eating pound cake that Carrie had brought to the table in a white box when Harriet heard the sound of a key in the lock. She looked anxiously at Carrie, who laughed and said, "That must be Dwight," and Harriet understood. She liked Dwight. He was one of Carrie's twin sons, and he sometimes appeared at the Roses' house and did yard work. The other twin, David, had always been more distant. He had a mustache, and Carrie had recently discovered that he also had a wife and child. Now they didn't "recognize" each other.

"That great big rusty boy, could you imagine he would do all that and not tell me I was a grandmother?" Carrie had testified in the kitchen at 23 Rutland Close, to Harriet mostly, as the child ate lunch while Carrie ironed. "I could have gone to my grave not knowing I had grandkids," she said more than once.

Harriet was not surprised at anything David had done behind his mother's back. He had always seemed shifty, and the mustache had seemed like a disguise that made him the false twin. Once, Harriet saw him closing her mother's handbag as she came into the kitchen right after he had gone in for a cold drink. He had slipped his hands into his pockets and winked at Harriet, who had pretended to ignore him.

Dwight was, Harriet thought, handsome. He had been a teen-ager when his mother had first come to work for the Roses; now he was twenty-five. He wore tight white T-shirts and he lifted weights. It wasn't clear to Harriet where he lived, and as he pulled up the third kitchen chair and helped himself to pound cake, she was concerned that by her presence she was somehow displacing him as well as Carrie. He asked the little girl questions about school while he ate. He tipped his chair back and reached around behind him with one hand to open the refrigerator door in a practiced gesture, but as his hand closed on what Harriet could see was a beer bottle, she saw Carrie shake her head and tilt it in Harriet's direction, and he let go of the bottle and groped toward a half-empty soda bottle instead, which he drained in one long pull. Harriet loved the way the skin on his forehead was shiny and perfect-looking. When Carrie said it was time for small people to have a bath, Dwight tweaked Harriet's nose, kissed his mother on the cheek, and left.

From her bath, Harriet could hear Carrie washing dishes, and then she could hear voices. At first she thought it was a radio, but she recognized Carrie's laugh and hurried to finish the bath and put on her pajamas before anyone came into the bathroom. As she dried herself with Carrie's flowered towel—at home all the towels were one blue—she was fascinated by the mottled green linoleum floor, which looked like marble or a myopic seascape. Harriet had never seen linoleum on a bathroom floor. She thought it was beautiful.

When Harriet emerged from the steamy bathroom, the air in

Carrie's living room seemed especially clear and cool. Two strange ladies were drinking coffee in the kitchen with Carrie. She introduced Harriet proudly, and as the little girl shook hands with them and said how do you do the way very polite children did, Harriet pretended that she didn't see them exchange looks over her head.

As there were only the three kitchen chairs, Harriet stood in her bare feet while the ladies chatted, unsure about what she was supposed to do next. Carrie drew her onto her lap, where she felt too big, but it was nice.

"So this is the child," said one of the ladies, looking at Harriet with momentarily sad eyes.

"What kind of car does your daddy drive?" asked the other one in a chirping, too bright voice, waving her hand in a warning gesture to her friend. Harriet had no idea who they were, but gathered they were also part of this project.

"Well, it's a Cadillac"—here, the ladies looked at one another knowingly—"but we got it for free from a man who owed my father money," Harriet explained, not wanting them to think the Rose family rich.

"L. T. just got himself a Pontiac last week," one lady said to Carrie, who seemed to know who L. T. was. Who was L. T.? "And I told him, I says to him, 'L. T.,' I says, 'L. T., do you know what Pontiac stands for?" The lady was already laughing before she could get out the rest. "And then I told him, 'Poor Old Nigger Thinks It's a Cadillac!' "

They all laughed uproariously. Harriet was shocked by the use of the word *nigger,* which she was forbidden to utter and had only whispered alone, experimentally, looking in the bathroom mirror. She couldn't believe that these three ladies were smiling and laughing. Hadn't they heard? Soon after, it was time for the visitors to leave, and they all did their polite handshaking routine again, and then it was bedtime.

Carrie made sure that Harriet brushed her teeth, and she

washed the child's face all over with a soapy flowery washcloth. Harriet had forgotten to wash her face in the bath. Then Carrie tucked Harriet tight into her bed, which smelled faintly of her.

Carrie asked, "Do you want to say prayers with me?" Harriet didn't answer, and Carrie murmured some sort of prayer with her hand on the small head that lay on her pillow. She sat with the child in the dark for a while, and Harriet listened to the tick of Carrie's bedside clock, and to the sound of a siren that passed nearby. When it had died away completely, Harriet startled her by saying, "Carrie?"

"Here I thought you were asleep. Did the siren wake you?"

"No, I wasn't sleeping. Carrie? That lady said 'nigger'."

"Oh, Alice doesn't mean no harm. L. T.'s an old fool."

"But, isn't it a bad word?"

"Sometimes it is, sometimes it is," Carrie said, smoothing the covers over Harriet.

Harriet thought the words a dozen times before she said them. Then: "What is a nigger?"

Carrie chuckled softly. Then she said, "It's a nasty word for black people."

Harriet gazed up into Carrie's face. She saw what she had always seen and never noticed. "You're black," she whispered, reaching up to touch a smooth cheek with one fingertip. Carrie smiled down at her and didn't say anything.

The next day, after a breakfast of cornflakes, they retraced their subway ride back. By the time they had walked from the subway station to Rutland Close, it was the time Harriet usually got up on school mornings. Harriet could hardly believe it was only early morning after all that. She was exhausted.

Carrie had worn her uniform to work this morning. She didn't always. Sometimes she arrived in a pretty skirt and sweater and changed into her uniform, which hung in a closet in the guest room on the third floor. She only worked a half day on Saturdays.

                                ★ ★ ★

Ruth Rose met them at the front door, a cup of coffee in one hand and a cigarette in the other. She was wearing the bathrobe she put on when she wasn't planning to get dressed at all. Harriet wondered if she had been crying.

When her mother bent down to kiss her, Harriet could smell on her breath the winey sweetness that was typical of grown-up breath when they came to tuck you in during a dinner party. Gay was different, though. Gay never had any bad smells. Harriet suddenly missed Gay and wished she wasn't in Paris for so many weeks.

"It's all done," Harriet's mother said to Carrie, then straightened and turned half away from Harriet. She took one last drag on her cigarette and stubbed it out on the inside of the cup. She dropped the butt into the inch of milky coffee and it floated there. She handed the cup to Carrie and added, gazing out the open front door into the middle distance, "There are some bags of things for your church. You should take a taxi today. Let me know how much it is, okay?"

Harriet stood close by Carrie a moment longer, not liking the feeling of change in the air. What was all done?

Ruth Rose hunkered down again and took Harriet by her shoulders. Carrie carried the cup past them toward the kitchen, and then Harriet could hear water running and the sounds of dishes being washed. "I've cleared out your brother's things," her mother said, staring into Harriet's face as if she was searching for something. Harriet avoided her gaze and looked down. "Harriet?"

"What?"

"Adam's things are taken care of. I'm leaving that room locked for now. I put some of his toys into your playroom. Do you understand? I don't want you trying to go into his room for anything. There isn't anything in there you would want. It's just a room now."

*   *   *

Carrie had the sink filled with sudsy water, and her gloved hands were dipping in and out with glasses and plates. The radio on the counter was playing softly. It was the kind of music that Harriet recognized as the kind Gay liked best, with a man singing about love while music tootled along.

The music reminded Harriet of the moment the previous week when the principal of the school, an old lady with bluish hair named Mrs. Gregory, had walked into the classroom. Mrs. Gregory had apparently been very impressed when she learned from Adam's obituary notice in the newspaper that Harriet was the granddaughter of Gay Gibson. Her condolence call, and her attempt to bring this into a conversation with Harriet's mother, irritated Ruth, who told Harriet that she now had a new, additional reason for avoiding Mrs. Gregory at PTA meetings.

Lately, whenever Mrs. Gregory passed Harriet in the hallways, she bestowed on her the smile she saved for her most favored children, the ones whose parents invited her for dinner or gave her nice presents for Christmas. Mrs. Martin was just then fiddling with the radio to find the music enrichment program to which they were supposed to listen when Mrs. Gregory arrived in the classroom.

"I thought I'd found the girl of my dreams / Now it seems / This is how the story ends . . . ," had poured out of the radio, sung by one of those men with a big, creamy voice.

"Harriet Rose will now tell us all who is singing," Mrs. Gregory had announced, astonishingly, pointing to Harriet.

"Bing?" Harriet had guessed, scrambling to her feet, knowing that it would have to be Bing or Frank or Mel. Those were the ones her grandmother liked best. Mrs. Gregory beamed at her, and Harriet was relieved to have guessed right. She never did understand why Mrs. Gregory had assumed that she would know something like that.

Matching

Barbara and Harriet could sit on their stoops and wave to each other, because of the curve of Rutland Close.

Harriet loved the way the eight houses on Rutland Close matched: she thought of the Roses' house as a right and the Antlers' house as a left. Both had nearly identical entry halls when you walked in the front door, but what Ruth Rose called her front hall Anita Antler called her "foyay." The Roses' sunporch was to the right of the front hall. The Antlers called the analogous room the music room and kept there an out-of-tune grand piano of which they were terribly proud. The Roses' piano was in the living room, "where a piano belongs," according to Harriet's mother, who disdained the pretension of a music room.

Harriet's bedroom window faced Barbara Antler's bedroom window. Harriet could hardly believe that their rooms were the same size, as Barbara's seemed somehow smaller. When Harriet stood in her own bedroom and looked across into Barbara's, she could see through the room and out into the hallway, where a few spokes of the third-floor stair banister always seemed to glow like illuminated organ pipes, despite the general gloom of the Antlers' dark house.

Harriet would arrange the door to her room so that it was a matching degree of openness. If one of the Antlers were to look in her window, the Roses' organ-pipe banisters would be equally, identically visible. When is a door not a door? Harriet knew: when it's ajar. The closet doors in these small front bedrooms had mirrors set into them. Harriet thought if she and Barbara both left their closet doors open wide at an exactly equal angle, then there would be an infinity of mirrored rooms mirrored forever. (It never happened. Harriet was always on the lookout, but Barbara, an untidy girl in so many other ways, always kept her closet door completely shut, for fear of monsters.)

The Roses' house seemed to have more sunlight. It was partly because the Antlers had enormous rhododendron bushes in front of their house, but it was mainly because Mrs. Antler was always reminding Octavia, the housekeeper, to "draw the drapes." Harriet knew from Gay that common people say drapes and well-bred people say draperies, or better yet, curtains.

Gay Gibson was a woman who had spent her seventy years mastering rules for others to live by, when she wasn't publishing light and witty verse about her many marriages and divorces. She found Harriet's reports of the Antlers' "foy-ay" quite hilarious. "Do they by any chance have those cut-glass crescent-shaped salad plates?" she asked her granddaughter. "I do sincerely hope so. What marvelous people." Harriet often accepted secret missions from Gay, and finding out if Anita Antler harbored such salad plates was one of many objectives she achieved with distinction. (Mrs. Antler did indeed.)

The Antler household was full of baby gates blocking free movement from one room to the next, and their living room was dark and shrouded in plastic. There were no windows in there because Mrs. Antler's idea of decorating the room had been to install an entire wall of smoky mirror panels.

The Antlers, it turned out, had moved to New York from Philadelphia because just around the time Mr. Antler's father had died and the older brother, Murray, was supposed to take over the family glass and mirror business, Murray had gotten into big trouble with the law. (Harriet could never figure out—could never overhear enough—to know what exactly that meant.) Murray Antler was uncooperative, whatever *that* meant (Harriet wondered if the word had another meaning; she knew that desperate substitute teachers applied the term to the worst children), so he wasn't going to be around to run the business for a long time. So Albert Antler, who had been forced out of Antler Glass and Mirror in the first place by his unscrupulous brother, had sold his fence company, packed up his family, and come back to New York.

The living-room mirrors had been installed by Antler Glass workmen, who had been anxious to please their new boss. Barbara told Harriet the mirrors were "top of the line." Harriet envisioned a thick black line on the wall, down where it met the floor, drawn by the two men she had seen delivering the panels.

The Roses' living-room windows overlooked the Antlers' driveway and faced the black windows blanked by Anita Antler's mirror wall. The Roses' windows were never covered because most of their curtains were so old and limp they had begun to shred. One curtain was in fact half-gone because it could be reached from the sofa, and for years Adam had sat on the sofa and swirled the curtain into a cocoon around his body while he sucked his thumb and caressed the satiny fabric.

Sitting on the top step of the Roses' stoop, Harriet placed her feet in front of her, two steps down. Her palms on either side, she pressed down on them until she was nearly suspended by her arms. Soon she would have deep prints of the brick patterns in striations all over her hands. If she could run to a fortune-teller fast enough, what would her fortune be?

Barbara followed Harriet's instructions and sat in the middle of the top step of her stoop. She was supposed to sit on the eleventh brick, but she wasn't reliable. Harriet ran over to check, then ran back to locate herself precisely on the corresponding spot.

"Don't move your feet! Don't turn your head!" Harriet shouted, turning her own head to see if Barbara was doing her bidding. Barbara was younger than Harriet by a few months, and she was not always obedient.

"You moved your head!" Barbara called out.

"You shouldn't have been able to tell! I had to, to check on you!"

Now Barbara was turning around and talking to someone else. Octavia had opened the Antlers' front door a crack and was peering out. When she played with the Antler children, Harriet often got the crawly feeling on the back of her neck that she was being watched. Octavia kept too close an eye on things.

"What mischiefy tings are you girls gettin' up to?" Octavia had an accent because she was "from the islands" (Harriet didn't understand how a person could be from more than one island), so that even when she was saying mean things, it all came out in a pleasant singsong. Octavia lived in a dark room on the third floor that was strangely cluttered with medicinal-smelling dolls.

"What's dis den?" Octavia emerged in her gleaming white uniform. She bent over to retrieve a dish towel and an empty mixing bowl that Barbara and Harriet had been using earlier in a failed experiment with caterpillars. "Where's my switch?" Octavia hummed melodically. "I'm going to start a switching, oh, yes, I am," she sang as she shook out the dish towel.

Octavia kept a switch in the corner of the kitchen, and the two older Antler girls got regular switchings on the backs of their legs. Rachel, the baby, was still too young to be punished this way, but Octavia had recently begun to smack her fat little hands when she made a mess with food on her high-chair tray. But Barbara waved a hand to Harriet to signal that this was only an interruption, not a serious threat to their activity, and after another moment Octavia went back inside, banging the door shut behind her.

Uppity, that was the word Carrie used for Octavia. Carrie would never say Octavia's name. Harriet rather liked the musical quality of the name, and she knew from Barbara that Octavia was so called because she was the eighth born in a family of nine girls. Carrie spoke of her as That One and had told Harriet several times that island people were a little crazy and believed in crazy things, thought themselves better than anyone else, and were not to be trusted.

Harriet had now noticed that Barbara was wearing sandals, which spoiled everything anyway. Harriet told her to go change into her red sneakers and white socks that were like the ones Harriet was wearing. While Barbara changed, Harriet got up and measured the width of the Antlers' stoop again. Four and a half stick lengths. Harriet measured her own stoop. It was exactly the same. Barbara came out wearing her sneakers. They were the wrong kind. Mrs. Antler bought shoes for her children without them, on sale at places where the shoes were tied together and dumped into bins and you had to rummage to find the right size, and how did you even know your right size?

Before Adam died, whenever Harriet got new shoes, it took the whole afternoon. Adam took a long time to fit because he was afraid of the music that was always playing in the shoe store. One salesman got to know the Roses and would turn off the music when he saw them coming.

In the shoe store, Adam would only sit in the fourth seat, and if someone was already sitting there, he would begin a high-pitched sound of anguish, like a noon whistle, which was generally quite effective in getting most people to move right away. Then, with the music off and the fourth seat his, Adam would only try on shoes that didn't have any red on them. Sometimes, while the negotiations for the fourth seat and no music were under way, Harriet would scout ahead for shoes without any red in or on them, or on the box either. By the time Adam had shoes that fit him, everyone was exhausted. Then it was Harriet's turn. She usually got the first pair of shoes that fit, no matter what.

She had gone to the shoe store with her mother several times since Adam died. The first time, two older salesmen had stared at them, and Harriet had the feeling they were talking about her and her mother when they stood murmuring, hunched over invoices behind the counter. A new salesman who hadn't been in the store when they used to come in with Adam fitted Harriet now, and the odd calmness of those afternoons left her with the feeling that she had forgotten something, or had left an important possession behind somewhere. Every time, Harriet had picked red sneakers.

All of her shoes had a picture of a boy and a dog inside, and you could put your foot in, too. She suspected that Barbara's shoes probably had no arch supports, whatever those were. Harriet's red sneakers were solid and thick. Barbara's were pointy, and the white rubber edge around the sole was already coming apart. What could Harriet do?

Harriet and Barbara sat on their stoops. From a distance of, say, the lamppost in the grassy patch in the middle of Rutland Close, you wouldn't have noticed the difference in their sneakers. They sat very still in their identicalness. Two little girls of seven with dark hair and bangs. Striped T-shirts and red shorts. White socks, red sneakers. Matching houses. If only there could have been six more little girls. They held still, as if for a time exposure. Then a cloud passing changed the light and they were both suddenly bored, ready to do something else. Bikes.

Harriet's mother drove into the Close, hunched behind the wheel of the Roses' old pale blue Volkswagen. She drove in a panicky slow motion that made some pedestrians back up and look around for high ground. She rounded the Close at this out-of-control snail's pace, and with much clashing of gears, she parked.

Harriet signaled to Barbara that she was going to get her bicycle out of the garage and silently Indian-walked up the driveway, backward. Barbara skipped away toward the Antlers' garage. Harriet's mother was taking grocery bags out of the front seat, where she had lashed them in place with the seat belt.

Harriet rolled her bicycle down the driveway. It was green, a Huffy with a banana seat, thick tires, and foot brakes. Harriet worried that it was too much like a boy's bicycle, but she was proud of it. Standing with her left foot on the left pedal, she pushed off with her right foot, coasted for a moment, bumped down the driveway ramp into the street, and then mounted the bicycle, swinging her right leg over the seat. If cowboys rode bicycles, this is how they would get on.

Barbara coasted down her driveway on her old Raleigh and bumped down into Rutland Close. They rode around the circle abreast, standing up on the pedals to pump as fast as possible. As they passed the Roses' house for the second time, Harriet's mother called out, "Harriet—please help me with these groceries before you go off."

Harriet and Barbara rode once more around the circle, coasting without pedaling, and then Harriet steered back up her driveway ramp and hopped off the still-moving bike and parked it on its kickstand in a practiced motion.

"Back in a minute."

Barbara would ride around the circle until Harriet came outside again. Sometimes, when she was alone, Harriet would ride around the circle fifty times, counting, before shooting out onto Middlemay Avenue, wound up in a knot like the double-twisted rubber-band motors of those balsa-wood airplanes. (Slide wing forward to loop-the-loop. Slide wing back for longer flights.)

Harriet lugged two brown paper bags full of cans into the kitchen and knelt down to stack them into the cabinets she called the round-and-rounds. They were revolving cupboards built into the corners of the kitchen. What fell off in back, nobody knew. There were mice.

Most of the cans were cat food. Harriet stacked them right side up, which nobody else ever bothered to do. She organized them by flavor. If she had had to, Harriet could have eaten some of the flavors, like Savory Stew. Just not the fishy ones.

"I'm going now, okay?" Harriet called up the stairs. She didn't know what to call her mother anymore. She couldn't say *Mommy*. The word just wouldn't come out, hadn't crossed Harriet's lips since Adam died. Harriet could still remember being in her crib, and she could remember how quickly Ruth used to come when Harriet called out "Mommy" from her crib in the middle of the night, but it was different now, and that was a million years ago. Adam always called their mother Mommy, and Harriet was afraid to remind her mother of him. She wasn't sure that her mother heard her just now, but it didn't really matter.

Harriet helped herself to a drink of water from the kitchen faucet out of her cupped hands. She wiped her hands on her shorts and skipped back outside. On the sidewalk, Barbara was sitting on her bicycle, rolling back and forth over the same spot at the foot of the Roses' brick walk.

Barbara's rusted black English racer was too big for her. The chain was loose, and the rear tire rubbed against a bent fender and made a noise. It had belonged to her older cousin Flora, who was slightly retarded and, in the words of Ruth Rose, "overdeveloped." At eleven, Flora had body odor, and mature breasts. She was still interested in dolls. Harriet thought that Barbara's having Flora in her family sort of lined up with Adam's being in the Rose family. Since Adam's death, Harriet had been waiting for Flora to die, too.

When Adam was alive, both girls were still riding smaller bicycles with training wheels. They had called him the Lollobobby Monster (so named because of Lollipop-brand flowered underpants, the wearing of which made one immune to the Lollobobby Monster) and always rode the hell away, away from the Monster, who would make a feeble attempt to catch on to the fenders of their bikes as they flashed by, too swift, too fleet. He could never catch them. Barbara thought it was a game.

Today they rode around the Close once, twice, faster, and

faster, and then out and down the block, across on Greenway North and over to the long blocks of Linden Terrace, where azaleas bloomed in every yard. People came from miles around to see the azaleas of Linden Terrace.

Harriet and Barbara reconnoitered at a corner mailbox. Harriet could hear Barbara behind her because of the squeak-squeak of the rear fender rubbing. They rode to the alley that dipped down steeply from both ends. You could pick up so much momentum if you pedaled hard on the way down one side that it would carry you right up the other side all the way to the top.

"Today we'll do something different," Harriet announced to Barbara. "Instead of going one at a time, we'll both start at the same time from opposite ends. That way, we'll pass in the exact middle at the bottom."

"Cool," agreed Barbara.

Harriet angled her bicycle down toward the bottom of the drop and pushed off. She pedaled furiously, leveled out at the bottom, and coasted up to the top. She rode her bicycle out into the street in a tight circle and returned to the alley entrance. She stopped her bicycle at the top of the drop and stood facing Barbara, who was waiting at the other end of the alley.

"Now!"

But Harriet's bicycle was faster, and her side was a little bit steeper. She passed Barbara when Barbara was still coming down and Harriet was going up the other side. Harriet had been wrong about how this would work: the two sides of the alley weren't the same at all.

The New Baby

Mr. Antler loved his roses as much as he loved his children. He certainly spent more time tending to the two flowerbeds centered on the lawns on either side of the Antlers' front walk than he spent with Barbara, Debbie, or Rachel. Harriet had never even seen him kiss them. The memory of the night Adam died, of the way Mr. Antler held her, seemed like a secret between them.

The May evening Mrs. Antler came home from the hospital with Jennifer, all the children who lived on Rutland Close and in the surrounding neighborhood gathered to play and wait. They rode their bicycles around and around the Close, a pack of nearly thirty children revved up to see the newest little Antler girl. There was something almost funny about the way the Antlers had all these girls, but it was something to celebrate, Harriet thought, unable to imagine what it would be like to have sisters, or even one sister. She thought about a pie, and having to cut it into so many pieces. But there was something missing also, some unspoken absence of a little boy baby to break up the monotony of all those girls, that made Mr. Antler, so big and tall and booming of voice, seem almost defective, as if his inability to duplicate himself made him not quite what he seemed.

Harriet rode her bike with the throng and whipped her head around each time she passed the entrance to the Close, straining for a first glimpse of the Antlers' car. Finally, as a cheer went up from the pack just ahead of Harriet, the avocado green Dart appeared, made the turn from Middlemay Avenue into the Close, and glided up the ramp into the Antlers' driveway. Mr. Antler liked to drive too fast, Harriet knew from her mother, who constantly warned her against standing too near the Antlers' driveway when Mr. Antler was arriving home at the end of his workday.

The Roses' lawn ran alongside the Antlers' driveway, and where the two met was the property line; a muddy tire track smudged this boundary, as neither of the Antlers was careful about honoring this border. Simon Rose was fond of pointing out (not that he cared about gardens or lawns) that they never drove on the grass on their own side of the driveway.

Mr. Antler sat behind the wheel after he had shut down the engine, staring straight ahead. Kids who had stopped astride their bicycles wheeled away, and there was a sudden quiet. Barbara, Debbie, and Rachel rose to their feet from the step on the Antlers' stoop where they had been sitting importantly, expectantly, and cleanly, having been scrubbed and threatened by Octavia. Octavia herself now bustled out the front door, with Antler children and others scattering before her.

Looking official in her white, starchy uniform, Octavia came around to the passenger door and opened it for Mrs. Antler, who held the tiny bundle that was her new baby snug in her arms. (Harriet noticed how cozy this looked, then remembered her mother's scorn for the Antlers' perpetual carelessness and lack of concern about safety, about seat belts, about the need for car seats for any of their children.) Mrs. Antler looked older and tireder and much smaller than when Harriet had last seen her, which had been behind an overloaded shopping cart at the A&P the day before "her water broke" and she was rushed to the hospital.

Cooing in her songlike island way, Octavia scooped the baby away from Mrs. Antler and carried it straight back into the house where she could make it her own. Mrs. Antler sat slumped and still in the car, like someone who had just given a speech waiting for the applause to die down. Her door was still open. Neither of the Antlers spoke.

The neighborhood children had all drifted off. The Antler

girls and Harriet remained standing on the lawn beside the car, and Harriet saw a sisterly "Now what?" look pass between Barbara and Debbie. It made her feel lonely. She tried to catch Rachel's eye, but Rachel, who was not quite three, was busy retrieving her tricycle from a bush. Once she had wrestled it out onto level grass, she plonked herself down astride the seat and gaped at her mother, who had disappeared three days before.

Harriet caught her own eye instead, reflected in the car window just behind Mr. Antler's head. She smiled and turned her head a little and dropped her chin down.

There was a girl in her class, a very fat girl named Mary Alice Balabar, who held her chin up very high whenever class pictures were taken. Harriet had noticed this for years and had only recently figured out that when Mary Alice (who wore matronly clothes unlike those of any other fourth-grader) tipped her head up like that, her double chin disappeared temporarily.

But Harriet was thin and liked the way her own face looked when her chin was dropped down, and she looked up from under her eyebrows, like someone with a secret. This was the way she liked to pretend she was being photographed. She tilted her head and turned a fraction, taking a small step back in order to fit more of herself into the frame of the car window.

"Harriet Rose!"

Mr. Antler's bellow startled her and she leaped away from the car.

"Harriet Rose, get the hell off there!" he yelled, jerking open his car door. She looked around her and saw that her feet were no longer on grass, but were instead pressing down on the clods of soil and bark that surrounded Mr. Antler's rose beds. She nearly lost her balance, but recovered and took a giant step back onto the lawn.

Mr. Antler rushed over and squatted down to pat the mulch and soil back into place. He straightened up then, squared his shoulders, shot his cuffs, and scanned first all of his roses and then the expectant faces of his children, before closing his car door with exaggerated care and striding around the car to offer his arm to his wife. At this moment, Rachel, having realized that her long-lost mother was not a mirage, rocketed straight into his legs with her tricycle as she headed for the object of her heart's desire.

The impact knocked Mr. Antler into the side of the car door, and Harriet heard him hiss, "Shit," as he sagged against Mrs. Antler, who sat down suddenly, banging her head against the window frame. Mrs. Antler burst into tears.

Rachel burst into louder tears. Debbie rammed her thumb into her mouth. Barbara glared at Harriet and said, "Look what you did, Harriet Rose. Why don't you mind your own business and get off our lawn? This is *our* new baby, not yours."

Mr. Antler helped Mrs. Antler from the car. She was sniffling and wiped her nose on the sleeve of her old beige coat, which was about a foot shorter than her maternity dress, which was printed with a sailboat design that made Harriet think of shower curtains. They hobbled toward the open front door together. Mrs. Antler could hardly walk because Rachel clung limpetlike to her leg and had to be lifted completely with each step. (Harriet's mother called Rachel "Anita Antler's potted ivy" and "Anita Antler's personal mink stole" and had predicted trouble over this new baby since winter. "Anita Antler should take up some vertical activities," she had sniffed, whatever that meant.)

The two older Antler girls followed them into the house, and the front door shut with a bang. For a long time Harriet stood still on the grass, like someone in a game of Mother, May I? until she realized that it was beginning to get dark and the streetlights were flickering on. She could hear Mrs. Murphy over on Summer Street calling the Murphy children for dinner.

"Patty, Bobby, Billy, Jackie!" Mrs. Murphy called in a high, sweet voice. "Danny, Mary, William, Thomas, Annie!" Harriet chanted the Murphy names along with her. "Lorraine, Christine,

Louise, Arthur, Donald!" they finished together. The Murphys' pie slices would be infinitesimal.

Harriet liked the look of Mrs. Murphy, a freckled, red-haired woman whose first name was Mary, like the sixth-born Murphy. When Harriet was five, the one and only time she had gone to church with her grandmother, she had misheard the words of a psalm, and had thought she heard the minister say, "Surely good Mrs. Murphy shall follow me all the days of my life." During the next hymn, when she asked Gay about this, Gay had laughed and offered her a Curiously Strong Peppermint and explained what he meant. When Harriet's mother heard that Harriet had gone to church, she was furious with her own mother, who had been expressly forbidden to "drag Harriet off to church" during Harriet's weekend stay with Gay in the city.

"It will only confuse her," Ruth scolded when news of this escapade leaked out when Gay had delivered Harriet back to Rutland Close. Gay had told Ruth about Harriet's confusion about Mrs. Murphy then and had succeeded in diverting Ruth's anger as they laughed together. Harriet, sitting on the stairs eavesdropping with Tobermorey in her arms, had buried her reddening face in his fur. Ruth Rose's nickname for Mrs. Murphy, to Harriet's agony, was from that point on Goodness-and-Mercy.

It was getting darker, and Harriet missed the sound of Mrs. Murphy's voice. All the Murphys must have come home. Did they really eat mackerel for dinner every night? Mackerel snappers, Harriet's father had called the Murphys long ago. Mrs. Antler's little suitcase was still on the backseat of the Dart. Lights glowed in the windows of most of the houses on Rutland Close, with the exception of the Roses', which looked completely dark, although Harriet knew that one light, her mother's bedside reading light, was illuminating a little slice of what used to be her parents' bedroom, though now it was just her mother's.

It was time to put her bike away. Harriet wheeled it into the garage and parked it against the wall. In the pouch mounted behind the saddle of her bicycle there was a small tool kit that came with the bicycle. In addition to the beautiful little wrench and screwdriver, Harriet kept her Swiss army knife there at the ready. She unbuckled the pouch now and reached in for the knife.

It was supposed to have been a present from her father, and she liked the way it felt to say those words, to say, "My father gave me a Swiss army knife." "My Swiss army knife? Oh, it was a present from my father."

Apparently, Simon Rose had bought it at some airport a long, long time ago, when he had been married to Harriet's mother for only two years and they didn't have any children yet and lived in an apartment in the city and Ruth was just pregnant with Adam. The knife was put away for a long time, and then Adam was born but had things wrong with him, and then he wasn't old enough to handle a knife, and then maybe he was but it wasn't a good idea because of the way he was, and then he was dead, and Simon had never even thought to give the knife to his son, because he had never had the son he had planned on having that day at the airport when he bought the knife.

One day, when Harriet said to her mother that she wished she had a pocketknife—because of a book she was reading in which one of the characters spent the entire winter whittling a chain out of a stick of wood—Ruth had simply handed it to Harriet. Her mother explained to her that it was something they had meant for Adam to have, and she might as well have it now that she was a responsible nine-year-old.

Harriet wondered if her father would have thought it was okay for her to have the knife. She didn't dare ask her mother. She had overheard several telephone conversations, and she had pored over various letters hidden in her mother's desk, and she knew her mother hadn't heard from her father in more than two years, she knew that the Christmas-light business had been sold to someone else, and she knew that a lawyer sent them money to live on but wouldn't say where Simon Rose was living.

Since Adam had died when he was nearly nine, Harriet thought her being past that age probably had something to do with her mother's willingness to give her the knife. It was as if her mother had held her breath waiting for Harriet to grow up, the way Harriet held her breath and gripped a button at the same time when she passed a cemetery. Her cousin Nina had taught her that, along with a song about worms crawling in and out your eye once you were dead and buried.

Was Adam still eight now that he had been dead for three years, or was he eleven? Would he always be eight? Were there worms crawling in and out his eye? Harriet had been given a rose to put on his coffin before it was lowered into the ground, so fast, like the way the Ferris wheel drops away from the top where you can see the whole fair, down, down, down to nothing.

The Swiss army knife had a big blade, a little blade, a little pair of scissors, a corkscrew, a screwdriver and can opener, a file and Phillips screwdriver, a little tweezers that fit into a slot, and a toothpick that Harriet planned never to use, not even in an emergency, because then no matter how much you cleaned it, it would still have germs on it and go back into its slot and it would be disgusting forever.

Harriet crept along the side of her house, brushing against the overgrown rhododendron bushes. She held the knife closed because she knew it was wrong to walk with any of the blades open. When she got to the Antlers' car, she opened the small blade and, crouching low, scratched back and forth in one spot on the passenger door. The metal underneath the paint was surprisingly shiny. Harriet wiped the blade on grass to clean off the avocado green paint grit—eliminate incriminating evidence, she thought—and rubbed it on her jeans, before folding it into the handle. She turned her head to study her face in the side mirror, to look into the eyes of a criminal. Her face looked back at her as if from far away.

She scooted around the car to the nearest flowerbed, the one she had stepped into by mistake. The scissors, she quickly learned, weren't strong enough to cut through the stems of the roses, but the big blade was, and laboriously she cut through every single stem, until nothing in the bed was more than six inches high. She left the stems and branches lying where they fell. Tightly budded roses and smaller, beginning buds that would never grow into flowers lay prettily on the brown background like an artful picture on the cover of a book her mother might read. The thorns were sharp, and Harriet's thumb was nearly blistered from the sawing by the time she was finished.

Safe in her own backyard, Harriet sat on the edge of her old sandbox and rubbed and rubbed the big blade with her shirt until it was shiny clean. She polished it in the damp sand, wiped it off, and closed it. She dropped the knife into her pocket and wondered, scared, what she was going to do next.

An old headless mop handle leaned against the trash cans beside the garden gate. She picked it up and weighed it in her hands, then went out the gate carrying it over her shoulder like a soldier with his rifle.

The blind, dark windows of the Antlers' living room looked out on the driveway. They must be eating dinner now, in the kitchen with a smell of frying onions and the television on and their new baby in the old baby carriage Rachel used to sleep in that always stood in the hallway.

Harriet aimed the mop handle up over her head like a spear and tapped against the black glass. Harder, and harder. Then the window broke with a startlingly loud crash, and then came the sound of glass falling and breaking on the pavement, which made it real. Harriet dropped the mop handle and ran into her own yard. She didn't feel real, but she was breathing fast, almost panting as if she had run a long way.

"Hey, you!" she called out tentatively. "You! Where do you think you're going? What are you doing?" She realized no one could hear her and repeated herself more authentically. "Hey! Stop!" she yelled as loud as she could. Lights were going on in her house, and the Antlers' driveway floodlights blazed on. "Stop! I see you!" she screamed out again. Her breathing was ragged.

Harriet could almost see him now, a boy maybe eleven or twelve, running away, easily climbing up the high, trellised fence behind their house, straddling the top for a moment where he could see everything, and then dropping down, down to freedom on the other side.

Harriet the Spy

Harriet Rose to the occasion, she told herself. Harriet crept out of bed and sidled noiselessly down the hall. Harriet the Spy. She ducked behind the bathroom door and waited.

She heard the rattle of her mother's bedside table drawer handle as Ruth Rose stored away her reading glasses and Angela Thirkell novel for the night. Harriet listened for the click of her mother's reading lamp. The pale rectangle of light that spilled from her mother's room and lay across the hall carpet vanished.

As Harriet's eyes adjusted to the darkness, she could hear the murmuring voice of a radio talk-show host flare momentarily before being extinguished as Ruth Rose searched the airwaves for a night baseball game from the West Coast, blipped past music and voices, found one, and tuned it low.

Harriet eased out of the bathroom, taking giant steps onto the hall carpet. She passed the closed door of Adam's room. She took a breath, held it, and reached out to test the doorknob. Locked, as always.

The door to Adam's room had been locked for nearly three years now, ever since Harriet came back from her one and only overnight trip to Carrie's a few weeks after he died. Whenever her mother was in the kitchen or talking on the telephone or otherwise preoccupied, Harriet methodically searched through every single drawer and riffled every known hiding place in her mother's desk and bureau and closets, but she had not yet come across the key.

In those days and weeks right after Adam died, after Harriet's father had moved into the guest room just across from Adam's room (a move Harriet now recognized was the beginning of his leaving), Harriet stopped being able to fall asleep at night.

Sometimes, after Harriet had lain awake for hours, when she wandered down the hall to the bathroom in the middle of the night, she would see light coming from under his door, and she would hear the impatient sound of newspaper pages turning.

Simon Rose couldn't sleep either, and Harriet would tiptoe down the hall, not daring to intrude but thinking, "We're two of a type," feeling pleased somehow to know that he joined her in wakefulness. How could her mother sleep through those nights? Ruth Rose seemed to spend enormous amounts of time sleeping. Harriet remembered how, when she was little, before Adam died, it was always easy to go to sleep and sleep all night until morning. It was a skill she had somehow lost, like forgetting how to ride a bicycle, no matter what people always say.

The door to the guest room was open and the room was dark. Sometimes Harriet worried that she couldn't remember her father's face or the sound of his voice. What if he had come back but hadn't told them and was living somewhere else? When Harriet went into the city for visits with Gay, she searched the faces of men she saw on the street, on the chance she might spot her father.

A couple of months after Adam died, Simon Rose said he was going to Yugoslavia on a buying trip. Harriet and her mother would have the house to themselves, he said to Harriet while he stacked shirts on the bed the afternoon of his flight. Harriet sat beside his open suitcase and ranked his rolled socks in order by color: six shades of dark blue.

He said he needed to hunt down the source near Zagreb for a unique small flashing lightbulb that he wanted to incorporate into his line, but later that night, before he left in the taxi for the airport, he stood in the doorway to Harriet's room and told Harriet, who lay in the dark room under her covers, that he didn't know where he would go after that and didn't know when he would be back. Harriet had lain there hoping he would tuck her in, but the taxi was waiting and the driver was honking the horn and then her father was gone, gone, gone. Harriet pretended to herself that her parents talked all the time on the telephone.

"Say Daddy's on a business trip," Ruth would coach, still, though no one ever inquired, before lunch at Gay's or any other occasional Gibson family gathering the two of them might attend.

Harriet paused at the bottom of the stairs that led to the third floor. Faint light from a streetlamp shone through the bathroom window. It was filtered through the leaves of a maple tree that had grown too close to the Roses' house. When the wind blew, branches brushed against the house and tapped on the windows. Good night, nobody.

Harriet could just make out the place on the wall in front of her, just below the light switch, where she had picked away at peeling paint until the bare spot, showing a queer brown color of varnished plaster, had begun to bear a strong resemblance to the map of South America that hung in the back of the classroom where Girl Scout meetings were held.

She began to creep up the stairs, whose risers were higher than any other flight of stairs she knew. She skipped the fourth stair, knowing its creak, and when she reached the landing at the turn, she froze like a statue and waited to be sure that her mother had heard nothing.

Harriet's feet were cold from the bathroom tile floor, and she sat cross-legged on the stair landing and rubbed them. She should have worn socks. Foot mittens. Something moved in the darkness of the third floor hallway and she felt a stab of fear. But it was only Tobermorey, who trilled softly as he strode up to her and butted his head against her thigh.

"*Shh,*" she cautioned him absently as he flopped at her side and began to purr. "*Mrkgnao!*" he trilled again, and began to knead her pajama leg with sharp starfished paws. She stroked him and pushed his paws away, gave him a final rub and got to her feet. As Harriet tiptoed toward the attic door, the cat stared after her, his green, unblinking eyes aglow in the dimness. Abruptly, he turned away and began to wash.

Harriet opened the squeaky attic door an inch at a time, quiet, quiet. Cold air flowed past her. She walked in, feeling in the chill blackness before her for the string that hung down from the bare bulb. It brushed her face, and she reached for the doorknob behind her with one hand while plucking at the string with the other, neither wanting to turn the light on while the door was still open, for fear of detection, nor wanting to close herself into the attic darkness. She always tried to tug on the light cord at the same moment that she shut the door.

Harriet hugged herself and looked around the riot of broken household objects, old toys, file drawers, picture frames, stacks of books, suitcases, yellow packing boxes with green Mayflowers on them, shadeless lamps, lampless shades, and trunks of old clothes. The smell of mothballs and camphor was clean and musty at once. Harriet liked the smell and took a deep, appreciative breath. It was almost as good as the rich perfume of mold in the garage.

Her old nursery-school blanket was rolled up and stuffed onto a shelf crowded with bundles of old magazines, nursery lamps, cheap vases that had come into the house with floral arrangements (Gay always deplored such vases on the grounds that only the lower classes send arrangements, while People Like Us send cut flowers). Harriet took the blanket down and shook it out, then spread it with care over the dusty plank floor. Next, she reached up to a shelf on which sat a row of hat-factory wooden heads that Simon had brought home when his uncle Zelig's hat store in Brooklyn had burned up. Harriet didn't like to touch them because their featureless faces bothered her; they reminded her of faceless hordes of distant dead relatives who had burned up in Nazi concentration camps, although these heads, some of them lightly singed, had eluded incineration, as had Uncle Zelig, Aunt Esther, and Uncle Meyer.

Behind the heads, Harriet knew, lay the box of photographs. It was a brown, nondescript, leatherette box, of about the same dimensions as the box in which Harriet's new ice skates had come. In gold script, over the catch, it said *Records*.

Gingerly feeling between two heads, she located the edge of the box. She drew in a big breath and held it, before picking up one head by the ears and moving it aside. She let out her breath with a sigh. Sliding the box out, she balanced it in her hands and lowered it onto her blanket, then settled herself comfortably cross-legged next to the box.

The catch was stiff, but not locked, as Harriet knew. She fiddled it open and lifted the lid. Here were the photographs bound in bundles by short lengths of old faded green velvet ribbon. Sorting past packets she had looked at before (most of which seemed to be tourist snapshots of unknown people standing in front of various monuments and fountains in cities that Harriet assumed were in Europe), Harriet selected a bundle that she hadn't opened before and released its ribbon. She allowed herself one new group of pictures per attic mission. A dozen black-and-white photographs, each about the size of a playing card, separated and fanned out on the blanket.

Unlike the photographs Harriet had examined previously, these pictures all had smooth edges. The tourist ones had crinkly edges. She picked up the top photograph. It showed a man, a woman, and a little girl standing alongside an enormous car. The man was wearing a big overcoat and a broad-brimmed hat, and the woman, turbaned and wearing dark glasses, had a big dark coat with a fur collar. The little girl also wore a hat, with a round brim that turned up. She had on a light-colored coat that had two rows of buttons, and a doll dangled from one hand.

Her other hand was clasped awkwardly by the man, who was reaching around and stooping down in order to be closer to her for the picture. His other arm was partly around the woman, who held a purse with both of her hands and seemed to be staring straight into the camera, although Harriet couldn't tell for sure, because of the dark glasses.

The next photo was of the same man and woman, without the little girl. Harriet examined the picture closely for signs of her. Maybe she was in the car, ducked down out of sight. The couple were posed in front of the hood of the car this time, and the grille of the car was like a grinning shark behind them. They were standing with their arms around each other.

Harriet pushed the photo off the stack and onto the blanket. She studied the next picture. Same woman, but without the sunglasses, same little girl, now sitting on the hood of the car. Where was the man? Harriet could see his shadow on the ground in the right-hand lower corner of the picture. The little girl was looking at him, but the woman was looking away, squinting into the sun.

Harriet could see the license plate on the front of the car. It had fewer numbers, a dark background and light numbers, not like the license plates Harriet knew. Was it from a long time ago or from another state, or both? She dealt herself the next picture. It was a close-up of the man by himself in front of the car, and he was smiling right at the camera as if he were in the middle of telling the punch line to a joke. His smile made him look familiar.

Harriet suddenly knew that the man was her father. She covered his hat and hairline with her finger. Yes. She moved her finger down to cover the man's dark eyebrows, too. Definitely yes. Simon Rose, now quite bald and eyebrowless in his fifties, had been a handsome young man with dark hair and bushy eyebrows.

She went back to the previous photographs, covered his hair line with her fingers, and turned the stranger into her father every time. His body looked different in these clothes. The hat seemed jaunty, funny even. His tie was loosened at the collar but still made him look as if he were going out to dinner at a fancy restaurant. His pants hung on him differently, somehow charmingly, confidently. His belt was wrapped around his waist as if he were more alive then.

There were two more pictures in the stack. One was a tilted attempt at photographing a moving black cat, whose head was partially cut off by the frame. The blurred body of the cat, punctuated by its upright tail, was crossing in front of one of the car tires, and reflected in the round shine of the hubcap, Harriet thought she could see the crouched figure of the man—her father—with the camera against his face.

The last picture was of the little girl sitting on the hood of the car holding the cat. Where was the doll? The black cat hung limply from the crook in the little girl's arm. Harriet studied her closely. She covered the little girl's hair with one finger, but the little girl didn't turn into anyone she knew. She reminded Harriet of somebody, though. She covered the little girl's hair again. Then she covered the little girl's rather pouty mouth. Now the little girl looked just like—Harriet Rose.

But I wasn't alive in the olden days when they took these pictures, Harriet thought, suddenly feeling panicky. She dropped the picture and swept all the photographs together. She shaped up the stack, first the sides, then the top and bottom, until it was even all around, with the first picture of the man, woman, and little girl on top. She gazed at them, trying to see into the black lenses of the woman's sunglasses. A moment later she rummaged through to find that last picture of the little girl with the cat again.

P.S. Your cat is dead, thought Harriet. It was the punch line to a joke she had overheard her father tell someone once. She didn't understand the joke. The cat would have to be dead because these pictures must be old, she calculated, studying her father's younger face in the photographs she held in the palm of her hand. So the cat would be dead and the little girl would be a grown-up. Harriet closed her eyes for a moment and tried to think of adult women she knew.

There was Mrs. Martin, her teacher. But Mrs. Martin was from Ann Arbor, Michigan. There was the lady who worked at the dry cleaner, where Harriet sometimes accompanied her mother when she had a new dress that needed to be pinned for hemming. Harriet remembered joking between her mother and the dry-cleaning lady about a twenty-fifth birthday not too long ago. But she was Italian.

And then there was the woman, the little girl's mother. Who was she? She would be old by now. Harriet sorted back through the pile until she came to her. The pouty mouth on the little girl was hers.

Simon Rose had been married to this woman and this was their little girl. That had to be it. Or maybe he was just friendly with them? Harriet peered at the picture in her hand, the one of the three of them together, and tried to make out a wedding ring. The woman seemed to wear several rings on both hands, but it was hard to tell from such small pictures if there was a wedding band on her left hand. Harriet knew her father eschewed a wedding ring and had heard him speak contemptuously of men who wore any kind of ring. His hands here seemed blank of jewelry, too.

Harriet stared at her father's hands for a long time, looking at one picture after another. In the cat picture, where she could see him in the hubcap reflection, one of his index fingers was crooked in the act of taking the picture. Something about that gesture seemed both touching and almost horrifying to Harriet. She swept the pictures together again, any which way, tied them together with the frayed length of velvet ribbon, thrust the bundle of pictures in among the others, closed the box lid and latched it, and stood to replace the box behind the wooden heads.

As she shoved the box up onto the shelf, it knocked against one of the heads, which wobbled against another head, which in turn fell against the next head. Harriet caught the last head as it slowly toppled off the end of the shelf, and she heaved it back to its upright position. Holding that last head with one hand, she reached across the row and carefully set the others back in place one at a time with her other hand.

If they had all rolled over the edge of the shelf, she thought, it would have sounded like someone bowling up here. The jig would have been up. Jig as in dance or jig as in saw? Harriet wondered automatically.

She pulled the string to extinguish the light while turning the knob to the attic door. Tobermorey was waiting just outside the door, and Harriet just managed to block his attempt to slither through her legs into the attic.

"Thanks, Tobe, that's all I needed, to hunt for you in there all night," she whispered in his ear as she carried him in her arms down the stairs.

In her room Harriet pauses in front of the full-length mirror on her closet door. The moon is high and the room is filled with tree shadows and patches of moonlight on the walls and rug. She shifts Tobermorey in her arms until his back half hangs down from the crook of her left arm. She attempts a pouty mouth and gazes into her own eyes, envisioning a man crouching down before her with a camera held to his face. His index finger is crooked over the shutter button with grace and wit as he tells her to smile. He is young, he knows how to do things, he is her daddy. He laughs as the cat begins to struggle free, and lovingly he presses his finger on the shutter button and takes a picture of his little girl.

November 12

After school, Harriet knocked on the Antlers' back door. It was a raw, gray November afternoon of one of those days when the sun never really seems to get all the way up in the sky before it starts to set again. Harriet's hands were cold because she hadn't worn mittens. Octavia answered the door with the littlest Antler, Jennifer, in one arm and a container of milk in the other. She didn't really greet Harriet so much as register that she was there before she turned away distractedly, leaving Harriet to close the door and hang up her jacket among the slightly dirty Antler outerwear that took up all the hooks in the hallway.

Harriet's jacket slid to the floor twice before she found a cranny between jackets in which to wedge a sleeve. Their mitten basket, which tilted from the handle of the laundry-room door, was overflowing with ragged, dirty, mismatched pairs that Mrs. Antler had mated with wooden clothespins. The Antler girls shared these mittens. Harriet couldn't imagine sharing the way they did: shirts, socks, underpants even. Harriet couldn't understand why they always seemed so cheerful, all crowded together. They didn't seem to realize how deprived they were in their shabbiness, how lucky Harriet was in the solitary splendor of her unshared drawers of folded clothing. She found the Antler children already seated at the kitchen table having their snack.

Carrie didn't work for the Roses anymore, and now some days there wasn't anyone home in the afternoon when Harriet got out of school. She wasn't sure where her mother was when she wasn't home. Harriet had started going over to the Antlers' on days like this one, when no one answered the doorbell at her own house, although it had never been particularly arranged. Harriet missed Carrie, Carrie who loved her and called her Rabbit and made tuna fish sandwiches just right. But only a few days after fourth grade had begun, Harriet now knew, there had been some kind of disagreement between Carrie and Ruth involving money.

One day when Harriet came home from school, Carrie was just leaving, earlier than usual. She grabbed Harriet and hugged her tightly and kissed her over and over again. Puzzled, Harriet hugged and kissed her back, but then Carrie abruptly turned away and left the house moments later. Only afterward did Harriet find out that Carrie was never coming back to work for the Roses again, that Carrie had been saying good-bye.

Not too long after that, Ruth threw away Carrie's old uniform, which had always hung on a bent wire hanger in a closet in the guest room. Harriet stole it from the trash and kept it hidden, wrapped in a plastic shopping bag under her bed. The pale green dress, which had always reminded Harriet of the uniforms on the waitresses at Schrafft's (where she had gone three times for lunch with Gay; on each occasion Harriet had ordered a club sandwich), gave off a faint smell of Carrie that was a mixture of sweat, deodorant, and hand lotion.

Harriet was secretly glad that her mother wasn't home this afternoon, because it was more interesting in the Antler kitchen than sitting alone at her own kitchen table with the glass of milk and cookie that her mother might tentatively offer—is this what you like?—before apologetically creeping back upstairs with a glass of sherry, her reading glasses, and a mystery novel.

The smacking sound that made Harriet jump was Octavia's big blue-black hand clapping down on Jennifer's pink sausagey arm. Harriet stopped crunching her graham cracker and tried to catch Barbara's eye, but with Octavia diverted, Barbara was furtively helping herself to a spoonful of grape jelly from the bowl Mrs. Antler always kept on the kitchen table.

The Antlers' jelly bowl, and the glass sugar pourer with the metal flap that sat next to it (both of which Harriet had reported to Gay, who seemed delighted to know of their existence), made Harriet think of luncheonettes. Harriet loved the word *luncheonette*. Carrie took her to a particular one a few times; at this lunch counter the food was delivered to you by an actual model train. There were plates bolted to the flatbed cars; train tracks circled around the counter and through the kitchen. Each hamburger or sandwich was accompanied by a miniature cardboard box that held two Chiclets. Harriet wasn't supposed to tell her mother about these outings, because Ruth Rose had pronounced the place both unsanitary and unsuitable. There was a black man, named Freddie, behind the counter who would joke with Carrie and refill Harriet's soda glass over and over. Harriet wondered if she were to go there on her own, now that Carrie was gone, if Freddie would even recognize her, let alone provide free soda. But maybe he knew all about the money disagreement, maybe he would be angry with Harriet.

Barbara watched out for Octavia while she licked the jelly spoon and reinserted it in the bowl. Jennifer had been happily flipping bits of gummed graham cracker from her high-chair tray onto the floor for the benefit of the Antlers' mutt, Archie. It took her a few seconds to react to Octavia's smack. She flapped her arms, drummed her feet, and screwed up her face, drawing a big breath. Then she began to scream in a long connected howl that went on and on and made Harriet want to cry.

Jenny seemed able to sustain her screaming while breathing in and out. Harriet was overcome with sadness the way she had been the time she stood on a Fifth Avenue curb with her grandmother while a parade of piping bagpipers inexplicably streamed by. (It hadn't been a holiday, as far as she knew.) That relentlessly sad tone, too, had brought her to the brink of tears.

Barbara, Debbie, and Rachel all continued cramming graham crackers into their mouths as fast as they could. Only Harriet had stopped eating; the other children had blank looks on their faces, as if they had agreed in advance to ignore this moment.

Octavia, still standing over Jenny with one hand raised, lowered it slowly while humming in the back of her throat. She sat back down in Mr. Antler's chair, the one with arms at the head of the table, and baring her mouthful of enormous teeth, she slowly turned her head to beam this spurious smile beacon around the table.

"You be nice like the other children. See how they are bein' nice?" The other children made no sound other than a steady crunching.

"Tavey, up me?" Jenny reached out and smiled cautiously at Octavia.

"How you askin' me?" Octavia cupped a hand behind her ear to pantomime her expectation.

"Tavey, up me, *pease?*" Jenny reached out again expectantly.

Archie sat gazing up with love at Jenny. At the sight of her upraised arms his plumey tail thumped hopefully.

Octavia's switch came from nowhere, dividing the air in two with a mean whistle, whipping Archie across the nose. He cowered and whined and slunk down onto his belly, then scrabbled across the linoleum until he was safely wedged behind the thicket of chair legs under the table.

"I do not tolerate a bad animal in this house!" Octavia declared.

For the rest of the afternoon, Harriet played with Barbara and Debbie. Anita Antler worked some days as a volunteer in the charity thrift shop on Healey Avenue, and this was one of her late Fridays. She came home sometimes just as Octavia was serving the Antler children their dinner, but it didn't matter, because Mr. and Mrs. Antler usually ate together after the children's bedtime. Harriet had heard plenty of her mother's dim views of these particular Antler habits; Ruth Rose did not approve of parents who didn't eat with their children. On the other hand, Harriet dreaded the dinner hour, when the two of them would sit grimly together with the portable television playing at what used to be Adam's place at the kitchen table. And Harriet certainly hadn't eaten with her own father in a very long time.

Harriet believed Ruth that in all ways the Rose family of two knew better, had superior and preferable methods for just about every aspect of daily living, compared to the arrangements next door. But Harriet craved something in the Antler household: the jolly carelessness, the sugar and jelly sandwiches, the friendliness of all those dirty jackets jammed together.

Ruth Rose was of the opinion that her next-door neighbor worked at the thrift shop mainly in order to skim off the most desirable merchandise for her own family before it was tagged and displayed for the shop's customers. This was possibly the case. When Harriet's old, beloved, outgrown red party shoes—a pair of shoes that had been controversial in the first place because Gay had taken Harriet to buy them without Ruth's knowledge or advance consent, and Ruth always said they were too pointy and didn't have adequate arch supports—were donated to the shop in a bag of clothing Ruth had culled from Simon Rose's closet when he had been "away" for the better part of a year, they had turned up on Debbie Antler's feet three days later.

Debbie Antler had very wide feet, and Harriet had rather narrow feet, and as a consequence the tops of Debbie's feet bulged and overflowed around the ankle straps, and the shoes looked terrible on her. She wore them for everyday, too, which made it even worse. Harriet hated to see Debbie slopping around in those prized red shoes. She wished she had been allowed to keep them in her closet just to look at them. At the very least, her mother should have just thrown them away.

Mrs. Antler's own feet were amazingly large, and her shoes, among rows of which Harriet now squatted as she hid in the mysterious undergrowth of Mrs. Antler's closet, were like cord-wood. Footsteps sounded on the wood floor, then more muffled on the bedroom carpet, and then the closet door creaked open and light trickled in. Mrs. Antler's belts and chains that hung on a rack on the inside of the door swayed and clinked together. Harriet held her breath. The door swung closed, though not all the way. Something moved toward her. The rustling dresses in their plastic shrouds parted, and on her hands and knees, Barbara slowly emerged next to her in the gloom.

"I thought you were here," she whispered to Harriet, and then scooted in next to her. They sat together breathing in the smell of camphor and Mrs. Antler's shoes.

"Debbie won't find us. We'll be here until it's time for me to go home for dinner," Harriet whispered back.

"She's a retard," Barbara whispered back, and then they both began to giggle as they heard Debbie calling for them downstairs. The slam of the kitchen door vibrated under them, and then they could hear her outside, in the backyard, shouting their names into the late-afternoon November darkness in a still-hopeful voice.

"Forget this," Harriet decided, and they both crawled out of the closet. "Doesn't she know any of the rules of Sardines? We wouldn't be *outside.*"

"She's a retard," Barbara repeated cheerfully. She had dragged a pair of her mother's shoes out of the closet with her, and she sat on the rug, idly inserting her sneakered feet into the gaping maw of these black-and-white opera pumps. She stood up awkwardly and wobbled over to see herself in the full-length mirror on the door to her parents' bathroom. Standing up in the shoes, her feet slid far down into the toes. Harriet stood up behind her, having helped her to her feet; holding on to Barbara's shoulders, she stepped into the shoe-space behind Barbara's feet. Astonishingly, her own sneakered feet just fit.

The two girls admired themselves in the mirror, stepping forward and back together, like a couple learning a dance step. They walked around the room, grandly stepping forward like part of a circus parade, like the tall Uncle Sam who waved his starred-and-striped top hat while striding along with stilts in his pants legs. Harriet's knees knocked into the backs of Barbara's thighs, and as she stood just behind Barbara in the uphill part of Mrs. Antler's shoes, her eyes cleared the top of Barbara's head in their reflection.

Octavia was coming up the stairs. They could hear her sing-song voice addressing Jennifer, whom she must have been carrying.

"You got de bowels, chile? You got de bowels, oh, yes, you do. Your Octavia gone make you fix-up, oh, yes."

The two girls made an instantaneous and unanimous decision to seek refuge back in the closet, which they did, stepping gracefully together in giant steps, there not being time to get out of Mrs. Antler's shoes, and they pulled the door shut just moments before Octavia arrived on the stair landing.

Harriet could hear the squeak of water faucets turning and then the gush of water filling a bathtub. She stood by the closet door, which she held open just a crack. Baths were usually just before bedtime in her experience, and the running-water sound made her worry that it was getting late, that her mother might be waiting for her at home.

"Does she give Jenny a bath before dinner?" Harriet wondered to Barbara, who was crawling around behind her, returning her mother's shoes to their spot in the lineup.

"She's really weird about baths," Barbara said, without further explanation. They stood together, debating if they could sneak past the bathroom without Octavia's notice. They probably could. Taking exaggerated giant tiptoe steps across the bedroom carpet, they reached the doorway and peered down the hall. Good—the bathroom door was closed, and Octavia's voice could be heard within, asking questions and then answering them herself. Harriet and Barbara tiptoed past.

There was a horrible, wet slapping sound that jolted Harriet like an electric shock. For a moment, all she could hear was the sound of the bath running, but then Jenny began to scream, and scream, and scream. Harriet had never heard anything like it.

"Come on, let's get out of here," Barbara urged impatiently from the top of the stairs. Harriet skittered down the hall, then stopped in her tracks at the sound of another slap. Jenny's screams ratchetted up a notch louder and more desperate. Harriet was frightened. She could hear, unbelievably, a singsongy crooning from Octavia, and then midscream, Jenny choked and coughed, and then, strangely, the bathwater was turned off, and only Octavia's humming and some splashing could be heard behind the closed bathroom door.

"Come on, slowpoke," Barbara called up to Harriet from the bottom of the stairs. Harriet stepped down a few stairs, one at a time, her head cocked to one side as she listened for Jenny. She stopped again.

She looked at her hand as it gripped the polished banister, a banister identical to her own next door except the tone of the wood was a shade lighter, and the varnish was sticky. Her knuckles were white. She couldn't feel the wood under her palm, which had become part of the banister. There was no way to breathe in air. The slow twirl of the ringmaster in the top hat, the lion behind bars, the elephant, the seal with the ball on his nose, the clown. Splashing, and then Octavia's syrupy voice: "Feelin' fainty, little lamb? Open your eyes, an' look at your Anty Octavia."

Harriet listened to the silence then. She could hear gunshots and squealing brakes, car doors slamming and police sirens, in the den downstairs, where Barbara, who had given up on her, was watching television with Debbie and Rachel. Somehow, she got free of the banister and backed up the steps, one by one. Past the bathroom door, she retraced her steps until she stood in the dark bedroom again. She circled Mr. and Mrs. Antler's enormous bed, promising herself that one sound from Jenny and she could swim up from the bottom of this pool, up into the air, she could go watch television with the other children.

In the bathroom, Octavia hummed a snatch of her inside-out island tunes and then murmured, "I do not tolerate de longheartedness of a child, no I do not."

Harriet picked up the telephone.

Ruth Rose in her Volkswagen, Anita Antler in her Dodge, and the police cruiser, silent but with lights flashing, turned into Rutland Close one after the other, as if in a planned, orderly sequence. Their headlight beams swept around the Close and all three cars stopped together. Harriet stood on her own dark front steps, hugging herself, her teeth chattering with a mixture of cold —she had left her jacket at the Antlers—and fright. The sight of the policeman walking up the Antlers' front steps with Mrs. Antler made it real. Ruth Rose, who had been eliminated from the scene by the policeman, whose abrupt questions made it clear that his interest lay in the Antler household, stood on the sidewalk holding two grocery bags and stared uncomprehendingly after them.

"Harriet—are you all right? Is somebody hurt? Are you sure you're okay?" Her mother's concern washed over Harriet pleasantly. It was unusual for her mother to be so focused. She just always seemed so sad. Harriet took a bag of groceries from her mother. Tobermorey was waiting by the door to get in. He meowed and stropped himself impatiently against Ruth Rose's legs while she fumbled out her key.

Inside, Harriet felt as grateful as Tobermorey for the warmth.

Like him, she followed her mother to the kitchen, hoping for sustenance.

"Did one of the Antler kids fall?" Ruth Rose began to break eggs into a bowl. Harriet was pleased that they were going to have an omelette for supper; it was one of the few things her mother was really good at making.

Harriet asked if she could break the rest of the eggs, then carefully added a casual, "I don't know—I was playing there earlier but I left when they were all watching television."

"Well, it probably isn't anything serious. The policeman said they had a report and he needed to see the children. I wonder what that means. Do you think Octavia would call the police for some reason?" Ruth minced an onion and chopped up a handful of mushrooms. "Don't just twirl the eggs, Harriet, beat them, please. Or let me do it."

"Octavia," Harriet replied, as carefully as she could, "would think the police should be called in if Archie peed on the furniture." What was going on next door? Harriet wondered. Her mother was tuning the kitchen radio to a station with music. She zeroed in on Fred Astaire building up to an awful letdown and went back to cooking. Harriet parked the whisk in the mixing bowl and wandered over to the window. Behind her, her mother gave the eggs a more thorough beating. Mother and daughter making dinner together, thought Harriet. If someone looked in the window, that's all that anyone could see.

She looked out the window again just as the policeman was getting into his car. He shut the door, then a light went on inside, and she could see him sitting behind the wheel, his head bent as he wrote his report. After several minutes, the light inside the patrol car went out, he started up the motor, his brake lights flared as he switched on his lights. The patrol car rolled slowly to the corner and without signaling turned right and disappeared from view. Wasn't anything else going to happen?

Harriet felt an icy stab in her chest. Which would be worse? To be right, that Octavia had done something horrible to Jenny, or to be wrong, to have made the whispered, anonymous report in error? Harriet didn't know what to wish for.

The next morning being a Saturday, Harriet's mother let her sleep late. She woke to the sound of Mr. Antler shouting outside her window, and she got out of bed to look out through the blinds to see what was going on.

Mr. Antler was standing in his plaid bathrobe in the driveway, waving his arms and screaming in the face of a policewoman, who stood next to another woman, who was holding a blanket-wrapped bundle—Jenny—in her arms.

"The hell you'll take this child anywhere. I told you I wouldn't take her to a hospital for no good reason, and I told you she's not going with you either! She's not going anywhere! This is goddamned America, and we're goddamned American citizens. Just who the hell do you think you are?" He was shouting so loud that even through the storm window Harriet could hear every word he was saying. The policewoman was saying something, but Harriet couldn't hear her at all. The other three Antler children, in pajamas and bare feet, Mrs. Antler, in an overcoat clutched over her nightgown, and Octavia, in her white uniform, were stationed on the lawn watching, like pawns on a chessboard. Barbara looked up and saw Harriet, and their eyes met for a long moment. Harriet dropped the blind and backed away from the window. She didn't know whether to feel triumphant or ashamed.

The policeman had filed a report that night stating that he had found Jennifer Antler asleep in her crib, in what appeared to be normal condition, and that the anonymous report of a possible drowning was therefore unfounded. However, owing to the anonymous report, and to some discrepancies in the way certain routine questions were answered by the adults in the household, he urgently requested an investigation within twenty-four hours by the Child Protective Services.

Harriet had seen the social worker removing Jennifer that next morning in order to take her to a hospital for a medical examination. Despite Mr. Antler's objections, this had been done. X rays revealed that Jennifer Antler had sustained a fractured skull within the last few months. She had a broken rib that was several weeks old, a healing fracture of her upper right arm, and a very recent burn on her back that was consistent with a burn from a lit cigarette. None of the other children had any injuries.

Harriet never saw the Antler children again, except for brief glimpses of them getting out of their car; or, sometimes, if Harriet kept a lookout for a very long time, she saw one of them in a bedroom for the instant between the time the light was turned on and the shade was drawn down. Octavia vanished instantly. Ruth Rose thought she had been deported because her papers weren't right, but she might have elected to go back to whichever island it was instead of facing prosecution. Her papers, it turned out, weren't really hers, but belonged to her sister. Octavia had never mentioned being a twin. She probably was quite crazy.

"You were always so funny," Ruth reminisced to Harriet over lunch, the day Harriet got up the nerve to ask her mother about the Antlers. Harriet was in her second year at Cooper Union and had just won the Hadley Prize—the international photography award that was a herald of all that was to come— and this was a celebration.

These days, Ruth Rose seemed like a different person to Harriet from the mother with whom she had grown up. This woman eating lunch with her was *here*. Able to focus. Mother and daughter having lunch together.

Throughout high school, whenever a social studies teacher had referred to the Great Depression, Harriet had automatically thought of those darkest days, the weeks preceding hospitalization, when her mother had lain in bed (seriously suicidal, she later admitted, unable to proceed with plans for her death only because of Harriet), and then of those glimpses of the stranger who was Ruth Rose, drugged and expressionless in that hospital room. Ruth's year in the hospital was like a dividing line in Harriet's personal history.

Ruth still seemed sad to Harriet, but in an ordinary way. The problem with the medication, for Harriet, was that with all the highs and lows ironed out, what was left had an inevitable flatness. Acerbity had been replaced by a kind of dull-normal niceness, and Harriet sometimes got the feeling that her mother was determined to get this right, to keep it up indefinitely. Harriet kept a wary lookout for signs of the old Ruth Rose, which she wasn't sure if she would welcome or dread. Every time they were together, after the first few moments Harriet would feel a surge of loss about this agreeable middle-aged woman's taking her mother's place. You've changed, she would think sadly, each encounter a fresh disappointment.

They were in the West Village at a tiny bistro of Harriet's choosing, which served only enormous tubs of soup with vast hunks of bread, and one kind of rough red wine, which she hoped her mother didn't mind.

"You were so funny, Harriet, when you would ask, 'How could Octavia be from more than one island?' "

"Well, how could she?" Harriet demanded.

The Antlers moved away that winter. The children and Mrs. Antler disappeared during the Christmas vacation, and one day in January, during that first hard week of school when you realize there's nothing much to look forward to until spring, Harriet had trudged home for lunch through the snow—she could have walked on the shoveled sidewalks, but preferred a meandering course across untrod lawns—and discovered a moving van in front of the Antlers' house. Mr. Antler's car was in its usual place in the driveway, which was in itself unusual, but Harriet never did see him again, as both his car and the moving van were gone forever by the time she came home from school again after three o'clock. Her jacket, long since replaced as lost, had been neatly draped over the ledge of the Roses' brick stoop at some point in the afternoon.

The mailman said the Antlers' mail was being forwarded to an address in Chapel Hill. That wasn't proof they had moved to Chapel Hill, though, as Mrs. Antler's mother lived there, and they might have just stayed with her for a while or had their mail sent there. Another neighbor, a woman who had volunteered in the thrift shop with Anita, had heard they were living in Minneapolis. No one seemed to know what had happened to Antler Glass and Mirror.

"So, did you think it was all Octavia?" Harriet asked her mother while they sipped coffee. They both studied the dessert menu, which Harriet propped at a tilt between them—it was a child's blackboard in a wooden frame, ridiculously large as there were only three kinds of bread pudding from which to choose.

Ruth sighed. "That's hard to answer. I wouldn't have had any doubts about either Anita or Albert—you know they were really good neighbors, they were friends of the family, and Albert especially was very kind to us that night. You know . . ." She trailed off.

"The night Adam died," Harriet prompted.

"Yes. Albert was always very fond of you. You used to play there all the time, I don't know if you remember that."

"I remember everything."

"So you say."

They sat in silence. The waitress came over to the table, and they declined anything further. She shrugged and plucked the blackboard from Harriet's grasp.

"Where were you, on those afternoons when I came home from school? It seemed as if you were never there," Harriet asked suddenly.

"Oh, I don't know. Out. Doing errands. Going to the therapist." Ruth sighed and scratched the back of one hand with the other. Harriet was startled to note how old and veiny and loose her mother's hands had become. When did that happen? Her mother used to have beautiful hands, small, like Harriet's. "I think I probably kept myself busy doing errands in order to stay away from the house. It was so gloomy, I was so depressed, and you were so angry. I couldn't bear to see the angry look on your face when you came home from school. I was a coward."

This was much more of an answer than Harriet had expected, and she was a little stunned at the discovery that her mother seemed to know quite a bit more about herself, and about Harriet, than Harriet had ever imagined.

Ruth looked at her. "Since it's truth time, let me ask you this: Where were you, when I was in Payne Whitney? You came to see me only five times that year. You were only a few blocks away, at Mother's. She came twice a week and gave me reports. She made excuses for you, talked about your homework. I begged her to let you make your own decision about coming—I told her you weren't to be pressured. But where were you?"

Harriet looked at her mother without speaking for a moment. Letting her thoughts and words form without the usual tumultuous rush, Harriet answered slowly, "I was a coward, too. I didn't want to see you there. If I didn't go, it wasn't as real."

"Did you miss me? Did it occur to you that I missed you? That I might have needed you?"

"I tried not to think about it. I think I didn't want you to know that I needed you." Harriet felt something painful coming

loose and breaking up. She went on doggedly, like someone
wading into deeper and deeper water. "I guess I felt betrayed by
a series of people disappearing: I mean, think about it. Adam,
Simon, Carrie, the Antlers, then you. You wouldn't admit to me
that Simon—Daddy—had disappeared. Sometimes I thought it
was my fault. Sometimes I thought you thought it was my fault
that he left us. I felt that I had the power to make people disappear. Though, in a way, by not going to see you, I was making
you disappear."

Ruth smiled faintly and nodded that she understood. She
shook her head and waved a hand between them as though to
clear away something in the air.

"About the Antlers," Ruth said, as if they had mutually agreed
to change the topic. "I would never have thought for a moment
that either of them were capable of hurting a child, but their
behavior was very, very strange. Do you know, after that day,
neither one of them ever called, or spoke to me, or to anyone
else in the neighborhood? They acted very guilty of something.
It was never very clear what the social workers thought had
happened, either. None of the other children had a scratch on
them, I remember that. But I don't know what the official theory
was. The records weren't public because there was no criminal
case. It was all in the newspapers at first, every day, right on the
front page, because Octavia's papers were forged, or something.
Her green card turned out to belong to her twin sister."

"I remember she was named Octavia because she was the
eighth child. I wonder what her older sister was called. Septice-
mia?" Harriet wanted to make her mother laugh, and succeeded.

"But something was forged, too, I'm sure I remember that,"
Ruth added.

Harriet thought about Octavia's dark room at the top of the
stairs and pictured Octavia, surrounded by her dolls, sitting under
an eyeshade, humming melodically while painstakingly creating
forged documents in a perfect hand.

"But then the whole thing died down, and you know how newspapers never follow up to tell you how a story turns out months later when it isn't hot news. There were plenty of rumors, though." Ruth seemed to remember more as she spoke.

"Like what?"

"Oh, I don't know. It was ten years ago. Some people thought Anita did it, and that Albert was covering up for her, that he had hired Octavia in order to keep an eye on the children, because she hadn't been managing well on her own, and there had been other incidents, odd accidents. But you know, he was the one with the temper. He used to spank those children over every little thing. Do you know I told him myself, when you used to be in their house practically every afternoon, that he was never, ever to lay a finger on you, no matter how he disciplined his own children?" Harriet didn't know this.

"And no one ever knew who made that call to the police that night—lots of wild stories went around. Someone, I don't remember who, once tried to tell me that you did it. Can you imagine? You were ten."

Harriet shifted uneasily in her seat, leaned forward, studying with great interest the brown sugar crystals this restaurant affected among its coffee condiments. She fiddled with the little wooden spoon standing in the bowl, flipping it back and forth.

"Did you ever try to speak to either Mr. or Mrs. Antler? I mean, they were probably embarrassed. Did you ever make a move toward them, offer them your friendship, or did you just let them keep their distance?"

"Harriet, that's a real 'Have you stopped beating your wife?' kind of question. I don't remember the specifics. I must have made an effort to get in touch with them. Why wouldn't I have? I was a friend of the family. I'm sure I did." Ruth balled up her napkin and put it beside her plate in a gesture that was identical to Gay's end-of-meal habits. She stood up and apologetically excused herself to find the ladies' room, saying, "My back teeth are floating. With all that soup, a meal here gives an entirely different meaning to the term *liquid lunch.*"

Harriet brought out her camera from the bag at her feet while her mother was in the bathroom and toyed with the lens. She idly tested out the light meter and studied her reflection in the warped old mirror with an ornate carved frame that hung beside their table, making the restaurant seem larger, airier. She took a picture of herself in the mirror, then another, and then she took a picture of her mother standing next to the table, gazing down at the top of her daughter's head. Harriet continued to look through the camera. She focused on her mother's expression in the reflection without really seeing it, and then she did see it, and what she saw was a deep and abiding love, a mother's absolute and undivided love for her child, a love that Harriet could swear had never been visible to the naked eye.

Part III

July 20

Anne was not by nature especially tidy. But in this cramped flat, and with fewer possessions in Geneva than the student-y accumulation with which she had surrounded herself in her New York life, she had developed routines that precluded a certain amount of mess. More important, neatness and order headed off a certain amount of criticism from Victor, who was obsessively neat with material objects, if not with the larger issues of his own domestic life.

These days, everywhere she looked in the flat there was evidence of Harriet's presence. Once, the mere sight of these objects would have sent Anne's spirit soaring. Now, it was a complication. Which wasn't because Harriet was traveling with too much stuff; if anything, Harriet had impressively small quantities of clothing and camera equipment and personal things for someone away for a month.

On Eighth Street, Harriet had always been the austere one, opting for order, attempting steady sensibility in order to counterbalance both Anne's habitual penuriousness and Anne's haphazard bursts of crazy acquisition. Sometimes the two of them would stall in an aisle at the supermarket, creating a traffic jam while they argued about Harriet's firm intention to procure one necessary can of tomato paste versus Anne's equally steadfast plan to fill the cart with two dozen because it was on sale. ("Sometimes, *more* is more," Anne had unsuccessfully argued.)

Now, here, the problem wasn't really the turnabout of roles, though it was a bit ironic; heretofore, Harriet had been the picker-upper and the organizer, while Anne had been the messy, clothes-heaped-on-the-chair-for-a-month slob. She had even been known to *wear* some of those clothes after they had languished thus.

The problem was Victor. And Anne saw no reasonable way to pass along Victor's repeated complaints to Harriet. Every time Anne and Victor met in the flat for their lunchtime assignation, from the second day of Harriet's visit, Victor had commented on Harriet's toiletry kit taking up counter space in the bathroom, her camera equipment taking up too much of the closet, her two small piles of clothing occupying too much of the shelf beside the bed that Anne had cleared for her.

He didn't care for the brand of breakfast cereal Harriet had put into the cupboard beside Anne's health-food-store muesli. Harriet's books (she was always in the middle of several at once; this month she was reading Anne's books as well as her own Saki and Henry James stories) seemed to perplex Victor when he encountered them splayed on various surfaces throughout the flat. He would pick up each one, examine the title with a distracted air as though hoping for some explanation of something, and then close the book (thereby losing Harriet's place) before putting it down.

The color of the miniature carnations Harriet had brought home from a flower stall and put into Anne's one vase, a blue, earthenware pitcher Anne and Harriet had selected with care one Vermont weekend long ago, was not quite right. Victor preferred solid tones of white or pink for carnations; he did not approve of the purple edging on these, which struck him as vulgar. It occurred to Anne that Victor had until now been the one source of flowers in her flat, and she noted a rivalrous tone to his criticism of Harriet's flowers.

Suspended between Victor's various reactions to Harriet and her own pleasure at the presence of Harriet, Anne felt herself caught in a crosscurrent. She had always been afraid of the undertow at beaches. She felt as though she were on the verge of being pulled apart.

Yesterday, when Victor let himself into the flat with his key moments after Anne's own arrival and hasty ablutions and preparations in the bathroom, he had winced at the sight of an abandoned cup of coffee on the table. Observing with some significance that it was still warm, Victor emptied it into the kitchen sink, washed the cup, dried it with a dish towel, and placed it in its proper location on a cupboard shelf, as if by doing so he could eliminate Harriet's presence from the flat.

Anne, slightly breathless from remaking the bed, did not remark on her own observation that Harriet's perfume, Amazone, lingered faintly on the sheets she and Harriet shared at night, the sheets she had just stripped from the tightly tucked mattress (a Harriet Rose trademark, such fantastically, symmetrically organized bedding) in order to replace them with the set of sheets she kept in a plastic Bon Marché bag (the only souvenir of a Paris weekend with Victor) under the bed. This done, she adjusted the louvered shutters until the noon glare was filtered down to a dim coat of luminous dust on the surfaces in the room.

Only when the room was made ready in these ways did Victor beckon Anne with a tilt of his head that she should come over to where he stood watching her with his arms folded.

She went over and stood facing him for a long silent moment. The expectable erotic frisson that usually charged these moments was curiously absent. Something was missing.

Anne found herself thinking, absurdly, of Christmas Eve two years before, when she and Harriet had found themselves at loose ends and had at the last minute decided to cook a turkey. It was late afternoon on Christmas Eve; all the fancy grocery stores in the Village were already closed. The only turkey they could locate sat alone in an empty case in a so-called convenience market, a seedy Sixth Avenue place with perpetually rotating chickens in the window and outdated milk in the leaking refrigerator case.

The clerks had hovered over them impatiently, sweeping and

turning off lights, anxious to close the store, while Harriet and
Anne debated the meaning of the tag on this scrawny, pathetic
specimen. The tag read PARTS MISSING. She and Harriet had
managed to create a decent dinner of the poor thing, and several
friends had been invited at the last minute, and they had all drunk
a hilarious toast to the roadkill, their bruised, wingless dinner.

PARTS MISSING, thought Anne grimly, *c'est moi.*

Victor raised a hand and reached out to touch under her chin
with an extended finger; as he drew his hand back, she let him
bring her face close to his. She willed herself to go blank, to have
no feelings of any kind about anything. Victor, mistaking her
expression for feigned resistance, laughed and pulled Anne toward him to begin what they had come there to do.

Today it was raining. Anne wondered for a guilty moment
about what dry place Harriet might have taken herself to this
afternoon. Anne's sozzled umbrella dripped on the stairs, and she
knew Victor had preceded her, based on the other drizzle of
rainwater that ran in a dotted line across the landing and down
the hall in the direction of her flat. She stood outside her door
for a moment and wasn't totally surprised by a fleeting notion to
retrace her steps back to the street, where she might find a quiet
café and have some lunch. Maybe she would run across Harriet.
Putting her key in the lock, she couldn't decide which was the
greater loss of nerve: retreating, or going ahead in.

"Harriet has certainly made herself at home, I see," Victor
observed, not for the first time, as Anne closed the door behind
her, double locked it, and slid the chain across. He emerged from
the bathroom, carrying his suit jacket in his arms as if it were a
sleeping baby. (Anne knew he kept several small notebooks,
assorted pens, his billfold, and various other items of importance
filed with precision in his jacket pockets.) He laid the jacket
down on a chair, then slid the knot low on his tie so he wouldn't
have to retie it when he put it back on later, lifted the loop of

yellow-and-black-patterned silk over his head, and hung it on the bathroom doorknob.

He unbuttoned his white shirt and very carefully draped it on the back of the chair. "Is she writing a novel?" Victor emptied the contents of his pants pockets onto the table. He turned over the facedown spiral-bound notebook that lay in the middle of Anne's table and leafed through several pages covered in Harriet's slashy scrawl, at the same time bending over to unfasten and step out of his suit trousers, which he gathered, turned upside down, and held by the cuffs. He slid open the top drawer of Anne's bureau, placed the trouser cuffs inside, and shut the drawer on them, so his pants would hang flat.

"No, she writes letters to her boyfriend, Benedict." Anne's reply was muffled inside the knit dress she was lifting off over her head. She stopped for a moment with her crossed arms raised and trapped inside over her head. It was pleasant in here, alone with herself. She could see Victor through the close black mesh pressed to her face, though he didn't know it.

"But some of these have dates of last week. Why doesn't she send them?" Victor, still wearing black socks and droopy underpants, turned his back to her and began turning pages in Harriet's notebook again. He had taken out and put on his reading glasses. He reached inside his underpants and absently scratched his bottom. "Look, she has reported all about us. This is very bad. Our day at the beach. Look." He turned around and was surprised to see Anne standing still, contorted inside her dress.

"Are you stuck? You look like someone in a straitjacket."

"Or someone in dire straits," muttered Anne from inside the dress.

"I don't know what that means. But I can tell you this, it's very sexy. I like it *very* much. Even though you have been very naughty, taking off your clothing without my permission. Let me." Taking off his glasses and abandoning them with the notebook on the table, he circled her with his arms and held her tightly. Anne could feel just how much he liked it. Held this way, she was, in fact, bound like someone in a straitjacket. She fought off the urge to fight off Victor. He rubbed against her while pushing her toward the bed. Anne allowed Victor to topple her backward onto the bed and closed her eyes in the shrouded dark.

It was nearly two o'clock, and Victor was brushing his teeth with the special English badger-bristle toothbrush that Anne kept for him in the medicine cabinet. He was late, due back at the UGP offices just then, which meant that Anne would have to be later still, as they never returned to the office together. Anne would also have to explain, should anyone inquire, a complete change of clothing since the morning; the black dress would certainly require a long soapy soak in the bidet before it could be worn again.

"I'm off. Don't forget the meeting with the Syrian contingent at half past four. Do you think you almost came that time? *Mnn?*"

"Mmmn," she replied, standing in front of her open closet door in her underwear, turning away so his perfunctory good-bye kiss grazed the side of her face and her hair. She was impatient for him to leave; her revulsion, now that it had arrived, seemed long overdue.

He put a fingertip under her chin and tipped her face up to meet his.

"Do you tell her about this?" He gestured in the direction of Harriet's notebook on the table.

"What *this* do you mean?"

"Any of it. All of it. What I like. Your new little problem."

"Why do you ask?"

"I thought it might be the sort of thing two such close friends might talk about, when they lie together at night."

"What is that supposed to mean?"

"Do you find her attractive?"

"Harriet? Do you mean do I think she's an attractive woman, or do you mean am I attracted to her?" Anne felt a jolt of panic, which she tried to ward off. If Victor thought he could pick up those vibrations, had Harriet detected them as well?

He raised his eyebrows and shrugged. "Do you think," Victor said softly, his fingertip still lifting Anne's chin, which she found increasingly irritating, "that she would be interested in joining us?"

"For dinner? In bed? Oh, please. Not funny." Anne pushed Victor's hand away and turned back toward the closet, where she began flipping through her clothing options. Just leave, Victor, why don't you. Something very similar to the morning's black dress, or something completely different?

"Think about it," Victor said into her hair as he kissed her good-bye for the second time. Anne neither answered nor looked around, and a moment later she heard the door to her flat click shut.

Dressed (a red-and-black-checkered dress with a wide black belt cinched tight on her narrow waist—a bold change that defied questioning, as opposed to a sneaky near-substitution), Anne scouted around the flat before leaving. The small German vibrator with its many attachments was stowed in its black leather pouch, pushed quite far under the low, remade bed, along with the Bon Marché bag of sheets and pillowcases.

Anne tried to remember how Harriet's notebook had been before Victor began leafing through it. She closed it and put it back on the table. Had it been facedown or faceup? Where had the pen been? On the notebook, or next to it? Until this moment, Anne had never thought to question the contents of Harriet's journal, or interminable letter to Benedict or whatever it was.

But Victor's words still hung in the air. What *did* Harriet think

was going on? What was going on? She really had no intention
of reading so much as a sentence in Harriet's notebook, let alone
every single word. But that, finally, was what she did.

Anne was quite late getting back to the office, and she had to
walk in on the meeting, which was already under way; she could
only hope no one on the staff would ask her where she had been
or why she had changed her clothes. Though usually armed
with elaborately thought-out explanations to cover her Victor
assignations, at the moment Anne had absolutely no idea how
she would account for her lateness or wardrobe change.

"Miss Gordon has decided to grace us with her presence after
all, I see," Victor announced when Anne slipped into the room.
He looked at her coolly over his reading glasses, which always
slipped down his nose. He was in the middle of summarizing
unanticipated losses for these investors, a subject that had been of
some concern to him for days. Anne had spent hours agonizing
over the wording and the numbers, though the report's official
author was Victor alone. "Will someone show Miss Gordon
where we are in the report?"

Anne took her seat and murmured her thanks to the tiny Miss
Sreenivasan—whose first name was simply, mysteriously "E."
on all listings—who worked as the assistant to Victor's opposite
number in risk management. Miss Sreenivasan had flipped open
the stapled document at Anne's place and was pointing with her
pen to the column of figures under discussion. Anne nodded and
then scanned the page in an attempt to look as though she were
familiarizing herself with the information.

She tried to focus on the issues of the meeting, but her
thoughts kept straying. It seemed to be going well; Anne had
developed a strategy for shrouding UGP's lapses in an impressive
array of statistics, and the Syrians seemed puzzled, but not angry,
which was ideal. She hoped Harriet would forgive her for what
she had done.

July 23

Before the appointments with Dr. Van Loeb, Anne had not been familiar with this particular Geneva street, despite its proximity to her own, and despite her proclivity for roaming all over the Vieille Ville. The first time she had encountered Rue de l'Etoile was en route to a shop that sold restaurant supplies, a tiny place in an alley down at the end of the block. Anne had gone there for dishes and glasses in her first organizational burst after finding the flat. After agreeing to the flat Victor had found for her.

She had been suspicious of his wish to locate her so far from the UGP offices—and so far from the Marks family domicile, which was in a suburban development of luxury high-rises near the U.N.—but the Vieille Ville truly was the most desirable part of Geneva.

Now it felt like home, as much as any place ever could. Anne savored the mixture of familiarity and alienation that she felt on every street corner as she walked to her appointment. She took pleasure in that sense of increasing competence one can develop as one becomes adept at the dailiness of life in a totally foreign surrounding.

She relished the way she had come to know Geneva bus schedules. The German delicatessen across from her building had roast chickens after four o'clock, but one needed to reserve by noon. The dress-shop window changed its display on Thursdays. The elderly cat who lived in the pharmacy was named Endormi.

Getting around this once-alien city, she had written to Harriet only a few weeks before, had become second nature to her. What was the difference, Anne wondered now, striding at her usual brisk pace toward Rue de l'Etoile, between first and second nature? That was the sort of thing Harriet would automatically know, or would make a point of finding out. Whatever it was, Anne doubted that she herself possessed either. Ordinary reactions—behavior, responses, just knowing what to do or say or think or feel—which came easily to other people, so far as Anne had ever observed, weren't the least bit automatic for her. It was all learned for Anne, like a language everyone else had been born knowing.

The Vieille Ville seemed to fill the same space in Geneva that the Village did in New York. *The* Village, never Greenwich Village, Harriet had instructed Anne in a rather Gay-like tone, early in their friendship. Moving in with Harriet on Eighth Street had felt almost like coming home after what Harriet called the "uptownitude" of East End Avenue, where Anne had been subletting a half-furnished apartment from an elderly Hungarian couple, retired doctors, family friends who spent most of their time in Myrtle Beach.

Dr. Van Loeb. Anne had read her most famous book, *Children Without Childhoods,* at Bennington during sophomore year, because it was on the reading list for a psychology course Anne dropped after one dreadful introductory class. The professor, a sweet young thing from Georgia, was striking both for her glossy beauty (she wore a revealing silk blouse with one of those dismaying power-slut suits) and for her inability to speak intelligently. It was rumored that she was sleeping with someone in the art history department. When Professor Bilkey described the papers she would expect throughout the term, she sounded to Anne as though she were addressing kindergarten students.

When Professor Bilkey was for the second time pronouncing the word *vignettes* with a hard *g,* so it sounded like *vig nets,* Anne was gathering up her books. She left before the class was halfway over, convinced that she could learn nothing from such a person.

Anne forgot to return the Van Loeb book, a slender paperback, when she returned the other, more expensive hardcover course books. When, months later, *Children Without Childhoods* surfaced under some Shakespeare paperbacks piled beside Anne's bed, she read it through in one sitting. It was brilliant. There was something so clear, so penetratingly right about Dr. Van Loeb's simple sentences. The book was written in English, though Dr. Van Loeb's first language was Dutch. It had the grace and precision that comes with adopted language, of Anni Albers writing about design, of Hannah Arendt writing about the banality of evil.

Anne had been startled to realize that the subject of the book was the psychology of children who had survived the Holocaust. Why had she never heard about this book? Even when she bought it for the course, something about the cover design, a stylized brick wall, had given Anne the impression that *Children Without Childhoods* was about the plight of children in contemporary urban ghettos or something like that.

Reading it that night was an epiphany of sorts. Anne allowed herself for the first time to think about what was never explicitly explained in her own childhood. Though Henry could be quite matter-of-fact about his experiences and about the facts of world events as they carried him along, he would never speak directly about his feelings.

Anne, and her mother, had been expected to honor those silent spaces. At the same time, Anne had always felt that her family was somehow bound together by Henry's tragedies. Not to be analyzed, just to be *known*. For as long as she could remember, Anne had carried with her a confusing mixture of pride that Henry had survived and a kind of shameful guilt over her privilege and comfort, over having been spared. How could she ever prove herself in such a bland and dangerless world as this? The Van Loeb book had no precise answers for Anne, but it did put into words some of the sensibilities, the questions that had always hung in the air, unasked.

Anne had had no idea that Nina Van Loeb lived in Geneva;

she wouldn't have been certain, had she thought about it, that Dr. Van Loeb was still alive. She must be very old. Anne remembered reading a newspaper article somewhere that had referred to Dr. Van Loeb as a survivor herself. She had waited out the war in the Dutch countryside, hidden in the hayloft of a Lutheran farmer who raped her from time to time in exchange for food, and his silence when the soldiers came.

Then Anne happened to spot a newspaper listing for a lecture by Dr. Van Loeb at the university in early June. At first Anne had no thought of attending the lecture, and was merely intrigued, having read the book, but she found herself thinking about it, and it seemed significant somehow that she had bothered to tear out the information from the paper. She realized that she was as much curious just to see Nina Van Loeb, now eighty-nine, to be in the same room and hear her speak, as she was interested in what Dr. Van Loeb might have to say.

Anne's evenings were usually unscheduled, in the event that Victor should get away, though more often than not her nights were uneventful, punctuated at most by a furtive telephone call. She had attended the lecture, which was titled "The Inevitability of Sadness." It was Sunday, the twelfth of June. Anne wondered if anyone else realized that it was Anne Frank's birthday.

The lecture hall wasn't where Anne had thought it was located —the building she had assumed it to be turned out to house some sort of international center filled with unhelpful exchange students who seemed to speak no recognizable language and who were barely capable of languid gestures to indicate their lack of knowledge about university geography—and she arrived late. The only seats left were in the front row.

Anne settled into a seat and looked around her. The audience all looked studious, serious. Many people sat with blank notepads and pens, poised to take notes. Apparently some very great and important things might be uttered by Dr. Van Loeb this evening. Or maybe they were all psychoanalysts, too, in the habit of note-taking? Anne wished she, too, had brought something with which to take notes. She felt unaccredited, like a fraud.

Dr. Van Loeb walked out onto the stage. A ripple of applause began and grew, which startled Anne. Did one applaud at lectures? (A colleague at UGP, a dreary accountant with a wispy beard and a passion for Gilbert and Sullivan, whose only life achievement seemed to have been getting into Yale, had described applauding the final lecture of a brilliant and renowned classics professor there. The professor had then disappeared through a trapdoor in the stage.) Perhaps it was a Swiss thing, or they were simply acknowledging respect by way of applauding.

Clapping seemed wrong to Anne, an intrusion, an insulting act of pity. Miming applause without actually making contact between her hands, Anne felt that she and everyone around her were doing something inappropriate, like clapping between movements. Dr. Van Loeb ducked her head in acknowledgment of the applause, which grew louder. People began to rise from their seats. Anne stood and began to clap in earnest, her face red with empathic embarrassment. Why are we doing this? Why not let the woman give her lecture? As always, she thought, I pretend to take part in something that for everyone else is genuine.

Dr. Van Loeb was small, not much taller than the lectern, which she stood beside. She looked like a wise old Chinese man, or a monkey, yet Anne found her beautiful. Having to sit in the front row suddenly seemed like another significant happenstance, like finding out about the lecture in the first place.

There was something wonderfully intimate about being able to gaze up at Dr. Van Loeb, who was wearing a schoolgirl's plaid skirt and a gray silk jacket that matched the color of her hair, which was so raggedly cropped around her head that Anne wondered if Dr. Van Loeb cut it herself, with nail scissors. The jacket seemed plain, almost militarily severe at first, but when Dr. Van Loeb moved, there were flashes of red lining, which caused Anne to revise her opinion of the jacket: it was subtly elegant.

Dr. Van Loeb spoke in English, in a soft, accented voice, for perhaps forty minutes, glancing down only occasionally at her packet of notes, index cards she held in her tiny hands. Everything she said seemed momentous, filled with many layers of meaning and truth, though afterward, when Anne was trying to summarize the ideas of the lecture to Victor (who was listening reluctantly and with showy patience, in bed at noontime on the following day), she found that she could no more do it than she could remember the details of her dreams.

Dr. Van Loeb looked directly into Anne's eyes once, near the end, at a moment when she was pausing to draw breath for her concluding points. The moment electrified Anne. It was charged with something she didn't understand. When Dr. Van Loeb had finished and everyone around Anne had jumped up and burst into steady applause of the sort concert audiences sustain in the hopes of eliciting an encore, Anne had picked up her sweater and handbag and rushed out, feeling that if she stayed for another moment, she would burst into tears.

For days after, Anne couldn't shake Dr. Van Loeb, the lecture, that instant when their eyes met. What was so important, so magical? Why did Dr. Van Loeb filter now into all of Anne's thoughts, why had she become an invisible presence hovering overhead?

It annoyed Anne, and it upset her to find her thoughts drawn repeatedly to the same moments, as if she were being compelled to look through a series of virtually identical photographs over and over. Photographs such as Harriet might produce. If Harriet were here, she would be satisfyingly intrigued by Anne's preoccupation. She would no doubt develop all sorts of abstruse theories about it, and some of them might even be right.

But Harriet wasn't expected for nearly a month, and until then Anne had no one with whom she could satisfactorily talk about Nina Van Loeb. About her obsession with Nina Van Loeb. Victor made it clear that he didn't want to hear one more inarticulate reference to this miraculous Van Loeb woman, either. The third time she brought Dr. Van Loeb into the conversation, at a clandestine dinner in a little fondue restaurant in the basement of a hotel, where only tourists went, Victor had looked up from his menu, gazed at her over his half glasses with a cold look, and said, "You sound like someone who's fallen in love, you know."

Anne was stunned, and embarrassed. She knew he was right. There was only one person in Geneva with whom she could pursue this. That night, after Victor had left in time to be at home when Annamarie returned from a weekend of hiking with the children, Anne looked up Dr. Van Loeb in the telephone directory. The next morning, when she knew she would be safe from interruption at her desk for a few minutes, she telephoned. Dr. Van Loeb answered on the second ring, which caught Anne by surprise, as she had only gotten up enough nerve to leave a message. Stammering, Anne explained herself badly, but finally she was able to choke out a request for an appointment.

"You do still see patients?" she asked, after explaining that she had attended the lecture the week before.

"Yes, my vision has not failed me," came Dr. Van Loeb's polite reply.

"No, I mean, are you still, do you still . . ."

"Yes, do I still treat patients? A few. Is that your question?"

"I, yes, I would like to make an appointment in that case."

"Ah. Perhaps first we should have a meeting to talk, Miss . . . did you say your name was Gordon? A consultation."

Anne thought that was what she had requested. But Dr. Van Loeb seemed to think they should meet in order to plan to meet. Whatever. (The precise literalness reminded Anne in a pleasant way of her dealings with Harriet, who wouldn't *make* coffee, though she would be happy to *prepare* some. Anne and Harriet frequently accused each other of being overly literal.) They agreed on an hour for the next day, after Anne was through with work.

The first time Anne saw Dr. Van Loeb's waiting room, which was up one flight, in a building entered through a courtyard like her own, she was struck by its spare elegance and timelessness. I could live here, she thought as she opened the unlocked door (which was marked with a brass nameplate), as per Dr. Van Loeb's instructions, closed it behind her, and went to sit on the oatmeal-colored sofa opposite the door.

The walls were rough, white plaster, and the late-afternoon June light streamed in an open casement window and fell across the worn Persian carpet in pleasing stripes. The room smelled of furniture polish, and something else, that crisp butter and linen smell of good restaurants. Maybe a faint coffee aroma. Would Dr. Van Loeb offer her coffee?

There were magazines on a small table, but Anne, who was ten minutes early, didn't want to read. She became aware of a soft roaring sound coming from somewhere underneath her. She ducked her head down and lifted the skirt of the sofa and saw that the sound was coming from a small machine. White noise. To block out other noise, to prevent her from overhearing the private conversation in the next room that Dr. Van Loeb must be having with someone else. Anne flushed with embarrassment, feeling caught out for having peered under the sofa, somehow accused of eavesdropping by the very presence of this device.

She jumped up and began to examine a print on the wall, feeling as though she were somehow onstage. It was the only art in the room other than a wild-looking wooden mask, possibly African, that loomed over the sofa and made Anne think with distaste of Picasso. The print, which hung beside a closed door, was a matted reproduction of van Eyck's *Wedding of Mr. and Mrs. Jan Arnolfini.*

Anne tried to remember what she had learned in art history. She recalled something about this being a document of a marriage. Was the woman pregnant, or was her rounded belly, over which her hand was placed protectively, a suggestion of future fruitfulness? The dog signified fidelity. What kind of dog was that? A terrier of some sort.

It reminded Anne of a stuffed dog she had been given by her mother after she had her tonsils out at age four. It had a key in its belly, which scratched Anne when she cuddled the dog, who never did have a name. When wound up, it played "How Much Is That Doggy in the Window?"

Where was that stuffed dog now? Anne supposed that thinking about it now must have to do with thoughts of her mother. Was she looking for mere mothering from Dr. Van Loeb? How tiresome and unoriginal. Maybe she ought to leave at once, telephone an excuse later.

Oh, and the painter was visible in the reflection, a fact she hadn't learned in class—or if she had, she hadn't retained it—but from Harriet, who had mentioned this painting en passant in a passionate discussion of her beloved Dutch still lifes. Still lives? Anne could never remember which was right. Jan van Eyck was here.

Having a wonderful time. Wish I were anywhere but here. Anne checked her watch. It was precisely six. She wouldn't leave now that she had got this far. She searched the print for other clues, trying to lose herself, trying to forget what she was here for. There were seven candleholders in the candelabra, which signified something or other. Seven sacraments. But there was only one candle: the sacrament of marriage.

The couple were a quite peculiar-looking pair, actually. Did people really look like that? They stood apart, joined only by their hands. The man's pale gaze seemed to penetrate the centuries. Anne felt that his eyes could momentarily shift from the middle distance to meet her stare.

The door next to Anne opened suddenly, nearly hitting her in the head. She stepped back. Dr. Van Loeb's face emerged in profile at the edge of the door and she peered around the room, not seeing Anne. Anne cleared her throat nervously.

"Oh. There you are. Miss Gordon?"

Anne nodded. Dr. Van Loeb didn't come out any farther or offer her hand, but simply tilted her head that Anne should follow her. So there hadn't been another patient. Unless there was a different way out? Anne closed the door behind her as Dr. Van Loeb sat down in an armchair and gestured in the direction of another. Anne sat down, too, feeling perplexed already over the unfamiliar etiquette. There would be no coffee.

She looked around the room. It was lined with bookshelves and had a more cozy, personal feeling than the waiting room, though it was a good deal larger. Anne wondered if this was Dr. Van Loeb's living room. Perhaps she lived on the other side, through the other door in the opposite wall. Dr. Van Loeb was watching her. Anne dropped her eyes and clasped her hands together, aware of her own nervousness. Neither spoke. Perhaps a minute passed.

"Could you tell me something about yourself?" Dr. Van Loeb murmured. She was looking at Anne with a sort of detached, almost blank curiosity. She was wearing a tweed suit that might have been fifty years old.

"I was at your lecture," Anne began hesitantly.

"Yes, in the first row. I remember you."

This startled Anne, and thrilled her, too.

"Some of the things you said . . . they were about me. I mean, not about me as a survivor, obviously, I'm not a survivor, but you see, my father was, is. He was there, at Auschwitz." Anne trailed off, feeling overwhelmed by a surge of sadness. She could never explain it all. She had counted on this connection too much. It was foolish to hope. She started to cry.

Dr. Van Loeb simply sat still, saying nothing. After Anne had continued to weep quietly for a few minutes, Dr. Van Loeb made a sudden gesture with one hand that seemed for an instant to Anne like a dismissal, a "get out of here," but in fact it was an indication toward a box of tissues on a small table.

"Miss Gordon, do you know what you want from me?"

Anne couldn't find any words. She was still crying. It no longer mattered if tears were running down her face. Though it was doubtful that anything would be achieved, there was actually a little bit of comfort in her sense that it felt safe to do or say anything while she was here.

"I think about death all the time," Anne whispered.

Over the course of that hour, and the next two, Dr. Van Loeb elicited from Anne a rudimentary history, a sense of Anne's cast of characters, and some tentative identification of what she called Anne's "conflicts." Anne managed not to cry continuously by the third hour. At the beginning of the fourth meeting Dr. Van Loeb proposed that Anne would be well suited to psychoanalysis. They discussed fees. They agreed that they would begin in the third week of July, after Dr. Van Loeb returned from a month in the U.S.

Today, letting herself into Dr. Van Loeb's waiting room after those four weeks had passed, Anne fought the urge to bolt. All momentum for this dubious enterprise had been lost. Harriet's presence had changed everything. Anne had gone too far to turn back. She had kept this appointment only because she hadn't canceled it. Well, maybe because she wanted to see Dr. Van Loeb one more time.

The room was familiar, yet Anne felt that she was seeing it through different eyes. Anne hadn't told Harriet about the appointments with Dr. Van Loeb, though she had mentioned the lecture several times. It wasn't that Harriet would disapprove or misunderstand. The risk, Anne thought, was that Harriet would understand too well.

The noise machine hummed under the sofa. Anne breathed in the familiar air and stood facing the van Eyck reproduction. Surfaces. It was all surfaces. And light. The couple loomed large

in the room, larger than life. The way they touched made Anne
think of the way Harriet talked about Benedict. There was a
future for them, Anne thought. But not for me.

Dr. Van Loeb opened her door precisely on the hour. She
didn't greet Anne with more than half a syllable before turning
away. Anne followed her, thinking ruefully, How was your trip
to the States, Dr. Van Loeb? . . . Oh, my month was fine, thank
you, I've done quite well to survive this far, considering that I'm
falling apart even as we speak. Oh, Dr. Van Loeb, offer me a cup
of tea. Help me. Hold me.

A pale blue paper napkin was spread on a pillow at one end of
the couch on the far side of the room. Anne had barely noticed
this couch at her previous appointments, as she and Dr. Van
Loeb had sat in armchairs nearer to the door. Now Dr. Van Loeb
was already sitting in a small upholstered rocking chair at the
head of the couch. Anne realized with a stab of panic that she
was supposed to lie down now. It was too late, she didn't know
how to tell Dr. Van Loeb that this was her last appointment, that
she had changed her mind. It would seem like a sudden decision
brought on by the anxiety of the moment. She would have to
go through with the hour.

Anne lay down slowly, feeling ridiculous and fraudulent, feeling Dr. Van Loeb's eyes on her. She had glimpsed a blank writing
pad in Dr. Van Loeb's hand. Anne lay there. She heard the sound
of a pen scratching on paper. What could Dr. Van Loeb be
writing when nothing had been said? A minute passed. What
was one supposed to do with one's hands? Anne closed her eyes.
She wished for sleep, oblivion.

"I don't know what I'm supposed to do," Anne said finally in
a strangled voice. May I go now?

"Just say what comes to mind. The only rule. Dreams, fantasies, whatever comes to mind." Dr. Van Loeb's voice sounded
different, floating facelessly. Anne wanted to sit up and turn to

see her. Instead, she flattened herself obediently on the couch and clasped her hands, like a body laid to rest, and tried to think of something to say.

Finally: " 'Last night I dreamt I went to Manderley again.' "

Long silence.

"I beg your pardon?" Dr. Van Loeb said at last, sounding reluctant to speak first. This can't be the way it's supposed to work.

"The second Mrs. de Winter. You know, *Rebecca.*"

"What comes to mind?"

Anne was startled that this was taken as a legitimate association, and she now felt a little foolish about her clever opening gambit. But maybe all roads lead to the unconscious, in the end. "I think," she said slowly, giving it some thought, "that Rebecca was a lesbian. Mrs. Danvers was in love with her, don't you think? But Rebecca was a monster, too."

Pen scratching. Silence.

"Do you feel that you are a monster for loving Harriet?" Dr. Van Loeb's voice seemed to come from inside Anne's head. Anne felt her face flush. She wished she hadn't told Dr. Van Loeb as much as she had. Again she fought the impulse to sit up and turn around so she could see Dr. Van Loeb's face.

"Yes," she whispered.

Neither of them spoke. Anne could hear the distant sound of an ambulance or police siren. Dir-ty, dir-ty, dir-ty. It came nearer, then faded.

"Can you say what you are thinking?" Dr. Van Loeb prompted.

No. Anne scrambled up a slippery mental slope and finally found a toehold.

"Can Queen Victoria eat cold apple pie?"

"?" Dr. Van Loeb made a Dutch-sounding interrogatory noise in her throat.

"I said, can Queen Victoria eat cold apple pie? It's the seven hills of Rome—Capitoline, Quirinal, Viminal, Esqualine, Caelian, Aventine, and Palatine. I learned it at school."

"And what comes to mind?"

"There are seven candleholders in the *Arnolfini* candelabra. You know, in the waiting room. I think that's why I thought of it. Seven sacraments. Seven deadly sins. Seven league boots." You want free association, you get free association. "Seven sisters. Seven brides for seven brothers," Anne rattled on. "Seventh heaven. Seven sleepers. Secret Seven. Seven seas. Seven wonders of the world. I've always liked the seven hills of Rome. I've always liked Queen Victoria, too. And apple pie, for that matter." Anne began to cry.

"Do you feel that in your present circumstances you are being made to eat cold apple pie?"

"Like Eve in the Garden do you mean?"

Silence. Pen scratching. Anne lay with closed eyes. She rubbed her tears with the back of her left hand. Her watch face felt cool on her forehead, and she kept her wrist there.

"Sometimes," Dr. Van Loeb said quietly, "forbidden fruit is indigestible."

Anne thought about this for a moment. Which forbidden fruit? Victor? Or Harriet? She wanted to ask, but there were no words. She rubbed her nose furiously with the back of her hand, then stopped when she remembered a Harriet theory about never rubbing your nose at job interviews. Something to do with it being a body-language signal of guilt.

Anne opened her eyes. She hadn't moved her hand, and the face of her watch was in front of her left eye, too close to read. She didn't want to check the time in an obvious way, so she tilted her wrist back just a fraction.

Suddenly, unexpectedly, Dr. Van Loeb's face came into focus an inch from her own, reflected in the watch crystal. Shocked, knowing that she was breaking a cardinal rule, Anne couldn't resist looking.

Dr. Van Loeb began to speak again. "You are obviously very anxious on the couch. That is natural."

Anne couldn't bear to keep looking at Dr. Van Loeb's face and turned her wrist a fraction until all she could see was an unexpected hand waving in the air.

"You have many pressing issues that are a source of worry for you. Perhaps we have moved too quickly to the couch. Do you want to consider returning to the chairs, so we can sit together for a while longer?"

Anne moved her wrist again and Dr. Van Loeb came back into view. Her face had an animation and liveliness that Anne had never seen before, when viewed this way. It was so intimate. Now Anne understood to what extent Dr. Van Loeb had concealed herself behind a neutral facade in their face-to-face meetings—and even at the lecture.

Dr. Van Loeb had finished what she was saying, and the sound of a question hung in the air. Anne hadn't been listening. She looked up at the ceiling for a moment and sighed, knowing the time had come to explain to this good woman with whom she didn't quite dare connect that she had changed her mind and was never coming back.

When Anne shifted her gaze back to the watch face for one last look, she saw there something extraordinary. Dr. Van Loeb's kind face was creased with loving concern. As she looked down at Anne with a tender intensity not quite like anything Anne could remember ever having known, their eyes met in the reflection for an instant.

An unbearable instant. The deeply focused look was overwhelming. Anne jumped to her feet, snatching up her handbag from the carpet beside her, and rushed to the door. She turned back to see Dr. Van Loeb still sitting there, watching her, the writing pad in her lap. The look on the doctor's face was gone, replaced by the careful blankness again.

"It's too late. I, I can't do this. I'm sorry," Anne choked out before she fled. As she closed the door behind her, she knew she would never come back. How could she? What Dr. Van Loeb offered, Anne didn't deserve, couldn't accept.

I am so much more like Henry than I knew, she thought as she walked the few blocks to her flat. Harriet would be there, expecting the usual mutual debriefings. Then they would go eat dinner. Harriet would chalk up Anne's mood, if she noticed it, to some Victor contretemps.

The chance, if there was a chance, is lost—it is much too late. I am just like Henry, Anne thought again, pausing in front of an old-fashioned dry-goods shop she had discovered when she was first needing things for her flat: coat hangers, dish towels, a toilet brush. I keep going and no one notices that I am already dead inside, no longer real.

July 26

I want to make images that seem like memories, thought Harriet, framing herself in Anne's mirror. Not a bad opening for the catalog essay, she noted as she changed her mind about the shutter speed. Stop posing, she scolded herself, reaching out with one hand to shift the blue pitcher of wilted carnations on Anne's bureau a few inches back. Stop watching yourself. She realigned Anne's hairbrush (in which sprouted a few of Anne's long blond hairs), and the pile of black-and-white snapshots, that mysterious deck of photographs she had found in the attic long ago.

Harriet focused the camera again and then carefully lowered it to her chest. Picture this. This pitcher. Her Girl Scout counselor at overnight camp, a probable lesbian called Tex, had noticed Harriet's interest in photography (Harriet had her first camera that summer, a cheap point-and-shoot with which she went around pointing and shooting), but whenever Tex called photographs "pitchers," Harriet had inwardly cringed, having been specifically enjoined from making that error in pronunciation by her grandmother, who was phobic about such dreadfully unattractive speaking habits. Gay had, in her amusing but persuasive way, deputized Harriet as a member of the pronunciation posse.

That summer, Harriet, twelve, had been both vigilant and contemptuous on each occasion that Tex said "pitcher" for picture, or when her tentmate, a boring girl from New Jersey called Karen Feldman who spoke with a lisp, boasted about her mother's subscription to a fashion magazine she called *Vogga*.

Now, as she studied her composition with satisfaction, she mentally captioned it *Picture: Pitcher* and then immediately wondered if Tex would have pronounced it *Pitcher: Pitcher,* and then wondered if Nolan Ryan would ever consent to sit for her for a portrait that might include in its composition a similar vessel, because in that case Tex could call the result, *Pitcher: Pitcher With a Pitcher.*

Poor Tex. Harriet hadn't thought about her in a long time. After that summer, Tex had written to Harriet from the University of Iowa, where she was in her last year of working toward a degree in library science, whatever that was. Harriet, in sixth grade, had momentarily imagined library shelves full of books interspersed with racks of test tubes and Erlenmeyer flasks. (Harriet had discovered Erlenmeyer flasks in science class that year, still loved to draw Erlenmeyer flasks, and even now would often doodle interlocking sets of Erlenmeyer flasks while speaking on the telephone.)

The letter, so full of unstated longing and admiration, was three pages of chatter about courses, a new kitten Tex had named Lone Pine in honor of their unit at Camp Claverack, and descriptions of Tex's plans for the following summer, when she intended to return to Claverack where she hoped she would be Harriet's counselor again. "Have you taken any pictures lately???" the letter ended. She had signed off with a troubling and uncharacteristic "Love Ya, Tex." Harriet never answered the letter, and Tex never wrote to her again, and as it happened, Harriet didn't go back to Girl Scout camp the following summer.

Harriet took the picture, changed the shutter speed and the aperture setting, focused again, lowered the camera, and cradling the camera between her breasts, took another picture. She stared unsmiling into the mirror both times, seeing herself for the moment as the camera would see her, as a stranger attending her show in the fall would see her. She wondered if Tex ever went to New York, ever went to photography galleries. What was Tex's real name? Probably something like Sue Ellen.

Harriet opened Anne's closet and moved the door back and forth until the mirror on the inside was angled properly. She stepped back to the dresser to where she had been standing and turned around. In the closet-mirror reflection she saw herself, the dresser behind her, the flowers, the objects on the dresser, and reflected in the mirror over the dresser, her own back, and the reflection of this reflection. The morning light lay like a layer of transparent film over every surface. She framed it, focused, and made several more exposures. In each picture her hands were on the camera in front of her as though it were an exposed organ of her body.

The doorbell was ringing. Harriet couldn't imagine who it could be and entertained the transient concern that Victor had come back with more buttons missing. She stood frozen on the spot, the camera dangling from the strap around her neck, deciding not to answer the door, deciding to answer the door. The buzzer sounded again. It wasn't in any particular pattern, not Victor's ring for Anne. Then Harriet heard an impatient Shave and a Haircut, Two Bits, and she broke free of her indecision, crossing the room toward the door while doubting her sudden impulse—it couldn't be—but surely no Swiss postal worker would ring the bell like that; it was probably forbidden under the regulations. She fumbled the door open.

Benedict filled the doorway. He put down his old beat-up suitcase and slung his jacket over a shoulder. "I thought I might find you here," he said, and grinned.

"Moholy Nagy!" Harriet cried out, and then stood there, gaping. She could actually feel her mouth hanging open, one of Gay's top-ten despised habits. She closed her mouth and swallowed.

"I know. Do you think I could come in, sweetie?"

"Jiminy H. Creepers, Benedict! Don't do this to a person!" She flung the door open wide so hard that it banged against the wall.

"A very grown-up, modern flat, indeed," Benedict said, kicking the door closed behind him and looking around curiously.

He parked his bag by the door and draped his jacket over the back of a chair.

"What?"

"I was agreeing with you about Anne's apartment. God, I've missed you."

Benedict circled his arms around her tenderly, gracefully. They kissed briefly, shyly. Harriet had dressed somewhat oddly for the pictures and was self-conscious about being found this way, like a child doing dress-up. She looked good, though, in an antique paisley skirt and a skinny, clingy black shirt. Anne's new persona, or whatever it was, was actually beginning to have an osmotic effect on Harriet. She relaxed into Benedict's chest and breathed in his smell: laundry soap, sweat, airplane, and underneath it, that true essence of Benedict she had only smelled elsewhere, once, on a newborn baby: a gingery, apricotty sweetness. She began to cry.

"Why the tears? If it's me after that flight, I promise I'll take a shower." Benedict pushed her back gently in order to lift her camera strap off over her head. He placed the camera on the table, and then folded her into his arms again, murmuring, "This is where you belong."

Harriet wiped her nose along his tattersall sleeve.

"I don't really know why I'm crying," she began. "But you won't be able to take a shower, actually, just a sort of squatty rinse. But you're not smelly, you never are." Harriet leaned back to look up into Benedict's lapis blue eyes.

"Hey—too much sun." She traced his sun-weathered hairline with a fingertip. He had the sort of tan that sunburns turn into, and his terrier eyebrows were bleached nearly white. He looked good, though tired. His nose was peeling. His hair was slightly too long. Until now, Harriet had always thought Benedict looked prematurely old for his twenty-eight years, in a weather-beaten, Steve McQueen–ish sort of way, owing mostly to the cumulative effects of years of summer sun on his fair complexion. He had tiny crinkles around his eyes when he smiled. But compared to the dryness, the brittleness, of Victor, Benedict seemed buoyant, boyish.

"Now that I'm beginning to believe that you're really here, and that you aren't a Fig Newton of my imagination, I'm getting worried," Harriet said. "What happened to Highland Lake Tennis Camp? Or are you here with such horrific bad news to tell me that you had to do it in person? What on earth are you doing here?"

"No bad news, don't worry. Sorry, I certainly didn't mean to scare you—I didn't think of that. Christ, no, nothing's wrong. I quit, and it's all worked out with the Hodgsons. They knew they had me on borrowed time this summer anyway. I told them the truth—that I had made a mistake letting them talk me into coming back this summer, that I was burnt out and impatient with the campers, that I needed to pursue my painting, pursue you. I'm going to go back after Labor Day and paint the cabins, as penance. In their Quakerish way, I think they drove a hard bargain, actually. It's rained a record-breaking amount this month, and the courts were unplayable a lot of the time. Two other counselors can take over my art program. They were slightly overstaffed this year anyway, so my going was actually helpful to them."

"Well, that's all fine, but I still can't quite believe you're sitting here. You know, I almost didn't answer the door." Harriet put her back against the wall and slid down to a sitting position.

"I was going to call from the airport, but the flight got in so early I didn't want to wake you, and then when I got out of the taxi on the street, I couldn't find a pay phone, and it began to seem silly not to just come looking for you. I figured that Anne would be at the office." Benedict glanced at his watch, which was still on New Hampshire time.

"Almost five A.M. my time." He reset his watch. "By my calculations, that means we have to vacate the love nest within the hour."

Harriet stared at him. She felt a wave of dislocation she hadn't experienced since childhood, and an old sense of lostness. It was hard to distinguish the floor from the walls. It was hard to figure out where she left off and the tilting room began. She put her head in her hands to try to slow her racing thoughts. Was anything as it seemed? Was her mind somehow leaking?

"How. Did. You. Know. That." Harriet spoke with her head still in her hands.

Benedict knelt on the floor in front of her and took her suddenly clammy hand between his. "I am so sorry," he began, and rubbed her hand between his, as though she had just come in from the cold. Harriet noticed and took comfort in the fact that he was wearing a pair of khakis they had bought at the Yale Co-Op a few months before, when they had driven up to New Haven to see some Fox Talbot photographs at Yale. "I've done this crazy thing of showing up, and you must think I'm playing mind games with you, and I'm not explaining anything very well. Hold on."

He turned and reached with one hand for his bag, keeping hold of her hand with the other. He dragged the suitcase close and slipped his hand gently out of hers, as though she were so fragile that he didn't want to risk doing her any more harm. Benedict rummaged for a moment in the outer zipper pocket. He pulled out a thick manila envelope and held it out to her. It was addressed to Mr. Benedict Thorne at Highland Lake Camp in Ardfield, New Hampshire, in thick block printing. Postmarked Geneva just five days before, the envelope was plastered with express-delivery stickers and Swiss postage stamps.

"I got this on Monday. Go ahead, look inside." Benedict still knelt in front of her, and when Harriet didn't make a move, he opened the flap and shook out the contents into her lap. Harriet's spiral notebook flopped out.

"My letters! Your letters. Whatever. How on earth—" Harriet snatched up the envelope and studied it for a moment.

"Benedict—this is Anne's handwriting, I think. Oh, shit. Oh, Christ. Oh, man oh Manischewitz. I'm so confused my head hurts."

"Harriet, can you take us to one of those cafés with the expensive pickles and coffee ice cream? We can figure everything out. It's all going to be okay. But we've got to get out of here before Anne and Victor arrive, don't we, and I'm starved. Aren't you starved? I've never known you not to be starved."

Benedict said he wanted to sit in the sun, because he was the kind of bone-cold you can be when you're jet-lagged. He had located one of his old cotton sweaters in his bag, and he was now wearing the sweater under his tatty old summer sport jacket, but it was a breezy day. Harriet sat at their little table in a chair that she hitched around the table to be closer to him. There weren't any other empty tables. It was early for lunch, but most of the tables were occupied by newspaper readers drinking coffee, or by pairs of women leaning together, talking avidly, their cups empty, their napkins frankly crumpled on the table. Few American women, thought Harriet, would be capable of the particular self-confidence necessary to occupy café tables indefinitely.

The moment Harriet crossed her legs, Benedict pulled her suspended foot into his lap and hugged it there, like a prized pet, saying, *"Brrr.* Warm me up."

The waiter, who was accustomed to serving her solitary lunches that she ate with her nose in a book (mostly oblivious to the student romances and intrigues surging all around her), beamed his approval at Harriet. She imagined him thinking the Swiss-waiter equivalent of *Finally landed one.* He wiped away a

few crumbs and dropped little Café Clemence menu cards on
their table. Never before had he bothered to clean anything for
Harriet before she actually ordered, not even disgusting plates of
other people's leftover food in which cigarette butts had been
stubbed out.

They decided on grilled marrow bones with toast, the waiter
responding with great animation to Benedict's questions. Harriet
had never ordered anything nearly so imaginative. With Benedict
here, being so lively and curious about everything, she was
mildly ashamed about her dull choices day after day. Why didn't
the range of possibilities so evident to him at all times ever seem
to occur to her when she was on her own? Why hadn't she ever
ordered grilled marrow bones? She was beginning to feel put
back together.

Benedict began to stroke the side of Harriet's foot. He unbuckled the sandal strap (Harriet never bothered with the buckle
and found this attention somehow touching) and dropped the
sandal under his chair. He stroked her naked foot and she felt a
shiver of pleasure go directly from her instep to *there,* and she felt
her face go pink. Her toes flexed involuntarily, and she murmured, "Benedict, you can't do that here."

"Carpopedal spasm. Look."

The waiter came with their place settings and Harriet sat up
and slid her foot back into the sandal. Before long the waiter
returned and grandly unfolded a white linen napkin to reveal the
grilled bones nestled within. He poured their mineral waters,
indicated the basket of toasted bread, and made a big show of
withdrawing discreetly.

While they ate, mostly in companionable silence, Harriet
found herself studying Benedict's face. She knew it as well as she
knew any landscape, but the moment she'd seen him in Anne's
doorway, she felt that she had forgotten some essential aspects.
Sitting here, she developed a retroactive missing of him that was
like an ache.

"Sometimes," she said, chasing a morsel of marrow around the inside of a bone with a doll–sized fork, "I think I take pictures because I have a fear of forgetting faces."

"Or a fear that your own face will be forgotten? Not a worry, in your case." Benedict leaned back and stretched his arms over his head.

He looked at his watch. "So," he said. "Are they At It right now? I thought of a palindrome for them on the plane: sex at noon taxes."

"I guess I can't be annoyed that you read all the letters."

"Harriet, I suppose you could, but there was no return address, and then I saw that the notebook was in your writing, and it was, after all, addressed to me. Not just the envelope, I mean, the notebook was. By the time I realized that you hadn't sent me the notebook—when your letter arrived on Tuesday—I had read it all."

"Amazingly speedy mail service, for once. But you must have thought it was a bit weird of me to send you the notebook with no explanation, if you thought I sent it."

"A little. But when I realized that you *hadn't* sent it was when I got even more concerned. I mean, think about it, Harriet. Why did Anne send your notebook to me?"

"Are we sure it was Anne?" Harriet said a little desperately, hoping for some other explanation. They both waited to speak until a matched pair of noisy motorbikes roared around the square and up the street in the direction of the university. The stink of their exhaust hung in the air.

"Aren't we? I think so. Where do you think she got the notebook? When you wrote, you said you thought you might have lost it somewhere out and about."

"That's true, but the last time I know I can remember seeing it was on the table, in Anne's apartment. Flat. Whatever."

Benedict turned his palms up. "Face it, sweetie, your friend Anne is a little, what shall we say, kookamoonis."

"Is that a diagnosis, doctor?"

"Harriet, don't be peeved. I don't know Anne, but I'm here because of you, not her."

"So, why exactly are you here? I mean, Benedict, I'm truly thrilled to see you, but what is going on? You didn't bring any painting supplies, did you?"

"Only a little pocket set of watercolors. No, not really. I didn't come here to paint. Put simply—and I almost tried to explain this to the unctuous creep at Swiss immigration, but then thought better of it on the grounds that he looked as though he would love an excuse to do a body-cavity search—I'm here to rescue you from rescuing Anne."

"Is that what I'm doing?" Harriet felt flattered and annoyed at the same time.

"Rescuing Anne? It seemed to be what you were headed toward. And I don't think your friend Anne can be rescued, by you, anyway. I don't think it's up to you. I think you could get in a lot of trouble for your trouble. It sounds as though she's building up to an awful letdown, to use one of your lines."

"Thank you, Benedict Thorne. It's really very grand of you and I am exceedingly grateful that you have gone to all this effort. It's a wonder I've survived all this time without you." Harriet was now really irritated. The café chair was suddenly flimsy and uncomfortable, and she felt restless. She had the fleeting thought of just getting up and walking away. But she had to ask herself: From Benedict? Or from what he had to say?

"You aren't listening. Harriet—please just listen for a minute." Benedict drained the icy dregs of his espresso, then reached over for Harriet's and licked out her cup, which had some sugary sludge in the bottom.

"Would you like another? They cost about a hundred dollars."

"No. Listen: Anne is involved with this toeless Auschwitz

person, and that is her choice. His wife either knows and doesn't care, or doesn't care to know. What would you be doing, really, to rat on them?"

Benedict sat back, looking reasonable and logical. Harriet felt with her whole being the sense of what he had just said. It was almost a physical sensation, as if a seal had been broken. She suddenly felt less certain of what she knew or thought she knew.

"So, Benedict"—when at a loss, Harriet could always look for logic—"I still don't understand why Anne sent you the notebook."

"Maybe so I would know what was going on, and going on in your head as well. I mean, I've never even met Anne, and we both love you madly. Really. Maybe she's trying to lay a claim on you in some way. Maybe she's trying to lay a claim on me in some way through you. It isn't just about this Victor screwing her, or getting into her knickers or whatever they would call it."

"They would call it the greatest love human history has ever seen," Harriet said dryly.

"Or not seen. I don't really know what it's about. I agree, it might be a cry for help. I'm just not sure what kind of help Anne could use. Do you realize what a mess of a person you've described in your own funny, original way? Sometimes you strike me as fantastically observant without being as perceptive as you might be."

Harriet sat for a moment thinking, twiddling with a spoon, something Gay had told her starting at about age six that ladies never do. Ladies never put milk in their coffee in the evening. Ladies breakfast on wood, lunch on lace, and dine on damask. Since getting here, she hadn't wanted to admit to herself that if Anne wasn't unnervingly transformed from their Eighth Street days, then she, Harriet, had been somewhat mistaken about who Anne was in the first place.

And she hadn't really thought through the consequences of

communicating with Annamarie. Had she expected Anne to leave her job and return to New York with her the following week? And what then? Harriet couldn't imagine resuming the life they had shared, pre-Benedict. Harriet assumed, though nothing was worked out, that her future lay, somewhere and somehow, with Benedict.

She thought about Anne moving back to New York, and it suddenly loomed as an oppressively bad idea. The Geneva Anne didn't even seem like someone she would want to get to know, let alone take on as a caseload of one. And had she considered the wrath of Victor? Was he capable of violence? And what if he got divorced from Annamarie—what if he actually wanted to marry Anne? That would be, to use a Gay Gibson expression, out of the fire and into the frying pan. So why had Harriet been so certain that action of any kind was called for? Now she couldn't remember why she had felt so compelled to rush into battle.

Benedict reached across the table and took her hand in his. "This isn't an entirely new story for you, is it?" he asked. She shook her head, tears welling up suddenly. The waiter arrived with their check on a saucer, the slip of paper weighted down with a five-franc coin.

"Do they tip the customers here, or what?" Benedict asked, fumbling in his pocket for money with one hand while squinting at the check with the other. "Do they make their sevens and ones like this to throw you off the track of the total?"

"I know. It seems so obscure and dramatic to write numbers that way. I guess I've gotten used to it." Harriet sniffled and wiped her face with her napkin. "I think the money is to prime the pump." She picked up the coin and studied it. "The guy in the hood is sort of butch, don't you think? Here, I've got dough." They stood up to go. Harriet felt suddenly self-conscious, unused to company, to the luxury of male company of her own. She looked at her watch.

"Well, Benedict, the coast being clear, what would you say to heading back to the Hot Sheet Hotel?"

"Do you think they'll have figured out that I'm here?"

"Depends." Harriet tried to imagine Anne and Victor coming into the freshly vacated flat every day, their routine, the details of which she did and didn't like to think about. It was like pressing a bruise. "I don't know why they would look in the closet, unless Victor always checks closets on the lookout for the Gestapo."

"You're very hard on the man," Benedict said after a moment. He put his arm around her and squeezed her shoulder to temper the remark. They waited for an ancient Peugeot driven by a nun to chug past them, then crossed the cobbled street. It was a breezy summer afternoon in a European city. "He did survive something we can't really imagine."

"Which gives him license to behave outside the rules of civilization now," Harriet retorted.

They were walking up a steep hill; they passed the corner pharmacy, in the window of which were several versions of the men's bathing trunks Victor had worn that day at the lake. The cat lay sprawled on top of a row of Dr. Scholl's wooden sandals that were stacked up in pairs like children's blocks. Neither of them spoke for several minutes. Harriet and Benedict, still holding hands, bumped together, first accidentally and then again intentionally, as they turned down the narrow lane that came out on Anne's street.

When they emerged and headed in the direction of the flat, an aproned butcher across the street recognized Harriet and waved as he hosed down the sidewalk in front of his shop. A few days earlier, when she had taken a series of self-portraits in the reflection of the shop window, through which were visible a dramatic array of pigs' heads, the butcher, Harriet realized, had been pleased and proud to think she was photographing him at his labors.

"I *can* imagine it," insisted Harriet. "Has it ever occurred to you that some of the people who survived the Holocaust might not be very nice? Not every child was Anne Frank."

"Look, Harriet, Anne Frank wasn't even Anne Frank, I know that. I just wonder if you could cut him some slack. Anyway. I look forward to meeting your friend Anne, and her partially evil consort."

When they got back to the flat, Benedict was suddenly exhausted and told Harriet he needed to sleep. Harriet pondered the etiquette of bed linens for a moment and decided she would deal with it later. The sheets on the bed were those she and Anne had slept in the past few nights, though Harriet suspected that they had already been stripped off and reapplied since she and Benedict had been out. Anne never tucked in corners as neatly as she, Harriet, had been taught to do by Tex that summer at camp. (Harriet could never understand why people called them hospital corners. In hospitals, the beds weren't tucked in at all, only along the bottom, as though a team of doctors might arrive at any moment to view the patient's body with such urgency that the bedclothes should be ready to be flung back at a moment's notice.)

They dropped their clothes on the floor and crawled into the bed—"This really is a good mattress; I must remember to thank poor old Victor for his bad back," said Benedict sleepily—and cuddled together like spoons.

Five minutes of this and Benedict was revived.

"I'm not sleepy anymore," he announced in a whisper to the back of Harriet's neck.

"Good, because I'm vibrating like a tuning fork," said Harriet, reaching for him.

It was after four in the afternoon, and the golden light that lay across the floor seemed to flow from some very old tradition.

"Look, they don't have old sunlight like that in America," Harriet pointed out to Benedict, who had come out of the bathroom clean and damp, wearing a towel around his waist. One of the things Harriet loved about this man was his universal competence, his ability to do things like wrap a towel around himself so it looked terrific and stayed up.

Harriet was waiting for Anne to answer the telephone in her office. It honked in sets of twos. She covered the mouthpiece and whispered, "If you want grapes, there are some in the fridge."

Benedict wandered into the kitchen. Anne picked up her line.

"Anne Gordon."

"Harriet Rose. Pleasetomeetcha." Harriet never found office phone calls with Anne relaxing, but couldn't resist mocking Anne's officious tone. It was like trying to distract someone who was in the middle of saying her lines in a play.

"Yes."

"Not alone, are we?" Harriet thought Anne sounded even more strained than she usually was when they had occasion to speak during the day.

"Precisely so. What can I do for you?"

Benedict came out of the kitchen with a quizzical look, holding up a rolled-up, dried-out tube of liver paste.

Harriet waved him off and turned away. "I have some rather astonishing news, Anne. Benedict is here."

"Yes, I see."

"So, I wanted to let you know, and we were hoping you, or you and Victor, could come out to dinner with us. I didn't know if there were any plans afoot for this evening."

"Yes, well, thank you for that information. I should be able to attend the meeting."

"Christ, Anne, who've you got in the office with you, Yasir Arafat?"

Silence.

"Well, I'll make a reservation for just the three of us someplace, okeydokey? Eight o'clock? Anne? I'll expect you some-
time after six here, then? Right?"

Anne uttered a muffled, "Fine then," and hung up.

Harriet was still holding the phone in her hand when Benedict
circled around her with the liver paste suspended betwixt thumb
and forefinger.

"Don't tell me this is the Anne Gordon quotidian comesti-
ble."

"Actually, it is." Harriet felt a wave of guilt for mocking
Anne, though she had to admit it was irresistible. "She has it on
those little circles of pumpernickel that are like chewing tobacco.
You know, they're not exactly food, they're provisions. They
never get stale, she says. I've always thought that might be because they were never edible in the first place."

"So what's the word on tonight? From this end it didn't
sound as though Anne was turning handsprings of joy over my
presence." Benedict returned the liver paste to the door of the
fridge and helped himself to the promised grapes. He walked
around peering at things with the grapes in one hand, popping
them into his mouth one at a time.

"No, she wasn't alone, and couldn't talk. We'll find out the
story tonight. It will turn out she was surrounded by six zil-
lionaire Kuwaitis or something. But it will just be the three of
us. Maybe Victor is actually going to spend the evening chez
Marks. Maybe it's parents' night at Lucien, Otto, and Minerva's
school."

"Maybe he's cheating on Anne," suggested Benedict, who,
having deposited the grape skeleton on the table with a neat
collection of grape pips beside it, was now digging through his
bag for a change of clothes.

"Even I hadn't thought of that," sighed Harriet.

★ ★ ★

Anne paused outside the door to her flat to pull herself together. The music she had heard floating down the hallway was coming from her own apartment—she didn't recognize it so it had to be *Django Reinhardt at Le Hot Club of Paris*. Harriet had sent the record to her for her last birthday, and Anne hadn't had the heart to remind her how little she cared for that sort of music. (She did, however, share with Harriet a stubborn preference for record albums over tapes or CDs, and they had often spent weekend afternoons in the East Village on the track of increasingly rare LPs, Harriet looking for Teddy Wilson and Lester Young, Anne hunting down Ravel, Debussy, and her passion, Rachmaninoff. ("It's the zen of the black grooves, knowing you're looking at the grain of the music. And liner notes!" Harriet had ranted the first time they had met for lunch, instantly endearing herself to Anne.)

Victor out-and-out despised jazz. ("Chaotic" and "vulgar" were his words.) When Anne had agreed, reluctantly, to go to a jazz club in Carouge one night with Harriet earlier in the month, Victor had been appalled. ("Sitting around listening to rhythmic bleating for smug ex-hippies is not entertainment," he said.)

At the jazz club, Harriet had ordered a *poire,* something to which she said Benedict had introduced her (Anne had then suggested that Harriet should be drinking Benedictine), and Anne had nursed a crème de menthe, having been mildly insulted when their drinks arrived and Harriet informed her happily that the recently deceased Gay, that oracle of social wisdom, had considered crème de menthe to be "a whore's drink."

Harriet had recognized nearly every tune the musicians played, sometimes identifying a song after the first few notes. She had rattled on to Anne about which shows the songs were written for, and by whom they were written, and who had been the original performers. Once this would have charmed Anne immeasurably. But Anne had been edgy, aware that she had made Victor cross by spending her evening without him and in this way. When Harriet identified an obscure song by Jerome Kern, Anne had murmured an impatient and belittling, "Who cares?" only to have Harriet sally forth on the history of the Gershwin song "Who Cares?"

As she unlocked her door, Anne realized guiltily that the un-touched birthday record had probably still been in its telltale original plastic wrapping. *Merde*. This had been a devastating day, and she was in no mood to meet this impossibly wonderful Benedict. She had a bad headache and would have preferred to come into an empty flat. It would be so much simpler. Time had run out, the play was drawing to a close.

"Hi, Anne—Anne, this is Benedict, Benedict, this is Anne. You guys. This is great."

Harriet was wearing makeup? No, she was just sparkling and animated, her eyes bright and her cheeks pink as she stood in Anne's hallway, gesturing with her hands as if she expected them all to join together in song.

Anne shook Benedict's hand, and when their eyes met, she was startled by the deep, penetrating blueness of his gaze. She wondered if he had already told Harriet about the notebook, if that was why he was here. It crossed her mind that it might not have reached him, if he was already en route to Geneva. She had no idea if Harriet knew he was coming—would Harriet have baked a cake?—and wondered if she were being ambushed. Mailing him the notebook now seemed more like a dream than a memory. Why had she done it? To stop Harriet in her tracks, to remove Harriet from the scene of this crime, to have this knight in shining armor come and spirit Harriet away to their land of happiness? Or to see if he was as wonderful as Harriet thought, to call the bluff? Perhaps the notebook would reveal to him a Harriet who was not so appealing after all. Or maybe, thought Anne, seeing him now, I was wishing that Benedict would come rescue me.

Well, here he was, his shining armor consisting of very American-looking khaki pants, a button-down, red-striped shirt, a slightly scruffy blue blazer, and most American of all, thick socks and brown loafers. He dropped a necktie over the back of a chair as he came forward to meet her.

"When did you leave your tennis camp?" Anne asked in an attempt to simulate polite conversation, still standing like a guest in her own flat, every corner of which seemed to be permeated by a conspiratorial atmosphere of connectedness between Benedict and Harriet.

"Two days after I got Harriet's notebook," Benedict replied coolly and evenly, keeping his eyes on her face, curious to see her response.

"Benedict calls a spade a shovel," Harriet interjected. She poked him in the back to make him stop, or at least slow down. "Hey, why are we standing here? You must be wiped out after the day it sounded like you were having. Are you okay? Do you want me to make some tea?" Harriet could hear herself nattering to fill the space.

"Your eyes are so blue," Anne heard herself saying as she let Harriet steer her into a chair. "Harriet never told me you had such blue eyes."

"Whatever," Benedict said.

"Knock it off," Harriet said crossly, and gave him a little kick.

"I'm sorry, sorry, sorry, sorry," said Anne, putting her head down on the cool table. Harriet thought Anne sounded as though she were talking to herself. Harriet and Benedict looked at each other over Anne's head. Harriet thought Anne looked like someone kneeling before a chopping block.

"You're sorry about . . . ?" Harriet prompted gently.

Anne raised her head and gazed at the wall. She spoke as if she

were dictating, in a monotone. "Everything, I suppose. Taking
your notebook like that. Ruining your time here. Being rude
today on the phone. Being the very bad person that I am . . . "
Anne trailed off.

"Life doesn't have to be an Iris Murdoch novel, Anne," said
Benedict after they had all been silent for a moment. "Nobody
is really keeping track of bad and good like that in real life. We're
not all on a quest for goodness."

"But they are! We should be!" Anne cried out. "I keep track!
You don't understand. I am *not a nice person.*"

"Yes, you are," said Harriet. "Hold on. Victor's not a nice
person, but you really are."

"No," Anne said in a faraway voice. She seemed quite definite
about this. "I'm a monster." She had tuned them out completely.

"Earth to Anne, come in please," intoned Harriet in an attempt to salvage the situation. "Hey—we have dinner rezzies
at a place with a name like the Laughing Mushroom that was
recommended in one of my guides."

"Surely not," said Anne in a more normal voice. She turned
to look at Harriet. What a wonderful face. She couldn't bear
Harriet's look of concern a moment longer. "It's Geneva. Are
you sure it isn't called the Calculating Mushroom?"

Benedict raised his eyebrows at Harriet, and Anne glanced his
way and caught him, and they all laughed, and the tension in the
room began to dissipate, like a morning fog burning off in suddenly strong sunlight.

July 26

Anne's desk was covered with little pink telephone message slips, though she was only ten minutes late for work this morning. Miss Trout had an irritating habit of organizing Anne's messages as though she were laying out a game of solitaire. Anne had asked her just to stack them in one place by the telephone, but this was apparently not a change of habit Miss Trout was prepared to undergo. She had stood patiently at the door to Anne's windowless cubicle, listening to Anne rant on about her message slips while looking down, pushing wisps of limp hair ineffectively behind her ear, and chewing the ends of her blue-framed eyeglasses. Her pale moonface, which was covered with a spray of freckles, had an innocent-schoolgirl look that was deceptive. Miss Trout did not like Anne.

Anne knew that Victor played to good advantage Miss Trout's slavish secretarial devotion in exchange for the very occasional lingering hand on her shoulder or passing caress of her surprisingly well-formed bottom. Miss Trout had referred more than once to the sole occasion nearly two years ago when she and Victor had worked late one night on a report and they had eaten sandwiches together at a conference table.

Miss Trout had nodded that she understood Anne's wish about the messages, but apparently the nod had not been meant to convey any intention on her part to change her ways. Anne suspected that Miss Trout was onto her affair with Victor; she suspected that Miss Trout deliberately spread the messages across her desk as a pink reproach, a silent but effective announcement to anyone happening by Anne's office that she had been away from her desk for a very long time, and who knew where?

"Damn Sonya Trout. Damn the spotted creature," Anne mut-

tered as she swept the slips into a pile, then pulled out her chair
and sat down at the desk before idly shuffling through them.
Most of the messages were from the day before, when the
Wednesday meeting with four field directors from the UAE had
run through the afternoon and she hadn't come back to her desk
before leaving for the day. Two were encomia about an American expatriate square-dancing group run by Mormons, who had
tracked her down as an American living in Geneva; these she
crumpled into the wastebasket at her feet.

    Dr. Van Loeb had called again. Anne studied the message for
a long moment. With regret, she finally tore it into tiny pieces
and sprinkled them on top of the square-dancing messages.

    One message was from her father, who had called to say he
was going to Orlando for a week in case she was looking for
him. There was a telephone number for his hotel. Anne was
annoyed that he hadn't made an effort to catch her at home, and
she didn't care for the irritating widow who lived down the
street with whom she knew he would be traveling.

    Florida in July? Orlando? She cringed at the idea that Selma
Glass might have a visit to Disney World on the agenda. Anne
had read more than enough about Disney World. A silly Cana-
dian secretary with whom Anne once found herself eating lunch
in the UGP cafeteria—when Victor was unexpectedly requisi-
tioned to entertain some sheikh and was unavailable for the usual
luncheon activities—had actually gone there on her honey-
moon.

    Maybe Selma's grandchildren were part of the scenario. Anne
could picture the unsmiling Henry Gordon stoically experienc-
ing Splash Mountain or whatever it was called. No, she couldn't
picture it. He would wait for them. He would be appalled at the
cost of the food, and he would analyze the gluten content of his
hamburger bun. He would carry his supply of sadness around
with him like a tank of oxygen, and he would take deep breaths
from it whenever he felt the need, whenever he felt at risk.

★   ★   ★

When Anne's mother died, Henry Gordon gave up. He had made his way to America, changed his name in a burst of cautious yet optimistic ambition, and worked his way up over many years from delivery boy to master baker, despite the ironic flour allergy. He owned and ran three thriving bakeries. He had established a reasonably good life for his young family. His wife, a wholesome, healthy young woman from Ann Arbor, Michigan, by all rights should have lived well into her eighties.

This comfort and prosperity had been achieved despite the sad knowledge that years he should have been learning and studying had been spent in a prison camp, and he would never have the education his parents had intended or the sort of profession they had hoped their only child would have. But when Elizabeth died, he gave up. Henry Gordon had survived Auschwitz but he hadn't survived the freakish, suburban death of a young wife and mother.

Anne thought her father had been waiting to die ever since. He had researched and organized the excellent Swiss boarding school for Anne, and then he had packed her off, sold the three bakeries, and retired to an ugly little house in Jersey City, New Jersey. He was fifty-three years old. He had money for the boarding school, he had money for anything he wanted, for two reasons. The bakeries were bought by a giant conglomerate that made a fortune out of Henry's mother's strudel recipes, adapted for frozen distribution nationwide. And there were reparation payments from the German government for Henry's various lost relations.

Sometimes Anne thought he had picked Jersey City because he didn't know anyone there, for its ugliness (in distinct contrast to the idyllic neighborhood of her early years), out of contempt, out of contempt for himself. She had hated visiting him there in this new living death when she came home from Switzerland on holidays, and when she was at Bennington (where she majored in angst, wearing black, and having an affair with her married, forty-eight-year-old French-literature professor), she hated coming home for the visits that grew shorter and more infrequent. She hated visiting him now.

She wasn't even sure if she loved him, if love was what they had for each other. Once, soon after the disappointing end of the affair with her professor, Anne had referred to her own deep unhappiness.

"Unhappiness is a stronger bond than happiness, isn't it?" her father had said to her with a sad smile. "You are very like me, you know."

His every moment of every day seemed a cynical mockery. He went through all the motions of living. He ate his meals, he read newspapers, he was always neatly dressed, his personal hygiene was impeccable, but Anne knew her father was merely marking time, simulating a life, that he believed it was all for nothing.

When he looked at her, she knew he saw her dead mother in her features. There were no photographs of Elizabeth Byers Gordon around—Henry had destroyed them all, or so he thought—but Anne had one little dog-eared snapshot that she kept in her jewelry box. She looked at it from time to time. It was startling to realize that she, Anne, was now approximately the age her mother had been at the time of the photograph, a stiff studio portrait taken at an Ann Arbor shopping mall shortly before she and Henry met.

Elizabeth Byers had come to New York for the first time with two college friends, and she had been seated next to him at a stirring performance of *Il Trovatore* at the Metropolitan Opera House. She had never heard opera before. Agreeing to go for coffee with this thin, accented stranger afterward—they had chatted during the intermissions, staying in their seats, her friends abandoning her for the chance to gawk at the crowds on the plaza in front of Lincoln Center—seemed like a continuation of the exciting pageant. It was the most daring thing Elizabeth had ever done.

The last time Anne had seen her father, shortly before she left New York for Geneva, she had taken the train to Newark, where Henry had insisted he would meet her with his car. At the station, she first thought he had forgotten her, but then she had discovered him, finally, sitting in his car out in front. They had driven to his house with minimal conversation, and then he had led her into his gloomy living room and introduced her to Selma Glass, who sat expectantly on his sofa. Selma had offered Anne food as though she were a guest and had later thanked her for coming. Anne wondered how Henry could stand keeping company with this talkative, dull-witted, monkey-faced woman who fancied herself to be Jersey City's Jewish answer to Gloria Vanderbilt. It seemed another way of punishing himself for having outlived so many people he loved.

Most of the other messages were routine, work-related communications. Clients had to be consulted, reports were due, budgets were in need of figures, audits had to be monitored. Anne was unexpectedly very good at this unlikely job. The one message from today, this morning, was not actually a telephone message, and it was not in Miss Trout's irritating, feathery ballpoint handwriting, Anne saw, when she reached it. The slip was not signed, but it was written in black fountain pen, in Victor's distinctive crabbed hand.

"I need to talk to you. Come to my office and see if I am free," it said.

Anne found him alone at his desk, with curling ledger sheets of comparative quarterly figures laid out in stacks across the surface, and he looked up quickly from his work when she stood in the doorway, as if he had been waiting for her. Victor had a corner office with a window, and it was a real room with a door that closed, not just a partitioned space like Anne's. He was in his shirtsleeves, and his sleeves were rolled up just a couple of notches. Anne knew just where, up near the elbow on his left forearm, Victor's number could be found, under the white cotton.

"Ah, Miss Gordon, do come in. Why don't you shut the door so we have quiet to go over the numbers?" This was for the benefit of any passersby, Anne supposed, though it was an unnecessary charade just now. The hallway was empty, and in any case probably everyone on the floor, if not in the building, knew all about Victor's protégé, Victor's piece of ass.

"Here I am," she said simply, and stood, waiting. How many times had she dreaded a similar summons, only to find that there was either a genuinely urgent question having to do with UGP business, or it was a playful ploy to steal a few intimate moments during the workday? But each time she met with him like this, unexpected dread stirred somewhere inside her.

"How are you?" Victor inquired.

"I'm fine. How are you?" Get to the point, thought Anne.

"I'm not really fine, since you ask," Victor said, and stretched out his arms over his head. "Oh, my, these old bones. Well, I am, and I am not. Anne, sit down."

Anne dropped into the chair that faced his desk. Now what? She felt blood humming in her ears.

"I have had some surprising news, Anne." He stopped and looked at her. Anne wondered for a nauseating moment if Annamarie was going to have another baby.

"I must stress to you what a surprise this is," he went on. Every time he said the word *surprise,* Anne heard something in his voice that was like a lie. Victor took off his glasses and rubbed his eyes. He left his glasses on his desk and leaned back in his chair. Anne knew that with his glasses off she had become a blur.

"I have received a promotion," Victor said, rotating his chair to face the window, then swinging it back. He tilted his head in her direction. He smiled. Afforded the privacy of Victor's myopic gaze, Anne allowed herself the luxury of letting her face go completely blank, making no effort to mirror his reaction with the expected duplicate mask. She thought of Dr. Van Loeb.

"Congratulations," she murmured. She waited.

"Thank you. I am glad that you are pleased for me. I must tell you something more, though. I am being put in charge of the regional UGP office in Cairo." Victor stopped twirling around and landed with his feet on the floor in front of him. He put his glasses back on and searched Anne's face.

She looked down. What would Harriet say? So this is how the story ends, Anne thought.

"Anne?"

"When do you go, if I may ask?" Anne asked in a hoarse voice. She knitted her hands together and clasped them so tightly that her ring gouged her interlaced fingers.

"Officially, I take charge there on September one, but what with housing and arranging for the children"—he looked vaguely apologetic for a moment—"it looks as though we'll go in perhaps three weeks, or even sooner, depending on Annamarie."

"Does it?"

"Does what?"

"Does it depend on Annamarie, Victor?"

He looked irritated. "She has a great deal to do, to organize, to pack, to arrange the children's school records and so on. It's possible that Lucien may go off to boarding school. Nothing is certain."

"Don't make me ask, Victor. Or do you want to hear me say it?"

"Don't, my darling." He got to his feet and came around the desk to where she was sitting. He stood behind her and put his hands on her shoulders. "You are a very, very brave girl. I have not forgotten you. I know this is quite difficult. Not what we planned, you and I." He stroked her bare neck with one finger.

"Victor, what will we do? What will I do?" Anne felt as though a trapdoor had opened under her feet. A trapdoor that had been there all along. Suddenly, this moment seemed inevitable.

"I have been thinking of that. I have already this morning put in a recommendation for a promotion for you—here, let me show you the letter." He stepped briskly over to the window behind his desk and pawed through a pile of manila folders lying on the table there. He found the right folder, opened it, and pulled out a letter. He rushed back to Anne and flourished it under her nose; Anne pushed it away, certain she would cry if she saw the words on the page. He ignored her and began to read:

"Blah blah blah, 'in sum, Miss Gordon has proved herself remarkably capable in all ways, and in the months of work for UGP under my direct supervision she has shown a diligence and trustworthiness that demonstrates how eminently qualified she is for a promotion to Senior Account Supervisor,' et cetera, et cetera.

"You see," he explained obliviously to the stricken Anne, "in a few months' time, as a senior account supervisor, it would be perfectly natural for you to put in for a transfer to Cairo."

"Why are you doing this?" Anne whispered.

"Doing what? Writing you up for a promotion you deserve in any case? You might thank me, you know. There are going to be a lot of people begging me for recommendations before I leave, once word gets out. The jockeying for power on this floor will be overwhelming. There will be a stampede for this office, I can assure you." Victor looked around his office and smiled as he considered the various power plays his leaving would occasion.

"How long have you known about this?"

Victor didn't say anything for a beat too long. "I got the call this morning," he said, not quite answering the question.

★   ★   ★

Back at her desk, Anne sat and stared at a blank note pad for a long time. She made a short list:

> transfer—Cairo?
> Stay at UGP in Geneva
> Find other work, Geneva
> Dr. Van Loeb?
> New York (Harriet? Benedict.)
> Henry, New Jersey

The last possibility on the list she crossed out immediately. Working her way up the list from the bottom, Anne drew a line through each item until she reached the top and had crossed everything out. Then she went back to work.

As lunchtime approached, Anne wasn't sure what to do. Her apocalyptic meeting with Victor had ended abruptly when Miss Sreenivasan had come in with an armful of faxes that needed urgent attention. Victor had waggled his eyebrows apologetically at Anne over Miss Sreenivasan's head as she bent over his desk, laying out the papers before him. Anne had fled.

Was their luncheon rendezvous still on? Anne didn't want to ring his office to confirm it, as that would seem too desperate. Yet she was desperate to spend the hour alone with Victor, to feel the one thing she knew was real, his skin against hers. The power she felt in his need for her was something for which she was hungry, and she needed proof of it today, proof that she was still powerful, that he was still hers.

Having heard nothing further from Victor all morning, Anne decided that this was a good sign and felt reassured. As the usual time for synchronized ducking out of the office approached, she returned one last call, typed up one last interim adjustment figure, and then left the UGP offices and headed to the flat.

She rushed through all the usual preparations of the bed and found herself nervously spritzing with cologne, brushing her teeth, changing out of her clothes and into nothing, under her slinky robe. Then, as time passed, she changed her earrings, washed a few dishes, filed a hangnail. Victor was late. Anne looked through Harriet's odd collection of old snapshots of a man, a woman, and a little girl. More time passed. Anne wondered miserably where Harriet was, aware that Harriet had cleared away from the flat to suit Anne and Victor's need to meet. Harriet's camera was on the table. Usually she took it with her.

Victor was very late. Anne decided to telephone his private line, clinging to the hope that he had lost track of the time or been held up by an unexpected telephone call from the field.

It rang for a long time, and then Sonya Trout picked up with her usual crisp, "Victor Marks's line. Miss Trout here."

"Is he there?" Anne did not identify herself.

"Is that you, Anne?"

Damn Sonya Trout. *"Mmmn."*

"Where are you, Anne? You're missing our little celebration."

"Sorry?"

"We're throwing Victor an impromptu celebration lunch; we're celebrating his promotion. I looked for you, but you had left. Are you feeling unwell? You looked as though you were coming down with something this morning. We're all in the conference room." Miss Trout sounded positively giddy. She must have held out the telephone to demonstrate, as Anne could for that moment hear the murmuring sounds of a party. "I've got champagne, and I ordered sandwiches—smoked salmon and cucumber, the kind he likes," Miss Trout added proudly.

"So, everybody at UGP knows about the promotion now," Anne asked woodenly, clutching her robe around her as though Miss Trout could intuit precisely what she was wearing.

"Yes, there was a memo distributed this morning. Of course,

I knew all along he would get the promotion when I typed up his application for the Cairo posting—when was it—about six weeks ago," Miss Trout said smugly.

"Well, you sound like the cat who ate the canary," Anne snapped at her, giving up all pretense of formality at this appalling, though not entirely shocking, revelation.

"The cat who has been approved as special assistant to go along with the new section supervisor to Cairo," Miss Trout virtually crowed.

"Oh, fuck off, you cunt on wheels!" Anne shouted into the telephone. "If you're lucky, he'll let you lick Tipp-Ex from his ass and you'll have the first orgasm of your life!" She slammed down the telephone, breathing hard.

While she dressed, jerked the lunch-hour sheets off the bed and remade it, and then left the flat to return to the office, Anne's mind was racing. I have no choice, I have no choice, she repeated to herself in rhythm to the click of her heels on the pavement as she sped along. No choice, no choice.

At the office, Anne avoided staff and stayed at her desk, and she got the distinct feeling that Miss Trout had publicized some version of their telephone chat, as even the usual flow of office communication seemed to pass her by. Her telephone rang. She let it ring for a while, then answered it. It was Harriet, calling from the flat. Out of the blue, Benedict had shown up, was here in Geneva. Would Anne and Victor like to join them for dinner? Anne was noncommittal, indicated that she would join them on her own, let Harriet think she wasn't alone, put up with Harriet's teasing about her stony manner, and rang off.

Benedict. Oh, God, the notebook. Brilliant timing.

The telephone rang again. Harriet again? Sometimes when Harriet sensed that Anne was in need of something, she would call back with a knock-knock joke, or something similar that would leave Anne smiling into her afternoon, although Harriet more often than not had to explain a lot of stupid jokes to Anne, who never got them. (Only the day before, Harriet had first told her about, then explained, the news that Cock Robin turns out to have changed his name. It seems it had formerly been Penis Robinowitz.) But it was Victor.

"Anne. You're there."

"Not really," she whispered into the phone, suddenly near tears at the sound of his voice. She bit her lip.

"I'm sorry about the schedule. I did not know what Sonya had planned. You had already left. And I am sorry that I did not tell you myself that Sonya is coming to Cairo. I didn't think it was important. I understand that you were upset when she told you about it."

"Yes, upset. Is that the word she used?" Anne was curious. She hadn't seen hide nor freckle of the darling Miss Trout since returning from her so-called lunch. Anne would be hungry if she weren't on the verge of throwing up.

"I think so," said Victor. "You might consider some sort of apology for your temper the next time you see her. I have given Sonya, Miss Trout, the rest of the day off, so she can see about her visa at the British consulate."

"How nice."

"Anne, don't be childish. You can handle this. We must talk. Shall we meet in our usual fashion tomorrow? I promise I will be there. I long to see you. To see all of you." He shifted the telephone, and Anne could hear sounds in his office of papers shuffling, then a male voice asking a question, and then Victor covered the phone, though not very effectively, and said to who-ever had come into his office, "Yes, aren't those all the figures? . . . Shit. I will attend to that. . . . No, they should match. . . . Yes, stay. I will get rid of this call." He came back on the line. "My darling? I must go. Tomorrow."

Anne hung up the telephone without bothering to reply, as he had already disconnected. Her head throbbed with the beginning of a nasty, migrainelike band of pain. Anne found it oddly good company. She could hear her blood roaring in her ears. It was like the ocean.

When Anne was five, she had spent a week one summer at a beach on Long Island (Lido Beach, a hilarious redundancy, as Harriet had pointed out at dinner only the night before when the talk had centered on Shrimp Scampi and other menu silliness). The first afternoon, while Henry and Elizabeth read books under their striped umbrella, Anne had stood just a few feet in front of them in the waves, facing out to sea, afraid of the slight undertow, immobilized by terror while the tide rushed in and receded, rushed in and receded.

Standing still, her feet had slowly sunk into the sand until they were completely covered past her ankles. She thought she would die there. She accepted that this was her fate, and so she stood, paralyzed, not moving, not asking for help. Henry had sneaked up behind her then and lifted her free, hoisting her up into the air and swinging her around. He had meant to surprise her, harmlessly, as a father teases his little girl, and was disconcerted when she burst into tears. At first, he thought he had startled her, but then he understood that she sobbed and clung to him at that moment because he had saved her.

"You are so little to know how cruel the world is, my pet," Henry had murmured into her ear as he held her tightly in the bright summer sun. He stroked her and whispered into her ear, while Anne studied his Auschwitz number. Little hairs grew around it. This would be Anne's earliest memory of Henry's number, her sense that she herself was invisibly marked as well.

At dinner with Harriet and Benedict, Anne skillfully deflected the talk away from herself by interviewing Benedict about his life. On the walk to the restaurant (which was in an out-of-the-way financial neighborhood in a part of Geneva even Anne had never explored before; the restaurant's name turned out to be Le

Champignon Outré) Anne noticed that Benedict didn't so much walk as lope. He was so distinctly American in every movement he made. Harriet and Benedict walked close together, holding hands, and Anne tried to stay abreast of them, but kept having to drop back because the sidewalk was too narrow in places. It crossed her mind that this was the way Harriet must have felt all month when out with her and Victor. As they reached the restaurant, Harriet stopped at the alleyway beside the front door, to talk to a ginger tomcat who was sitting imperiously atop a rubbish barrel.

"Handsome puss," she told him admiringly, and he butted his head up under her hand appreciatively.

"Has Harriet told you her racist theory of cat personalities?" Anne asked Benedict.

"Harriet has told me many of her theories, but I might have missed that one."

Harriet was annoyed that Anne was putting her on the spot in this way, demanding a performance and at the same time demonstrating to Benedict her own closer ties to Harriet. She obliged, however, with a summarized version: "Ginger cats like this fellow are the most reckless. Black-and-whites are dumb. Gray tigers have the highest IQs. Persians are gay. Siamese are schizophrenic. And so on."

"Mrkgnao," said the cat.

"Doze was certainly reckless," Benedict said after another moment. Harriet continued to stroke the cat, who had begun to purr.

"Doze was mine, you know," Anne said.

"That's not true!" Harriet argued. "They were both yours and mine together."

"Whatever you say," said Anne.

Harriet thought of a moment in Central Park, years ago, when she and Adam had been taken by Gay to watch the seals. They had just bought two identical green balloons, and Gay was standing still, holding them, the string wrapped around her gloved hand, while both children, who were sitting on a park bench, finished up their ice cream cones. (Gay loved ice cream, but would never have dreamed of eating ice cream with her hands and thought ice cream cones were only for children in any case. At Gay's, ice cream was served on a plate and eaten with a fork and spoon.)

One balloon suddenly exploded with a bang. "Look, Harriet," Adam had screamed out, ice cream smeared around his mouth and dripping down his chin, "Your balloon popped!"

Benedict's bony hands—dusted with fine golden hairs and sprinkled with freckles like some wonderful spice—as Anne studied them discreetly at the table, were beautiful to watch in motion. The way he held his water glass, the way he sipped from it. He kept touching Harriet briefly, lightly. From the moment Anne had come into the flat a couple of hours before, she had felt that the sum of Harriet and Benedict together was a solid, substantial thing, an object, like a gold ingot. Her romance with Victor—whatever it was, whatever it was to be called, her affair, her passionate connection to the man—now felt tenuous, faintly ridiculous, artificial, insubstantial.

I am bleeding to death and nobody has noticed, Anne thought. The blood is invisible, but I feel lighter and lighter as it drains from me. Soon I will be gone. Her headache had settled in for the night, and it throbbed behind one eye, but she didn't care; it was a punishment Anne welcomed. I am getting to be like Henry, she thought once again, as she did now several times a day.

During drinks, she extracted from Benedict his basic life story: Benedict grew up in a small Massachusetts college town, his father an American-history professor, his mother a frustrated cellist who had given up a promising career in order to provide her husband and three children with a wonderful life and homemade bread in their Victorian farmhouse. Benedict was the youngest, an afterthought, he discovered during an adolescent conversation with his father about the perils of unprotected sex.

"You were a train whistle in the night," his father had said. "A most delightful surprise, however," he had added hastily and somewhat unconvincingly. Benedict had been named for Benedict Arnold, a remote ancestor on his father's side, through marriage. Benedict's father's doctoral thesis was a consideration of that cousin, Margaret Shippen, Mrs. Benedict Arnold, and her relationship to Major André.

Harriet interrupted here to point out the coincidence of her being represented by the Shippen Gallery, and Benedict said that he had often wondered if Gloria Shippen was a distant cousin.

"It's probably why we met," he said. "I don't think I've ever admitted to you that I crashed your opening that night. I wandered in the door basically because the name Shippen has always intrigued me."

"Well, whatever. We would have met sooner or later," said Harriet.

"Probably so," Benedict agreed, gazing at Harriet fondly.

Anne watched them look at each other and remarked, "In certain cultures, there is a belief that when people look into each other's eyes, their souls travel out of their bodies and meet halfway, to join together."

"What if a bus were to come along between them just then?" Harriet inquired brightly.

Benedict laughed, and Anne smiled briefly. There was a self-conscious lull, and then Anne asked Benedict another question about his family. Benedict's two sisters were married and had children. They lived in towns not too far from the Thorne ancestral manse. Benedict was the only one really to leave, which he had done by going off to New York to study painting at the Studio School, on Eighth Street. Anne, Harriet, and Benedict reckoned that they just missed overlapping on Eighth Street.

By the time Harriet and Anne were living in the apartment just a block away from the Studio School, the apartment Harriet shared now only with Bask (who was staying at Gloria Shippen's for the month), Benedict had finished school and had moved away from the Village to the sunny top floor of a brownstone way out west on West End Avenue, where he lived now, the tenant of an eccentric picture framer who was occasionally willing to take art in lieu of rent money.

They had sorted out their parallel time lines to this point when the waiter came back for the third time to see if they were ready to order. They decided to share a fondue and a big salad, and Benedict selected a spicy Alsatian wine, though not, Harriet and Anne were separately relieved to note, a Gewürztraminer. Harriet's and Anne's eyes met, and they both grinned.

"You two, no private jokes," Benedict complained good-naturedly.

"I think that all I have done in Geneva is eat in restaurants," Harriet said.

"It may be the only meaningful activity here, actually." Anne returned to Benedict's life story. "Are your parents living happily ever after, then?"

Harriet and Benedict exchanged unhappy looks. "No, God no," Benedict said after a moment. "My dad had an affair with a student two years ago, and he and my mother are still in the middle of a stupid divorce."

Harriet was uneasy, knowing that this was a sad subject for Benedict. He had believed in his happy golden childhood, and in his wonderful family, and this turn of events had been grindingly horrible for him. Telling her about it the first time, he had wept in her arms.

Anne flushed, thinking of her college affair with the married professor. She had been desperate for him to divorce his wife. She had even planted incriminating evidence in his coat pockets, twice, in the form of incendiary love notes full of explicit references that she hoped would be discovered by his wife, but nothing had ever resulted. The affair had ended when he went off without warning for a sabbatical year in France. *Here I am again,* Anne was startled to realize, *repeating history.*

"Does your father still see the student?" Anne asked.

"No, that ended badly, and then he got involved with my mother's best friend. Now they've broken up, but he's going out with someone else, I think. I don't know. I'm not in touch with him at the moment."

"From worse to bad, then," Anne said, feeling sorry for the student who had pried him loose, only to lose out to another woman.

"Well, my mother is pretty depressed, as you can imagine. She's gone to work in the public library now. Look, can we get off this subject?" Benedict's mouth was turned down at the corners, and Anne thought he looked as though he might cry. *What a sweet soul.* Harriet had taken his hand and was squeezing it.

"Speaking of marital infidelity and betrayal," Harriet said brightly, "what's up with Victor? Where is he? I do want Benedict to meet him."

"I'm sure you do," Anne replied. The waiter brought their fondue just then, and for a while they dealt mainly with strategies for dunking the bread in the molten cheese without losing it. They all three burned their mouths in the first few minutes, despite mutual avowals and warnings to avoid doing precisely this.

"The Old World evolutionary forerunner to pizza mouth," Benedict pronounced ruefully.

"To love and friendship," Harriet said suddenly, picking up her wineglass. Benedict and Anne picked up their glasses. They held them up together, clinked simultaneously, and drank. Anne burst into tears.

Benedict and Harriet exchanged puzzled glances. Anne looked up and said, through her tears, "Stop giving each other secret looks." She wiped her face with her dinner napkin and slowly folded it into a neat square in front of her. After a long pause, Anne quietly said, "I'm all right now," having swallowed back down her anguish.

"What's up?" Harriet asked.

"Oh, I've had a bit of unpleasant news at UGP," Anne said lightly.

"Are they in trouble? Is an international oil cartel looking for you because you missed a decimal point? Have you embezzled from the Kuwaitis? Have you been a spy for the State Department? Do you need to enter the Witness Protection Program?" Harriet began one of her freewheeling tangents.

Benedict nudged her. "Let Anne explain," he said gently.

"Victor has been promoted. He's going to head up the Cairo office," Anne said in an even tone.

"Oh." Harriet studied Anne's unrevealing face for a signal. "So, what does this mean for you? Are you off to Cairo?"

"Possibly, but if I do go, it wouldn't be for months. Meanwhile, I'm going to be left at UGP in a rather awkward position, once Victor leaves. People there know that I wasn't exactly brought in for my great expertise with international oil markets." Anne seemed to grow more tired-looking by the moment, as she spoke. She pressed the heel of a hand to her left eye.

"What, exactly, does a barrel of oil look like, anyway?" Harriet asked. "I've always wondered. I mean, do they actually have big barrels lined up that they roll down a gangplank, or is it an imaginary, theoretical sort of measurement?"

"I haven't the foggiest," Anne said. "I've never thought about it."

"So when does Victor leave for Cairo?" Benedict asked. He put his hand on Harriet's arm to keep her from going off the tracks again.

"Quite soon. Weeks. Days, maybe," was Anne's clipped reply. "As soon as his wife makes the arrangements. For the children."

"You poor soul," said Benedict. His pity made Anne feel close to tears again, and she fought them back.

"Oh, my god," Harriet said as Anne's situation dawned on her. "And you just found this out today?"

Anne nodded miserably, a tight smile playing on her face. The waiter came and asked if they wanted a sweet, which they didn't, or coffee, which they did.

Harriet rose from the table. "I shall return," she announced with a forced laugh. "But I *must* get to the loo."

Anne and Benedict sat in silence for a moment, both of them watching Harriet's back as she crossed the restaurant and then turned out of sight to follow a sign that indicated toilets were down a steep flight of stairs.

"She's very happy," Anne observed. "You're both very happy. Are you going to get married?"

"Don't you think that would be a good idea?" Benedict asked.

"I do, actually, and I'm not a great believer in the institution. I was prepared to despise you, but I don't. I think you're perfect for each other. I really do. You possess each other. You provide a kind of ballast that she needs, and you're both madly in love."

"You're very generous. I mean that. Your blessing, or approval, or whatever it is, it means a lot to me. I thought you were a nut case, from Harriet's descriptions, to which, thanks to you, I was treated in one toxic dose."

"The notebook."

"Yes. I'm still not sure why you sent it. Though I'm glad to be here. I had worked up quite a scenario in my mind's eye, you know. You can do that when you're far away from a situation, and you feel helpless."

"What sort of scenario?"

"Oh, I had you in a suicidal agony, things like that. Here's our coffee, no, it's not ours, it's for those people. What's taking Harriet so long, I wonder. I hope she found the bathroom and didn't fall down a hole somewhere."

"I was once in a restaurant near Lausanne, with my father, when he came to visit me at boarding school," recalled Anne. "A big fat Italian woman who had been sitting at the next table got up and left, though her sweater was still on the chair, and she didn't come back. Her lunch was served, and it just sat there. No one seemed to think much about it.

"All during our lunch, I could hear a woman's voice calling, '*Aiuto! Aiuto!*' but not knowing Italian, I thought I was hearing a mother calling her little boy named Aiuto. It must have been an hour before someone noticed that the fat Italian woman had somehow locked herself into the bathroom, and she was calling for help all that time. *Aiuto* means 'help,' in Italian. I didn't know."

"Well, there's no reason you would."

"No, I suppose not. But I felt terribly guilty about it. And I just couldn't believe that not one person in that restaurant knew Italian, knew she was calling for help."

"And that's why you have returned to Switzerland. Drawn back by your love of the warmth and generosity of the Swiss people."

Their coffee was served.

"Where *is* Harriet?" Benedict said, slightly anxious.

Harriet had really needed to use the bathroom, and she had also wanted to be by herself for a moment. As Anne's situation began to sink in, she had begun to boil with rage at Victor. She emptied her bladder, which was a relief, having not been able to find the right moment to leave the table before now. She washed and dried her hands, studied her face in the cracked mirror over the sink, and wished she had brought along her camera to take a fractured self-portrait in the bathroom, as the light was rather weird and the striped wallpaper made her think of Matisse.

On the wall just behind her was a framed antique circus poster that reflected in the mirror and reminded Harriet of something. It was sinister, like a Max Beckmann. There was a ringmaster in a top hat, a seal with a ball on its nose, an elephant, a lion behind bars, and a tumbling clown. She remembered: the circus-parade night-light of her childhood. On the way out, the sight of a pay telephone stopped Harriet in her tracks.

With a plan that had been half-forming into inevitability in some part of her mind for days, she looked up Victor Marks in the directory. He was there, which somehow surprised her. He seemed like the unlisted type, just as a matter of principle, as it would make life more complicated. She dug out a coin and dropped it into the slot of the telephone. Harriet had kept a finger on the line of the directory page, and now she dialed his number. Her hands had gone slightly cold and damp. She *would* do this.

Telephones don't ring in Europe the way they do in America, Harriet observed with irritation. They honk and bleat significantly, like their damned police and ambulance sirens. Everything always sounds like a dire emergency here, like an air raid warning. I've been here too long.

"Hello?" The accented voice must be Annamarie. Harriet was startled that the woman had answered in English, but then remembered that Annamarie was Polish, and French or English were the common languages of the household. And Victor wanted Lucien, Otto, and Minerva to speak perfect English, Anne had told her, so they could get into good American universities.

"Hello? Is somebody there?" Harriet could hear classical music in the background, and children's voices. She suddenly didn't know what she wanted to say. The half-rehearsed sentences were gone. Her voice dried up in the back of her throat. She had nothing to say. She was somehow content just to hear Annamarie's voice.

"Hello? Hello? Look, if this is a joke, I am hanging up now.

If this is a bad connection and you can hear me, I cannot hear you." There was a burst of noise and Harriet could hear a child's excited voice asking, "Mummy, Mummy, is it Daddy?" and Annamarie must have taken the telephone receiver and pressed it to her bosom for a moment, because Harriet thought she could hear the thump of a heartbeat along with a muffled, "No, sweetheart, I told you, Daddy will be home soon. This is a bad connection, or a prank." Then, Annamarie was back on the line, saying politely, "If I cannot hear you and you are trying to reach the Marks residence, please call back, but only if that is the case." Annamarie hung up.

Harriet put the receiver back on the hook carefully. She felt suddenly unburdened, as if she had achieved something. Having heard Annamarie's voice, having heard that little fragment of family life in the apartment, Harriet realized that these were real people, not just ideas, not just characters in her head, but actual people, with beating hearts. And something about Annamarie's voice told Harriet that this woman knew exactly what she was doing, that she was eminently capable and didn't need the sort of aid Harriet could offer, now, or ever.

When Harriet returned to the table, her espresso cup was empty. She looked at it in exaggerated disappointment.

"We drank it because it was getting cold. We assumed you had died. Here, I'll order you another," Benedict said. He automatically stood as she pulled out her chair to sit.

"My, my," Anne murmured. "We do have manners." She turned to Harriet and said, "Based on everything I know of her, Gay would have adored Benedict."

"I think so," Harriet agreed, touched by the observation. It made her think of stories she had heard from Ruth about Gay's lack of love for Harriet's father. Simon Rose: Jewish, from a poor family in Brooklyn, devoid of "breeding" or blue blood. (It seemed ironic to Harriet that Benedict came from—had more or less fled—the world Gay most highly valued, the world of those who were socially registered, the world that knew instinctively how to center perfectly acceptances with pleasure of kind invitations to attend. The acceptance world.)

When Simon Rose proposed to her daughter, Gay was appalled. Ruth, the styleless, drab antithesis of her mother (whose friends discussed endlessly the astonishing near-impossibility of Ruth being Gay Gibson's daughter), who had never before been the object of anyone's affections, listened stoically to Gay's harangues.

"You can't just marry him, my dear. He is the only man who has ever asked you out. Surely you're not going to marry your calling list of one?" Gay hated to lose control, hated to lose, period. Years earlier she had been caught off guard when Graham Gibson divorced her to marry a younger, richer socialite from Grosse Pointe, and she had forever after seen to it that she was the first one out the door from all subsequent marriages and affairs. She regretted her inattentiveness to the issue of finding Ruth a husband, and now it was too late. And Simon Rose, of all people. "He's no one, he's nothing."

Ruth knew that wasn't so; Simon Rose was everything that Gay disliked in a man: not particularly tall, not suave, not overtly witty or chivalrous, and not particularly attentive to her. He was, in fact, the first man Ruth had ever encountered in her nearly thirty years in the background of the life of the glamorous Gay Gibson who seemed to prefer her to her mother. He was also the smartest man she had ever met.

"What did Gay think of your father?" asked Anne.

Harriet gave her a look. Anne did still have the knack for intercepting her wavelengths.

"She didn't approve of the marriage for all the obvious reasons. But then, I think he sort of grew on her." Harriet thought a moment. "I've never really understood my parents' marriage. I grew up believing that Adam—the way he was, and then his death—both drove them apart and held them together. But that might not be fair to either one of them."

Anne thought of her own parents' marriage, as she remembered it, and then she thought of Ruth Rose, whose subdued presence was so unlike the cheerful midwestern heartiness she remembered of her own mother.

"There was never a particular moment when my father left," Harriet continued. "He just never came back. And I guess I've always wondered if I was somehow responsible, if there was something I could have done, or something I did. And then when my mother got worse, and worse, I felt responsible for her, too, and guilty at my relief when she was finally in the hospital and not my problem anymore."

"Harriet," Benedict broke in, "you don't have to assume that everything that has ever happened has been your fault. It's sort of adorable, but it's also sort of narcissistic."

"Oh, but that's just the point! Don't you see? That's why marriage is something I worry about. I mess things up. I make mistakes."

Anne twisted the thin gold ring off her finger and held it out to Benedict. He took it, not quite understanding her intention, and studied the ring.

"My father's parents were murdered by the Nazis," Anne said in a low voice. "This was his mother's wedding ring. A neighbor of theirs took it from her body before the Nazis came back to loot the apartment and dispose of the corpses."

"How do you come to have it now?" asked Harriet, intrigued, having never seen the ring before Geneva. She had noticed it the first day and had assumed it had something to do with Victor; perhaps it was useful when they checked into hotels. Did they ever check into hotels?

"After the War, when my father went back, looking for family, he happened to meet the son of the neighbor, and he was given the ring. It's the only thing left that was his mother's."

Benedict passed the ring over to Harriet, who held it gently in the palm of her hand as though it were a tiny living specimen.

"Do you suppose the neighbor took it for safekeeping, or was he just stealing a gold ring?" Anne didn't answer, and sensing that Anne thought the question tactless, Harriet shifted her focus.

"When did your father give it to you?" Harriet had often tried unsuccessfully to imagine Anne's father at the beginning of what was meant to be living happily ever after, but the Henry Gordon she knew was old and desiccated and defeated.

"It was my parents' wedding ring. He never gave it to me. I took it from my mother's finger before she was buried." Anne looked at Benedict, and then at Harriet. They stared back at her. Harriet stopped turning the ring between her fingers.

"He doesn't know I have it." Anne stopped again, and then finished, "I can wear it here because I don't know anyone."

No one said anything. Harriet was disturbed by this image of Anne taking the ring. Had her mother's body been in a coffin? Was it difficult to remove the ring from death-stiffened fingers? How could a child of twelve pull off such a maneuver? Anne had never told her about this, either, and Harriet realized again how little she knew her friend.

The waiter arrived with the new round of coffees and was placing them on the table when Harriet felt a hand on her shoulder, simultaneously saw a hand on Anne's shoulder out of the corner of her eye, and heard the voice of Victor say, "I apologize that I was delayed until now. This must be the painter."

Harriet turned her head to gape up at Victor.

"How do you do that?" she asked. "Really. How do you manage to track Anne down and materialize that way? Did you put a little homing device on her bra strap?"

Victor smiled a tight smile and put out his hand to Benedict, who rose in his seat and shook Victor's hand politely.

"Are you joining us?" Benedict said, clearing his jacket off the fourth chair at the table.

"We can only stay a moment," Victor said, and lowered himself carefully into the chair. Your back, thought Harriet. We all know about your back, and you really could have sat down more normally, I'm sure. And what's with the royal "we"?

"We?" said Anne.

"Yes, I thought you and I should go somewhere quiet and talk, tonight," said Victor.

"This is a quiet place, and I'm already here, talking with Harriet and her fiancé. Feel free to join us."

Fiancé? thought Harriet.

"Anne, do not punish me for inconveniencing you this afternoon. I am here now. There is not much time. Do come." Victor appealed to her, and when she didn't reply, he turned to Harriet and Benedict with a shrug for confirmation of his reasonableness.

Benedict met Victor's gesture with a shrug of his own, a subtle mimicry that Harriet recognized as an ominous sign that Benedict's hackles were rising. Benedict sat completely still. The coffee spoon flipping back and forth in his fingers made Harriet think of a cat's lashing tail.

"Don't you think a private talk is in order, my dear?" Victor addressed Anne again.

"Everything with you always has to be private, doesn't it?" Anne said with irritation.

"I think the word you mean, actually, is *clandestine,*" chimed in Harriet.

"I do not understand your childish games, Anne," Victor persisted. "It is not unreasonable for me to want to talk with you tonight. But you prefer to play with me in front of your friends. I cannot let you waste any more of my precious time. I have many urgent plans that require my attention, at home and at UGP. I really shouldn't even be here now."

"Where, exactly, *should* you be right now, Victor?" Benedict's quietly frigid voice brought them up short, and no one said anything for a moment. Harriet had never before seen the indecipherable look that was now on Benedict's face.

Victor smiled his lizard smile at Harriet, saying, "Ah, yet another asker of questions! You two must enjoy living up to one another's standards, my dear."

Benedict's coffee spoon skittered across the table and landed in Anne's lap. Anne placed it back on the table. Benedict leaned forward, started to say something to Victor, then stopped. Harriet put her hand over one of his, and he turned his hand over to grasp it. He sat back in his chair, shaking his head.

"You know, you really are an asshole, Victor," he said, in a tone appropriate for respectful compliments.

Victor lurched to his feet, a look of self-righteous hurt on his face. "Anne, come," he commanded. "Let me take you away from these unfortunate people at once. They are not your friends."

Anne stood up. "I'm just walking Victor outside," she said to Harriet and Benedict. Victor turned on his heel and left, looking furious. Harriet held out Anne's ring, and Anne took it. She followed after Victor. Her sweater was still over the back of her chair, and Harriet was relieved to note that Anne hadn't taken it, or her handbag, with her. Anne turned and looked back at them from the doorway, and Benedict and Harriet waved to her.

"Come back in two minutes," Harriet called after her, "or we're coming after you."

"Don't worry, I can do this." Then Anne gestured a throwing motion, and then she threw the ring. It arced through the air, and Benedict reached up and caught it.

In front of the restaurant, Anne crossed the empty street and stood with Victor next to the Citroën, which gleamed in the dark. She put her arms around him, and they embraced. They kissed. She felt like a scientist in a laboratory as she explored the moment from a distance. As his tongue probed her mouth, she invited old familiar feelings to surge, to take over; she waited for the rush of heat, but none of it happened. Victor didn't seem to notice. The experiment was an interesting failure. Anne felt the last piece click into place.

"Shall you escape with me now?" Victor inquired. "We could go back to the flat. We would have enough time." He took her wrist and guided her hand down the front of his trousers and pressed it there, where she could feel the pullulating evidence of his interest.

"No, I think not. We haven't sorted out the sleeping arrangements or anything. It would be terribly rude if I were just to take off now," Anne said lightly, extricating her hand.

Victor snorted. "You can hardly be rude enough to someone like that gangster your friend Harriet has produced."

"Benedict, you mean. Look, Victor, are we on for tomorrow?" Anne pressed herself against him. I really am getting to be like Henry, she thought in disgust.

"Mais, oui, ma chérie," murmured Victor.

"Usual time?" Anne persisted. "I might not get a chance to see you at the office in the morning. I've got those Saudis coming with their damned complaints."

"Yes, yes," Victor agreed, impatient, irritated, but still drawn to her.

"Until then. Ciao," and Anne quickly crossed the street, hugging herself against the chill of the evening air, and hurried back inside the restaurant before Victor could say another word.

When she reached the table, Benedict and Harriet looked relieved.

"You had another thirty seconds on the clock," Harriet told her, "and then we were coming to rescue you."

"Funny, Victor was trying to rescue me from you," Anne said.

"Well, that's what we were going to rescue you from," Harriet said, and they all laughed. Benedict held out Anne's ring to her, and she slipped it back on her finger, feeling its warmth from his hand. Harriet thought of Victor driving home to his family, and then she thought about Annamarie's voice, and the children, and she wondered if she would ever tell Anne about the aborted telephone call. Someday we will all laugh about this, she thought, but she was wrong.

"What *are* you going to do?" Harriet asked when they were lying in the dark, falling asleep. Anne had insisted on giving Harriet and Benedict the bed. They had argued about it the whole way home from the restaurant. They had made a nest of blankets for Anne on the floor beside them, Harriet pointing out all the while that if sleeping on the floor was to be done, then she and Benedict ought to be the ones to do it. Lying on the floor, Anne fought the sudden urge to get into bed between them. She squeezed her eyes shut so tightly she saw swirling sparks. They reminded Anne of magnified dust particles—microscopy. Random motes. It all seemed so random.

"It's really amazing that we met, any of us, isn't it?" Anne said into the darkness. "I mean, what are the odds of anyone meeting anyone else?"

"Oh, the stealthy convergence of human lots," Benedict intoned. Harriet giggled. There was a rustling of bedcovers. Anne wondered what they were doing.

"No converging of human lots, please, with a third party present," she chirped in a flawless simulation of cheery wit. It was quiet in the room then. After a long while, when Anne thought Harriet and Benedict had fallen asleep, Harriet repeated softly, "What are you going to do?"

The question hung in the darkness unanswered.

July 27

Victor had let himself out while she was still getting dressed. He had a meeting and was already late. Business as usual, only more so. Victor seemed relieved that Anne wasn't going to make any more scenes, and in fact she had been unusually passionate this afternoon. Anne imagined Victor descending the stairs, pleased with himself for his vitality, feeling quite the fellow. From the few stray remarks that had been dropped about her predecessors, Anne had concluded that Victor regarded his relationships with young women as something akin to a finishing school, a learning process from which all involved shared the benefits.

Anne had watched him in the mirror on her closet door as she took her dress off its hanger. He straightened his tie and smoothed his hair, looking in the mirror over her dresser. He was going bald, gray wings of hair flared at his temples, his nose showed signs of developing the slight red bulbousness that presages old age, and yet, and yet, there was still something attractive about him to Anne—in a repulsive sort of way. He was a man the way a lizard is a lizard, Anne thought. D. H. Lawrence. *Pensées*. Pansies. Victor Marks had a lizardlike vitality, an awareness, an aliveness.

He had picked up the bundle of old photographs that Harriet seemed to be using in some way these days in her reflected portraits, and the brittle rubber band that held them together had broken in his hands.

"Who are these people?"

Anne hadn't answered him, hadn't turned from the closet, and Victor had flipped through all the photographs before laying them down carelessly. He had kissed her on the back of the neck and walked out a moment later without another word between them, typically neither angry nor concerned, just distracted and in a bit of a rush, now that the sex was over.

Anne washed her cereal bowl from breakfast, jammy plates and coffee cups from Harriet and Benedict's breakfast, which had taken place after she left for work that morning, and Victor's just-used teacup and plate. (She had fed him the usual liver paste on rounds of pumpernickel when he said he was hungry.) She did the washing up under running water, not bothering with the dishpan, an uncharacteristic squandering of her hot-water supply. When the dishes were drying in the rack, she wiped out the sink and folded the red-checked dish towel into a neat, damp square, which she left in the middle of the tiny kitchen counter.

She brushed her teeth at the bathroom sink. The two other toothbrushes leaning companionably together in the tooth mug next to hers gave Anne a fleeting sense of warmth on this day when she felt an icy glaze forming on her skin. Their happiness was like a bubble, so perfectly formed, so complete, so impossible to get inside. She liked the sight of Harriet's books and small duffel bag on the chair under the window. Benedict's bag in the hallway. Benedict's shaving things. They made her feel a little less alone. She felt very bad about Harriet.

An hour earlier, when Anne came into the empty flat a few minutes ahead of Victor (Harriet and Benedict having departed for a day of exploring the galleries and looking at the meager art in Geneva museums), she had been greeted by the sight of a bunch of roses, roses that were her favorite shade of coral, filling the bidet. For an instant she thought it was a gallant gesture on the part of Victor, but then she was disappointed to recognize Harriet's writing on the note left on the table, which read, "You need a vase! I'm using the blue pitcher: sorry. Will rectify later. L.y. & l.y.—H and B."

Anne had held the note to her lips for a moment before crumpling it in a ball and throwing it away before Victor's arrival.

Let him wonder about the roses a little bit, she thought. (Victor had in fact raised his eyebrows when he saw the roses in the bathroom, but he had said nothing.)

Feeling comforted by Harriet's things, Anne realized that Harriet's presence was something she had always relied on—as long as she had known Harriet—to keep herself from herself. Since coming to Geneva, Anne had found it even more desperately necessary to avoid being alone with herself.

Once, in early spring, Anne borrowed Victor's Citroën in order to save delivery charges on the table for her flat. In an unpleasant warehouse district somewhere on the outskirts of the city, near the airport, she had taken a wrong turn and been stuck in a narrow alley, surrounded by huge trucks, with the table hanging out the back of the open car, the trunk lid bobbing because Anne's ineffective knots had come loose. Barely able to manage shifting gears under the best of circumstances, Anne had been near tears when a nasty truck driver had gestured obscenely and shouted at her that she was a stupid bitch and needed to reverse all the way back up the street, immediately.

This she had done, terrified of backing into another car or a lamppost, attracting attention, damaging the table, damaging Victor's car. She had survived the moment by conjuring up Harriet, imagining Harriet beside her in the front seat, making witty remarks and offering clever, useful advice about when to turn the wheel and how much clearance she had as they slowly careered backward, the Citroën's reverse gear grinding in protest.

Anne examined her skin under the glare of the bathroom light, then wiped the mirror of a few dried white specks she thought at first were on her face and not the glass. Over everything lay a sheen of inevitability.

Not why, but why not.

She made up the bed with fresh sheets. The used sheets, still warm to the touch in places, still damp in places, she stuffed into the trash under the kitchen sink. The small white hand towel

(Victor always preferred a small towel deployed precisely beneath them to absorb the moisture), a rather elegant one, with a delicate scalloped edge, she washed out in the sink and hung up to dry. It was Harriet's. Anne had taken it when she left New York, despite embarrassment both at her petty thievery and at her need to have some talisman of Harriet.

She smoothed the bedspread in place—not as perfectly as Harriet might have done—and knelt beside the bed, her hands folded in front of her for a moment. She felt momentum gathering.

Once, when she was little, her parents had taken her to play with some children of friends of the family, somewhere on Staten Island. They had found a heavy, straight-sided cardboard barrel in a dump, and all afternoon the children had taken turns rolling down a hill inside it, out of sight of the grown-ups.

If you braced your arms and legs, it was exhilarating, you were in control, turning magical cartwheels all the way down. If you just sat in the barrel and didn't prepare for what lay ahead, as the barrel picked up speed you were thrown around until you were completely battered and limp, broken into pieces by the time the barrel careened into a parked car at the bottom.

Poor soul.

Benedict.

He would see Harriet through.

It *was* brilliant timing, actually, to summon him in the way she had.

Love you and leave you.

Under the neatly made bed was a plastic carrier bag, for which Anne groped, on her knees. She had pushed it quite far under, and she finally had to lie prone on the floor next to the low bed in order to reach it, her shoulder just fitting the narrow gap between the bed frame and the cold wooden floor.

She drew out of the bag a coil of blue nylon cord, the same sort that people used to hang up their washing in poorer neigh-

borhoods. Anne didn't know why she had never seen any laundry lines in her courtyard, but she had sensed from the first day
she moved into the building that hanging her laundry out the
window on a line would somehow contravene the prevailing
customs. While she missed the fresh-air smell of line-dried laundry, she had developed a makeshift method for drying hand
laundry by draping it in haphazard clumps around the bathtub
and bidet.

In the basement of the building there was a gloomy little room
equipped with a washing machine, though no dryer, and if one
remembered to amass enough single-franc coins in advance, it
was possible to do one's wash. Anne indulged in having her
sheets expensively processed at the laundry down the street; they
were returned to her in three days' time, pristine and smashed
perfectly flat, wrapped in brown paper.

But where, Anne wondered, did other people dry their laundry? Another of Geneva's unsolved mysteries, like the way nobody ever even seems to think of stealing from the city's open
newsstands. Anne hadn't been able to stop thinking, from the
first day, about the way everyone in Geneva seemed to honor
the system of those newsstands. Just before Harriet's arrival she
finally began to take newspapers and magazines. She did it every
day now, though she often deposited them unread on café tables
just a block or two later. No one seemed to notice or care.
Another rule broken.

Not why now, but why not before now. Long overdue, really.
When you borrow time, sooner or later you have to give it back.

There were no ceiling fixtures in Anne's flat, just an expanse
of unblemished, white plaster, but a sturdy brass hook screwed
high up on the back of the bathroom door would do. It would
do. She could do this.

She was overdue at the office now.

Anne took one end of the cord and let the rest drop in open

loops at her feet. She had bought too much, but had never been good at guessing lengths and distances of things, in feet or meters, and it was the amount, she supposed, that the helpful man in the little dry-goods shop down the street had assumed she would need for a clothesline when she purchased it, the afternoon she fled Dr. Van Loeb's office. She placed the little crumpled receipt from the carrier bag on the table and weighted it with her gold ring. Let no one think this was an impulsive decision.

She knotted the end around the hook and, mindful of the table fiasco, tied three or four additional square knots to secure it there. Left over right and right over left. Such a good Girl Scout after all. When she and Harriet first met at the Shippen Gallery—an occasion Harriet insisted had something to do with a bunch of carrots Anne was washing in the sink in the back room, and Anne remembered distinctly as an introduction to Gloria's newest acquisition, a brilliant young photographer, at an opening for a show of photographs by mental patients (they agreed about the opening, but Harriet was certain they had already met by then)—their shared Girl Scout histories had been a source of instant early rapport.

How had it come into the conversation? Gloria Shippen had referred to someone at the *New York Times* getting "brownie points" for writing a review of a show by a mediocre artist whose paintings some Sulzberger was rumored to collect. Harriet had remarked to Anne, once Gloria had rushed away to greet a client, that of course the phrase had nothing at all to do with Girl Scout Brownies; the expression was derived from brownnosing. Anne had never heard that expression, though, she offered, she had been a Girl Scout, briefly, in Hastings-on-Hudson, before she went off to a Swiss boarding school after her mother died.

Anne and Harriet had talked about why they both felt like misfits in the Girl Scouts, and then Harriet told a long, funny story about a girl from Great Neck, Karen something, whose hairbrush had fallen down the camp latrine but she still wanted it back, because it was made with genuine boar bristles. The other people in the original conversation had fled long before this point.

Such tall doors, Harriet had observed that first morning in the flat, when she came in from the airport and Anne had been up for hours, pacing and arranging poppy-seed cake on a plate. Was it only three weeks ago? Such high ceilings. It makes you feel small and insignificant, doesn't it? Harriet had asked.

Yes.

Harriet's grandmother, the mildly famous Gay Gibson, whom Anne had heard of because she was often referred to briefly in other people's memoirs of New York life, had lived in an apartment on Sutton Place with impressively high ceilings. The first time Harriet brought Anne to meet Gay, it had not been a total success. Anne had started off with a panicky reference to those various footnotes about Gay that she had read, and Gay had replied dryly, "That's me—always the footnote, never the foot," and Anne hadn't been sure if she should laugh, and then when she did laugh—Harriet had chuckled—it came out as a nervous chirp, too late.

Harriet then told Gay about photographing Anne at the Central Park Zoo, where Harriet had spent so many childhood afternoons with Gay. Anne had obligingly posed against the glass in the monkey house, but she had been completely unable to make the funny monkey face that Harriet required, though Harriet demonstrated it for her innumerable times. Anne was desperate to please Harriet—she would have done anything to please Harriet—but she just couldn't get it. They had both been a little testy with one another by the time they were walking to Gay's. Harriet, Anne had begun to notice, had no idea of the effect she had on other people sometimes.

Tea had been served in pretty little pink and gold cups, along with stale Pepperidge Farm cookies, by an elderly and perhaps slightly inebriated maid in a green uniform who grumpily shoved the tea tray onto the table in front of them as if to say, "Here's your goddamned tea!"

Anne had been treated to a series of funny, brittle stories about Harriet's forebears. One among them, an Avery on her mother's father's mother's side, or something like that, had ridden for the pony express. But he had been on the wrong side of the law. Gay, who was having a "good day" as she teetered on the cusp of senility, had recounted all this while gazing steadily at Anne in her bright, birdlike way. He eventually came to his end, Gay explained, having settled into the comfortable grooves of this well-worn story, "when a platform gave way at a public event."

Seeing Anne's blank look, Gay had added a well-rehearsed "He was a horse thief, you see." Still nothing. Disappointed, Gay pursed her lips and sipped her tea, leaving Harriet to explain, "They hanged him. He was hanged."

Anne carried one of her chairs over to the bathroom doorway and stood on it. So far, so good. She stepped down and around the chair, pushed open the bathroom door, and gathered up in her arms the tangle of cord that hung down onto the floor. She heaved it all up in the air, like a child throwing confetti against the wind. Some of it caught on the top of the door, but the rest of it came down on the same side again.

"Merde," she muttered. "Shit." She pulled the door open wider, and it stuck and dragged on a snarled loop. She yanked the cord free, and the bundle that had hooked on the top corner of the door fell down on her head. She sobbed a frustrated laugh and dragged the chair around the door into the bathroom.

Anne twisted the rope around her wrist and down to her elbow and then back again several times. She bound it into a short hank, wrapping the final spiral slowly and carefully. How did people know how to make this particular sort of knot? She figured it out. It wasn't particularly difficult. Neatness doesn't count. This isn't going to be nice. Not the Lily Bart now-I-lay-me-down-to-sleep way. A private event. A private disgrace.

She stood on the chair and pitched the now-compact bundle of cord over the door. The weight of the cord on the other side pulled it down, and it was all gone except the knot around the hook and the length that ran away up and over the top of the door. She dragged the chair around to the other side of the door and pulled the door closed, squeezing the rope over the top of the door. The loop of rope at the end of the knot was more than high enough off the floor.

How could she do this?

How could she not do this?

No note.

August 18

Harriet looked over at Benedict, who lay on a chaise with his book tented on his chest, too sleepy and comfortable in the sunlight to read.

"Listen," she said, "are you sleeping? Listen to this: 'Parallax is the apparent difference in the position or direction of an object caused when the observer's position is changed.' I like that. I think I'm going to use it. It's amazing what wisdom lurks in a set of poorly translated instructions for a camera."

"Use it in your statement for the show, or use it to think about the recent events in your life?"

Harriet put the camera manual down and got up from her chaise to sit on the end of Benedict's.

"Move over." He shifted his legs and she picked up his feet and put them in her lap. She put one hand lightly on his ankles and neither of them spoke for a long time. The late-afternoon light glinted on the Mediterranean water; one minute the sea was sparkling, emerald, and luminous, and a moment later it was flat, metallic, opaque. Harriet couldn't figure out when it happened. She couldn't see the changing light, she could only see that it had changed.

They had come to Amalfi, to this former monastery perched elegantly on the side of a cliff, ten days before, a week after the funeral.

Looking out at the water, at the pretty little village below, Harriet felt empty. She tried to get outside herself, to look through her eyes as if they weren't her own in order to savor the moment. She knew these days were a barely affordable luxury, time out of time, that at the end of the week they would leave this elegant place and drive up to Rome, look at art, and try to

find Benedict's once-experienced rustic restaurant in Ostia that
served grilled fish (which Benedict thought had a name like
spiegel) at big wooden tables under trees. The next day they
would fly back to New York, and they would be back in ordinary time, back in their lives.

Harriet moved so she could put her head down against the
space under Benedict's chin, where she could lay her face on the
soft heat of his neck, and tucked the rest of herself into place
alongside him. She put an arm over him, and he put both arms
around her. Harriet sighed and allowed the tears that were always
just behind her eyes to spill over. It was a kind of crying she had
never done before, not when Gay had finally died, not when
word came about her father's mysterious death in Paris. Harriet
had cried tears of rage on countless occasions, she had cried over
dead cats, she had cried in anguish for an entire weekend when
Jack Richardson had broken off their romance. But she had
never cried this way. She actually wondered if she could become
dehydrated from it.

Crying seemed to be her default mode. She woke up from
deep sleeps with tears saturating her pillow. She cried when
something made her think of Anne. She cried when she realized
that time had passed and she had not thought of Anne. She cried
at the recurring image in her mind of Anne's body hanging
impossibly still on the bathroom door. She cried when she
looked at the dinner menu in the restaurant that was part of this
hotel, where she and Benedict were intrigued by the Fellini
extras who ate dinner around them every night. They had names
for some of them: White Suit, Lipstick on Teeth, Stavisky, Judge
Crater, The Executive Secretary, The Collaborationist.

Benedict had been the one to find Anne's body that day. At
the end of the afternoon, both of them tired from walking the
streets of Geneva, Harriet had handed him the key to the flat,
and they had split up to do a couple of errands. Benedict got

there only five minutes or so ahead of Harriet. He had already telephoned for the police and vomited in the kitchen sink. He had waited for Harriet in the hallway outside Anne's door.

Harriet whistled as she climbed the stairs. (A rule of Gay's she ignored was the one about whistling girls and cackling hens.) She was a very good whistler and liked to amuse herself by whistling appropriate tunes, so at this instant she was whistling "Stairway to Paradise."

She saw Benedict in the gloom of the hallway and called out to him as she approached, "Did you have trouble with the key? Sometimes it sticks. Let me." But then she had seen his face.

Benedict did not want her to see the body.

"I need to," Harriet said.

"You absolutely do not need to," Benedict insisted. "I do not want you to see this."

But then the police had come, and in the confusion that followed, everything happening fast, but in slow motion at the same time, Harriet had indeed seen beyond the door, just for an instant, but it was a sight that remained fixed in her thoughts, like some hideous snapshot that a sadistic lunatic might insist on showing you, over and over.

The funeral was arranged by Harriet. Henry Gordon had been on vacation in Florida; the efficient Miss Trout at UGP had a telephone number for him. He had listened to Harriet in sad silence, and Harriet had the feeling that he was not surprised, and that he was more concerned about her own feelings than anything else. He declined to make the trip to Switzerland, giving no reason, and agreed at the same time that a funeral there made as much sense as a funeral any other place. He was thoughtful and efficient as he provided Harriet with information that she would need and made arrangements to pay for everything. He insisted on wiring her a generous sum of money for her own expenses, as well. This trip to Amalfi was Henry's gift.

Harriet had no idea if there was a synagogue in Geneva, but in any case, Anne, like Harriet, had been neither fish nor fowl when it came to this sort of thing. "I'm a half-caste woman, and so are you," Anne had once said to her in New York, around Christmastime. So Harriet made her choice on the basis of aesthetics.

The service was held in a small chapel that was attached to an ancient Calvinist church just two streets away from Anne's flat. Anne had shown it to Harriet on the second evening Harriet was in Geneva. Anne had loved the unusually severe church facade. Inside, when she stumbled on the uneven flag floor, Anne had muttered, *"Merde,"* and had then giggled, gestured to their surroundings, and whispered, "a lapse in an apse."

It was almost exactly a year before that Anne and Harriet had wandered into a Catholic church in a slightly seedy neighborhood on the Upper West Side. It was a rainy Saturday afternoon, and they were on their way to a Cary Grant film festival at Columbia, for which they were much too early. Harriet was then working extensively on a series of available-light portraits, and the dismal church interior was a challenge. They had filled the offering box with coins and a five-dollar bill and had then lit every votive candle that wasn't already burning.

Harriet had moved Anne this way and that, edging her closer and closer to the candles until she was quite close to the holy blaze. Anne closed her eyes and took on the glow of a Madonna. Framing the first picture, Harriet had been startled to see a shadow of grief in Anne's face that reminded Harriet of Henry. When she took the camera away from her eye, it was gone, but when she focused a moment later, there it was again.

An elderly priest in an old-fashioned cassock had emerged

then and had chattered crossly at them in Spanish, waving his arms in the direction of the candles. He was mollified somewhat when they gestured at him to inspect the collection box, but he had stood there with his arms folded, waiting for them to leave, and so they did. Harriet had taken only the one picture and would later come to think of it as her best portrait of Anne.

Harriet couldn't bear to stay in Anne's apartment; that first night, it wasn't even clear if the police would have permitted it, anyway. Harriet and Benedict stayed in a hotel that was a short walk in the opposite direction from the church. The hotel, thanks to the generosity of Henry Gordon, was quite pleasant, though Harriet later couldn't remember very much about the place, other than the design of the telephone, on which she spent a lot of time making arrangements. She was dimly aware of the unusually gentle treatment she got from the annoying woman at the front desk, who made a sympathetic clucking sound with her tongue against her teeth every time Harriet came into view.

When Harriet came back to the room one afternoon after a long and mindless walk through the streets of the Vieille Ville, about which she could remember nothing, she had been startled to find Benedict lying on the bed, weeping. She had rubbed his back and stroked his head and whispered "It's all right, it's all right," into the back of his neck, and they had fallen into a deep sleep together.

"I don't even know what I think anymore," Harriet said to Benedict as they lay together in the darkness much later that night. Neither of them was able to eat much, or sleep through the night during this time, and they were both haggard. "I mean, I am simply tired of words, of my own thoughts, of my own mind."

"You were her best friend, Harriet, and you were good to her," Benedict said, reaching for her hand.

"Was I? I don't think I knew very much about Anne, or our friendship. I think she loved me more than I loved her, or more unequivocally, anyway."

"There's no way to measure that."

"Yes and no. I mean I don't think I was ultimately as good a friend to Anne as I said I was. I didn't understand her love. I basked in it, and at the same time I was oblivious. Do you see what I mean? I don't think I recognized her pain, I was blithely critical, I thought everything could be solved if I took her away from Victor. I thought I could dictate changes in her life. I thought of myself as the grown-up, and I treated Anne as though she were my apprentice. Maybe she really did love Victor. But there was something grim about it all, as though it were a sentence being carried out. It was as if Anne was absolutely compelled to do everything the way that she did it, starting long before I ever laid eyes on her. She was on some track that I never saw, and I thought I knew better. Oh, Benedict, who the hell did I think I was?"

"Harriet the spy?" Benedict kissed her forehead and hugged her tightly.

"More like Harriet in vain." Harriet sighed.

"My Harriet the brave," Benedict whispered.

The service would be more of a memorial than an actual funeral, without a body in a coffin. Harriet wasn't sure where the dividing line lay between a funeral service and a memorial service. It was soon enough after Anne's death to qualify as a funeral. Gay would have known.

In one of several telephone calls with Henry Gordon in those numb days, he had asked Anne to have his daughter's body cremated and the ashes shipped to him, so that he could scatter them on her mother's grave in Ann Arbor, Michigan.

"Henry, I think scattering human ashes in a cemetery is illegal," Harriet had whispered hoarsely into the telephone, through streaming tears.

"Then they will arrest me and put me in jail. Perhaps they will put me in the electric chair for such an offense," Henry had replied, his voice ever civilized as it traveled the distance between two continents that he himself had journeyed in his lifetime.

Harriet found a string quartet at the university who would play—Brahms and Schubert, which seemed like a reasonable compromise that she might have made with Anne: neither Rachmaninoff nor Lester Young.

A young minister met with Harriet and agreed to conduct the service. He urged Harriet to speak, to give a brief eulogy herself, but she told him she couldn't do it. He was unusually flexible, for a man of the Calvinist cloth, and he promised to include a minimum of religion. He asked Harriet a lot of questions about Anne and looked at Harriet with sad eyes. He insisted that she call him Lucas. His English was quite good, and when Harriet complimented him on that, Lucas told her that he had American cousins in Indiana, and prior to divinity school, he had gone to a community college for two years in South Bend.

"Sounds like dancing," Harriet had replied automatically, and he had smiled politely.

Harriet and Benedict closed up Anne's apartment in one long day of packing and sorting and discarding. Lucas helped, and Harriet gave all of Anne's furnishings to him, either for his personal use in his sparsely furnished quarters or for appropriate distribution. Harriet couldn't believe that there were any needy people in Geneva—she had glimpsed none—but the minister, clad for the occasion in faded American blue jeans, assured her that in the parish there were families who could make use of the clothing, who would be glad to receive such nice dishes, such a good mattress, and such lovely linens and bedding.

Harriet selected a small group of books and a Rachmaninoff record, the horsehair shawl, and a handful of other things, and Benedict packed up a box to ship back to New York. Henry had made it clear that he wanted nothing, but said that he hoped Harriet would keep anything of Anne's that meant something to her. As she listened to his voice, Harriet had thought about Anne's ring, which she had strung on a gold chain and was now wearing around her neck. She decided he didn't ever need to know about it.

Before they dismantled Anne's stereo to box it for the parish-house youth center, Harriet demonstrated its workings. At the first notes of the Django Reinhardt record, which had a light coat of dust from having sat on the turntable for a week, Lucas began to beat time with one hand on his thigh, while playing air clarinet in accompaniment.

Benedict, who was carrying bags of rubbish past them to take down to the bin in the cellar, grinned and asked, "Does Calvin know about this guy?"

"Who?" Harriet asked, straightening up, uncharacteristically slow on the uptake.

"Calvin. You know, Calvin and the Calvinists."

"Do you know Alvin and the Chipmunks?" Lucas asked eagerly.

The service was held late in the afternoon, to accommodate the workday at UGP. A surprising number of people attended, perhaps twenty. Everyone sat quietly while the quartet played to the conclusion of *Death and the Maiden*.

"Lucas looks sixteen years old," Benedict whispered to Harriet. He gripped her hand tightly. "Are you sure he's allowed to do this?"

"We are here," Lucas said, "because Anne Gordon made a decision. We are all very sad to be here. We might not like the decision. We might be very angry at the decision. But we have to acknowledge that it was her decision." He had gone on to say other things, things Benedict told Harriet about later that were reasonable and appropriate, and for which she was grateful, but Harriet hadn't been able to listen at the time. She sat, uncomprehending, until she heard the minister's pleasant voice launching into a concluding reading of the Twenty-third Psalm. She listened for Good Mrs. Murphy.

Afterward, while the quartet played the heart-piercing second movement of Brahms's String Quartet in B-flat Major, a movement that sounded to Harriet like death itself, people filed past her in an impromptu sort of receiving line. Harriet had decided against arranging anything in the way of a gathering afterward because she had no idea how many people would show up or who they might be. Thinking about what came next after this moment had just seemed like an impossible additional task.

She had telephoned Victor as soon as she had thought to do so, that first evening, at his home number, even before she tried to call Henry Gordon. When Annamarie had answered, Harriet had simply said, "I need to speak to Victor Marks," and Annamarie had put the telephone down without another word and gone to get him. In that moment, Harriet first had the crazy notion that he wouldn't be home because he was out with Anne, then could not believe that it was only twenty-four hours earlier that she had dialed the same number and listened to the same voice. What a difference a day makes.

Telling Victor, Harriet felt confused. She wanted to hurt him, but at the same time she knew that he was shocked, upset. The conversation had been over in a moment. "I'll call you tomorrow," he said. "Okay?" Harriet had no idea what they would talk about.

In fact, he hadn't called, and they hadn't spoken again. Harriet had next phoned the famous Miss Trout for assistance in locating

Henry Gordon, and it was Miss Trout to whom Harriet had
provided information on time and place for the funeral service.
Miss Trout had assured her that she would personally prepare a
memo that would go on every desk at UGP.

The people filing by and grasping Harriet's hand treated her as
Anne's family, Anne's chief mourner. Many of them approached
Victor, who stood alone, and spoke to him in soft voices, discreetly acknowledging his loss. Harriet was numb, having wept
through the Schubert, and the service, and could barely register
the series of faces as they occurred before her. Most of them
were from UGP, and a large group of them seemed to have
come en masse and seemed to leave en masse. A tiny elderly
woman had sat alone in the back, and Harriet had hoped to meet
her; she had a kind face. But Harriet never saw her again, as she
slipped out immediately after the service.

A short, stocky woman with an incipient mustache, wearing
an incongruous straw boater, introduced herself to Harriet, and
when Harriet didn't recognize her name, the woman explained
that she hadn't known Anne, but was with a Mormon square-
dancing group that had been in touch with Anne recently in the
hope that she would join.

"We might have been able to help her," the woman said
sadly, and she pressed some pamphlets into Harriet's hand.

Victor loitered in the aisle until he was one of the last. He
shook Benedict's hand and greeted him stiffly while Harriet en-
dured the Mormon square dancer, and then he approached Harriet and put his arms around her. It was genuine; she could smell
his grief. He felt old and brittle in his suit as she hugged him
back. She had never realized how small Victor was.

"We mustn't feel guilty, you and I," Victor murmured in her
ear. Harriet stiffened and pulled away from him. "Listen to me,
Harriet," Victor persisted. Benedict, who was talking politely

with some woman, looked over, concerned. Harriet put up her hand to indicate that it was all right. "You could not have prevented Anne from taking her life," continued Victor in her ear. He grasped her arm, almost as though he were feeling for a pulse, in precisely the spot Harriet knew his Auschwitz number was located on his own left arm. "Your time with her may have prolonged the inevitable. Haven't you realized that?"

"And why shouldn't *you* feel guilty?" Harriet asked.

Victor smiled. He seemed genuinely amused at her question. He tightened his grip on her arm and led her partway up the aisle of the chapel, toward the open doors, beyond which lay Geneva going about its usual business in eye-blinking brightness. He stopped and turned to face her for one last moment.

"I should not feel guilty," he explained, "because I do not believe in guilt."

The musicians filed past Harriet with their instrument cases, each nodding to her. The last person in the chapel, other than Lucas, who lurked respectfully, was still talking to Benedict. She approached Harriet and introduced herself. It was Sonya Trout.

"I was very fond of Anne," she said. "She was a lovely, lovely person. All of us at UGP are terribly sad at her passing away so unexpectedly." Talking to Miss Trout, Harriet was able to stop her tears for the first time in hours. She wished she could report to Anne about this encounter. Miss Trout was wearing a beige suit. She carried gloves. Her shoes—she had hilariously enormous feet, like pontoons—were a matching beige. Her legs, Harriet noted automatically, were of the unfortunate English type that Gay called "beef to the heel."

Miss Trout turned and gestured toward the front of the chapel. Two great bouquets of coral roses, for which Harriet had gone with Benedict to Place du Molard that morning, floated above their graceful glass bowls on either side of the apse. In front of the altar, there stood an enormous cylinder of artifical-looking white gladiolas. They had caught Harriet's eye during the service, and underneath her paralyzing grief she had wondered about them.

"I selected the flowers. They're from all of us at UGP."

"Thank you," Harriet said politely, making a mental note that Anne would have been as amused at Miss Trout's declaration of fondness as she would have been appalled by the gladiolas. Miss Trout still seemed to have something more to say.

"I just want you to know," she said, looking from Harriet to Benedict and then back to Harriet, "that whatever you may have heard, my relationship with Victor Marks is entirely platonic."

The air on the terrace was getting chilly, and Harriet was suddenly cold. At the same time she could feel heat radiating from her shoulders; she had got too much sun on the beach during the day. She unfolded Benedict's arms, which he reluctantly permitted, and stood to go inside.

Far away, down on the beach, two little children of five or six were throwing stones into the water. They were too distant for Harriet to tell if they were boys or girls; all the little children on the Amalfi beach wore the identical sort of colorful little underpants and nothing else. A wave chased them back up onto the sand. They advanced again as the sea retreated. Another wave chased them back, and one of the children, whom Harriet guessed was probably a boy, lost his footing and fell to the wet sand. The wave lapped over him, and as he struggled to get up, he called out joyfully to the other child, *"Aiuto! Aiuto!"* in a high, sweet voice. The second child ran back to him and helped him to his feet, and they joined hands and ran away from the sea together, out of Harriet's sight.

The heavy crimson bedspread had not yet been turned down; invisible staff came to do that while Harriet and Benedict were at dinner each night. Their bed was an enormous, high, canopied bower, and the four posts and headboard were swathed in the same rich material as the bedcovering.

The room was an odd mixture of severe and luxurious. The floor was simple wooden planks, but an unusual Persian carpet was beside the bed. Benedict followed Harriet into their room and examined his nose in the round mirror that hung on the wall in a worked-metal frame that looked like an enormous, medieval cog. The mirror was slightly convex, which gave him a funny reflection. He peered at his face.

"I'm burned to a crisp, but nevertheless it's only love," he said. "Do you want to shower first? Why don't you. I'll try to call this guy from art school, Corrado, at that number in Rome, to see if he can tell me the name of the fish restaurant under the trees."

When Harriet emerged from the shower, she realized for the first time that she had begun to feel like herself again. She wrapped herself in one of the enormous mottled-green bath towels from the luxurious supply the hotel seemed to replenish twice a day and left the steamy bathroom. She pressed the towel to her face; it was like a myopic seascape, and she thought it was beautiful. The air in the room was cool, and evening light was coming in through the terrace doors. The sun was low on the glistening horizon. Benedict was just hanging up the telephone and turned to face her, saying, "Corrado was home, and the restaurant is called Nanni. He gave me directions."

"Did he tell you what the fish is called?" Harriet was rubbing her hair dry with a small ivory-white towel she had removed from Anne's flat. It was actually Harriet's—it had been one of a set that she had permanently borrowed from Gay's apartment, at the point when Gay was just beginning to falter, before Anne left New York—and it matched several others on Eighth Street;

it must have got mixed in with Anne's things by mistake when she packed for Geneva.

"No, I forgot to ask. It's something like *spiegel,* or *spigola.* It doesn't matter, we'll figure it out."

"I look forward to eating spiggle-fish with you. Just don't give it that German pronunciation, or they won't let us have a good table." Harriet thought for a moment and added, "Or they will: remember the Axis."

Benedict smiled at Harriet and crossed the room. He reached for her hand. She held it out to him, palm up, as though he were going to read it, tell her about her future.

"Do you know," Benedict said, "that you have the most wonderful clavicles? Look, and tell me if you don't agree." He turned her gently by the hand he still grasped, until she was partially facing the weird convex mirror. "I adore those clavicles."

"Do you think it's a sixteenth-century hubcap?" Harriet couldn't believe she hadn't noticed the mysteries of this mirror until now. Her camera wasn't loaded, hadn't been used since that last afternoon with Benedict, before. She wondered where her film was, in which bag.

"You will marry me, won't you?" Benedict asked her suddenly, anxiously, his other hand raised in an almost religious gesture. "You will live with me and be my love?"

"Oh, I think that would be a good idea," Harriet said easily. "Soon, don't you think?"

They gazed at their reflection in the mirror. The entire room radiated out behind them, the glass panes of the terrace doors curving off on one side, and on the other side loomed the bed, gravid with its crimson overstuffing.

Harriet pushed aside with one foot her wood-soled sandals that lay on the bare floor. (She had impulsively bought a pair, the morning of Anne's funeral, out of the window of the chemist's shop where she had gone that day with Anne and Victor to buy Victor's ridiculous swim trunks. Things bear mute witness to our lives; she had suddenly wanted something from that window.) She said to Benedict, "Don't trip over those."

"Mr. and Mrs. Arnold Feeney," Benedict observed, looking at their reflection. "I love you, Harriet."

"Love's the only thing that matters," said Harriet.